NIGHT S'

Darbo looked around at the sem. had spent so many centuries. It was spaciu room for one person. His console and selection left-hand wall. For the first time ever they were a. dred blank grey stares greeted his. On the right was n. sleep was one thing humans had never managed to do wit. d up against the wall now, and his wardrobe, also set flush to the wall, .g with a row of cupboards for any personal possessions he may once have had.

The Goddess' body lay stiff and pungent at the centre of a brilliant white sweep of tiles.

NIGHT SEEKERS

LAUREN HALKON

Cosmos Books

Night Seekers

Published by:

Cosmos Books, an imprint of Wildside Press
PO Box 301, Holicong, PA 18928-0301
www.wildsidepress.com

For more information, contact Wildside Press
www.wildsidepress.com

ISBN: 1-58715-394-7

Chapter One

Dil-ya stepped out of the swirling dark and into the unlit room. Immediately she knew that something was wrong. She could feel the darkness calling her back, desperate to save her, and she cried out, turned to flee, but it was too late. It had gone.

It had others to think of.

Heart pounding, breath thundering in her ears, Dil-ya turned her head this way and that, straining to pierce the gloom. With the nurturing darkness gone, her magic seemed also to have left her. She had only her body to rely on.

She felt hot, burning, as though a million eyes were upon her. Her limbs felt weak, she knew there was someone there, there had to be, always was, always sleeping, yet this time . . .

"You didn't expect me to be awake, did you?" someone said conversationally.

"Who's that?" Dil-ya asked, cursing the quaver that edged into her voice. "Where are you?"

"Oh, you know me. I'm where I always am. Only this time I'm not so obedient."

"Obedient?" A chill slipped through her. What were those dreams Sahla had been having lately? Were they truly beginning to remember? And yet, this was not the way it was supposed to be, surely? "What do you mean? We never asked you for obedience. We came merely to love."

"Love?" The voice sounded as though it should have been amused, but the tone stayed the same. Flat, emotionless. "You expect me to believe that? To understand that? You, who took everything from us?"

The room moved, a presence closed on her. Dil-ya screamed, she couldn't help it, then the blow fell and her blood flowed.

She was dead before she hit the floor.

*   *   *

"No!" Sahla screamed, woke, looked up at Kai-ya.
"I know," he said and the tears fell.

*   *   *

Kai-ya walked slowly, head bent, hands folded behind his back. He had

5

spent the last hour softening Sahla's mind so that she could sleep dream-lessly for once. The others would stay with her, care for her should she waken again, and she may well do so for he remembered the horror writ large in those deep blue eyes. She was young, barely nineteen, and so recently come into her full powers. Forced to, perhaps, more quickly than she should have been, but the Dark Ones matured early and they needed her.

They knew how precious she was even as they feared her.

So precious, so all-knowing. Why then had he not listened to her? Why had he not stopped his wife, Dil-ya, from leaving this night? Why had he not kept her close by his side, safe in the darkness that gave them all home?

But he knew why, didn't he? Knew it as well as he knew why they lived as they did, deep in the slumbering darkness, the dreaming mind, the swirling landscapes of a sacred mountain that would soon breathe its last.

It was for this that he had let his wife go, had let her be the first to die, so that maybe, just maybe, they could all begin to live again.

He and Dil-ya were the last of their race, known only as the Pale Ones, tall, delicate people, with limbs and hair of brilliant silver and eyes as deep and dark as their souls. The Dark Ones, of whom Sahla was one, were more numerous, though never so much so as the Others. His Dil-ya had born only one child, and he had died a long time ago.

Kai-ya thought of his son as he neared the end of his journey. The land about him was one of deep forest and chattering animal life. The ground was springy with fallen pine needles, the air redolent with rich green life, chill and damp around him. Now, at least. Next time it may be desert. Such was the way of things when one lived in dreams.

Hi-ya had been a beautiful boy, strong of mind and body, his talent at moulding the darkness would have been great if he had been given the chance to grow. But he hadn't. He had died, as had the rest of the Pale Ones, as had so many of the Dark Ones, all because the Others could not stand the truth.

Once the Pale Ones and the Dark Ones had lived in the real world, had roamed the sacred mountain, a mountain so big, so all encompassing, that its ends could never be seen. It was their whole world and they had lived in harmony with its tides, birthing only the children the land could support, feeding from plants and seeds, game won in the chase, sharing the knowledge they acquired over the years. The nocturnal Dark Ones were the first to discover how to mould the darkness inherent in all things, a magic that could be used to shape mind and matter, to enhance life. This they had learned from the spirits of their ancestors and the Old Wise Woman of the Bones. They had many powerful shamans in those days, not just the one they had now in Sahla, and they had passed this knowledge on to the Pale Ones, who combined it with their machine magic to great and wondrous effect. Soon the two races intermarried and a new race was born of their union. The Others.

Humans.

Kai-ya stopped at the rim of the crater. It was always the same, despite the many different journeys to reach it. A vast gouge of rock that sheered away below him, blackened and jagged from unimaginably old eruptions. Hundreds of miles across, the trees stopped abruptly at its edge, as though their thick expanse had been cut away by a mighty sword. Only air filled the crater, its bubbling heart long since gone, yet often Kai-ya fancied he could see the smallest of flames in its depths, flickering defiantly, full of remembrances.

Like he could see it now. Like he could see it rise slowly from the pit, eager to greet his arrival.

"Hello, my friend," Kai-ya said, long since past feeling foolish for talking to air. He was the only one who knew of this place anyway. "And how are you today?"

The flame shivered in answer. He thought he saw a face, eyes full of sadness.

"Thank you for your grief, my friend. Only you can know how much I will miss her."

And so he would. Dil-ya and he were the only ones to remember the war all those years ago. They were the only ones to know the true horror of seeing children killed by their human siblings, Pale and Dark parents murdered by human offspring that could not accept such mixed heritage, could not accept the dark magic that gave them the land they lived upon.

"And for this," Kai-ya slumped to the ground at the crater's edge. "For this we live on only as dreams. Perhaps it would have been better to die. And yet what could we do?" He clutched at his hair, wailed his pain into the air. "What could we do, my friend? What could we do!"

Desperate to save those few they could, he, Dil-ya and their son had rushed to the shamans only to find them dead in their tebas, gutted and left to bleed amidst the smoking fires that had once been the huts of many families. Fleeing through a land quickly become a wilderness, the hunting cries of the humans ringing in their ears, they charged the machines one last time and called the darkness to them. There had been so much of it, a whole world screaming unheard for mercy, and from this monstrous surfeit they moulded a gateway, used their own despair-fuelled powers to catch up all those who still lived, to welcome them into the shattered dreams of the land they must leave behind.

It had worked. Would have been perfect if not for the arrow that had taken the heart from their son and left him dead and cold at the threshold where the darkness had sniffed at him, mourned and closed behind him, saving those that it could.

And now this was how they existed. The short-lived Dark Ones still birthed children at the chosen intervals and Sahla was the first shaman to be born since those terrible years. Dil-ya and he had kept the dreams alive around them as best they could by sending people through the gateways be-tween this world and the world of reality. They influenced the humans while they slept, hoping against hope that maybe they could alter these tortured minds, help them to welcome the darkness they so feared, help them to see the mountain as a living being. But it was all for nothing. Kai-ya had not been to the real world for a long time now. What he heard from those who did go was enough. The humans had almost completed their destruction. Now they were immortal and no longer in need of any emotion. They lived in the old rock spires, drained the sacred mountain of her last pools of life to sus-tain their own, and soon, when all were dry, the dreams of the land would cease and so would they.

"What could we do?" Kai-ya wiped his tears away. He knew. He dreamed, too. Though whether they were his own, or those of this flame that didn't exist, he did not know.

"Sahla," he whispered. "I'm so sorry. But you must go."

He looked to the flame.

"You must."

Chapter Two

The corpse was still there in the morning. It surprised Darbo, he had entertained the notion that perhaps it would have disappeared, like Gods and spirits had once been supposed to do.

He rose from his pallet and walked towards it. He was still wearing the same clothes he had last night. The blood on them had stiffened over the hours, but he paid it no mind, it meant nothing to him, after all.

He knelt beside the corpse and looked at it more closely. The early morning light streamed through the narrow windows of his spire apartment, casting the creature's—the God's?—face in brilliant relief.

It was female, this he could tell by the swellings of the breasts beneath her shirt, though to all other intents and purposes she was sexless. He had expected them to be male, the records had said they were, but then he supposed they could be wrong, so many other things were. Her face was long, the skull shaped differently to his, stretched at the top, like a crest, giving her a high, intelligent forehead covered in silver-white skin. The eyes, fixed in death, were completely black, no iris, no pupil, just black. Her hair curled down to her waist, in colour as pale as her skin. Her limbs were long, too long, and slender, yet he could tell they had once possessed considerable strength. He turned her over, cataloguing the caved-in section of skull, the seeping brains, the rusty blood, noticing that it was all the same as human matter, despite her unfamiliar appearance. In this, at least, the records were correct.

He let her head fall back to the ground. It made a soft and muffled thump. A brief thought as to what he would do with her crossed his mind but he disregarded it as unimportant. Soon there would be no one left to discover the body.

Darbo returned to his console and opened the main screen at the page he had been studying last night. There were three rock spire cities on the mountain, or so he had discovered. He doubted that anyone else knew. Most of the records he had found over the last month were so old that they had not been opened in many millennia. If he had been able he would have been curious as to why he had found them, and why now? But he was not able, neither he nor anyone else on this mountain. They were all caught in an emotionless state of life—needing neither food, laughter nor love, merely waking each morning and plugging into their consoles, pursuing endless useless knowledge, occasionally coming across the electronic tracks of another human soul, usually ignoring it. They had eradicated all need for anything else many centuries ago when they had finally discovered the secret of immortality.

The rock spires in which they lived provided a direct link to the living heart of the mountain via ancient machinery that wound in silver vines through hidden compartment walls. These vines, they had eventually learned, could be connected to the human body and used to sustain and continue life indefinitely.

No one knew when emotion had died, maybe it was part of natural evolution, maybe it was forced upon them when they defeated death. Whatever, research had been funded and soon the vines were found to store the mountain's energy and so were cut from the rock and implanted in each human so that they were no longer forced to spend hours each day hooked up to the vine-walls of their homes. Yet the stage had been set, each person was completely independent, had no need of human interaction, no need of outside aid, no need of anything anymore.

Darbo had never seen a fellow human being in all his six hundred and thirty years of life. He had been one of the last children to be born, a final explosion of blood before even this lone revulsion died out and came to be replaced with encelled humans locked within the spires whose outsides they had never seen. Clean, uncaring automatons.

The screen flickered before him, displaying the images that had awoken him to the past.

Tall pale creatures, small, dark, creeping devils, flames and water, shattered rock and bodies, the catastrophic downfall of those who had created the human race and cast it out into something the records called hell. A race with no purpose, no reason to exist.

Darbo knew it all had to go.

"All their fault." He tried the words for size, but could detect no bitterness in them, no hatred, only a hollow emptiness that had once, perhaps, held something.

He looked at the dead Goddess, thinking that maybe this would inspire some emotion, but it did not, merely made him consider the possibility of finding more of them and seeing if they all died so easily.

And along with this he considered whether their creations could also die.

*   *   *

Sahla awoke to find that the fires had burned low, the shadows had grown and her hut was empty save for one. Kai-ya's gentle face stared down at her in place of those of the unfortunate Dark Ones who had watched over her sleep. It was a face she knew well. Kai-ya and his wife had taken her under their wing when she had been born, recognising the power within her even as her mother had been caught between agony and gratitude at the handing over of her shaman-child. It was always hard on the clan-family of a blessed one; more so now, for people feared these unusual children as much as they had once honoured them. The powers they held, including the guiding of the dead to the spirit world, were—or had been—vital for clan life, but set them apart from all others forever. Sahla had been doubly cursed, or doubly blessed, in that she had been born long-limbed and almond-eyed, two things that made her physically repulsive to the squat Dark Ones with their huge, protuberant eyes all the better for seeing in the dark they roamed. Sahla had spent her entire nineteen years outcast from the society she served, tormented by fearful peers throughout her childhood and treated with a strange mixture of horror and awe when she grew and took on her full role. She often wondered what scared her people the most, the fact that she had powers they could could never know, or the fact that she looked so similar and yet so profoundly different to them.

Kai-ya and Dil-ya were the only ones who had not feared her. They had seen the bodies of her ancestor-shamans and they alone still possessed one of the old powers, the dark-moulding that she so excelled at. They had taken her tutelage upon themselves, treated her as their equal, perhaps making up for the loss of their own child. Sahla knew that Hi-ya approved of her relationship with his parents, she talked to his spirit on some rare and precious nights in her dreams, but she had never mentioned this to them. Some wounds should not be reopened.

Now she had a wound of her own.

"Kai." She struggled for a smile and reached out a hand to him. She had not seen him for many months before this day.

He grasped her hand and pulled her up into a quick embrace, crushing her fiercely against his chest as though he could reclaim his lost wife in so doing. Sahla wondered if he would die, too. She hoped not. She had heard whispered tales from other Dark Ones that Pale Ones bonded for life and when their mate died the one that was left behind would soon follow. It was a difficult concept to grasp for the Dark Ones who saw love as a wonderful gift that should be shared with many.

He released her suddenly, as though regretting such a display of emotion, and held her out at arm's length, looking at her with his intensely dark eyes. She felt a small shudder run through her.

"Your dreams were peaceful last night, Sahla?" he asked her.

"More so than usual. The ancestors are good friends, but very demanding at times."

"I know, Sahla. But be glad of them. You will need many friends in the future."

He turned away, but Sahla felt his tears, even if she could not see them. One did not spend nineteen years with someone and not learn to read their emotions.

"Kai." She reached out to touch him, to send a curl of gleaming darkness into his heart to ease the pain. He drew away. The movement was so minute only she would have noticed it, only she who wondered why the people who had once loved her now seemed so distant. Both Kai-ya and Dil-ya had drifted away from her in the last few years. Dil-ya she could understand in a way, she spent so much time in the land of the Others, but Kai-ya . . . well, Sahla had no idea why Kai-ya did not wish her company any more.

"We all miss her." She struggled against her tears, tears that could have been for herself or for Dil-ya, she wasn't sure. "We all loved her." She hung her head. "Oh damn it, it was so late, when I saw how it happened it was already over. I just wish I could have told you sooner, we could have done something to save her, I don't know . . . Maybe . . ."

Kai-ya turned, too quickly, brushed away her concern with a short, sharp laugh. "There was nothing you or I could have done. You told me all you could, but it wasn't enough. The true-seeing dreams are often unreliable; there are so many possibilities. It was, perhaps, meant to be. So many painful things are."

He turned away again, stared into the shifting shadows, unable to face her. Sahla frowned. Something told her that this moment was incredibly important. As if to echo her thoughts, the wind howled outside and a log shifted in the central fire, sending glowing sparks dancing across her lap. "What do you have to say to me, Kai?"

He looked back at her, smooth silver face gleaming in the flames. "Your dreams have been changing of late, haven't they, Sahla? Becoming more chaotic, hard to understand? Not just those about Dil-ya, but others, too."

This was not what she had expected, but she recognised that he was leading to something and so played along. "Yes, I see many images of the other world. The rock spires lying shattered, the humans dead alongside them, yet they can't be true-seeing, because all know the humans are immortal, they cannot die."

"Yes, that's what I thought. But, Sahla, I have true-seeing dreams of my own."

She almost gasped, stopped just in time.

"Oh, not like the others, not of love and anger, not the turning of re-membered cycles, mine are like yours, they reveal secrets, prophesise. I can't tell you where they come from, not the ancestors, I think, but I know they mean something."

"What do they tell you, Kai?"

Even as he spoke the words, she knew they were true. Knew them even as she hated them.

"You must go to the world of humans, Sahla. You must go fully and you might never return."

Chapter Three

Darbo looked around at the semi-circular apartment-cell in which he had spent so many centuries. It was spacious, providing more than enough room for one person. His console and selection of screens took up the entire left-hand wall. For the first time ever they were all turned off, and a hundred blank grey stares greeted his. On the right was his sleeping pallet—sleep was one thing humans had never managed to do without—folded up against the wall now, and his wardrobe, also set flush to the wall, along with a row of cupboards for any personal possessions he may once have had.

The Goddess' body lay stiff and pungent at the centre of a brilliant white sweep of tiles.

Her form was etched in the red ochre she had carried upon her person.

He had drawn her oh so carefully.

It was something he had discovered in the records.

He left her and walked to the door. It seemed surprised when he tried to open it, groaned and shrieked in its fittings, and he had to force it in the end. Darbo had always been strong.

He did not take anything with him. He did not look back. The word home meant nothing to him.

Out in the space beyond, the first thing he did was stare for at least an hour.

The inside of the rock spire reared above his head for nearly a mile, sheered away below his feet, stretched before him like a gaping mouth. There was no end to it. Red rock spun endlessly about him, inset with tiny white doors like a beehive, the workers diligent no more, locked away in eternal hibernation. In the centre of this stood a massive scaffold of metal pipes, interlocking, winding their way up and down the centre of this one of many spires in a city of over a thousand, in a world of three such cities.

And around these climbed the silver life-vines.

Darbo considered the possibility that these vines were a recent addition. No one had been out here in his lifetime and the vines were supposed to exist only in the compartments between the outside and inner walls of the spires. He stepped forwards, his feet clanging hollowly on the metal-gauze platform suspended outside his cell.

On closer inspection the vines did not look healthy. He was unsure whether they were the simple machinery all knew of or organically alive, like humans. Whatever they were, they were falling to pieces. Grey scales covered their outer sheaths and thin spines emerged from their unknown depths, waving at him as though a gentle breeze were blowing through the still air.

Darbo pondered the possibility that the shard of vine inside his body looked like this also, but quickly decided that this could not be so because he was still strong, still intelligent, still immortal.

He let his hand drop from its inspection of the vine. A few shreds of tattered grey material fell away and drifted slowly down into the spire's depths. Maybe it was one of those portents. He had discovered this from those old records, too.

He had discovered a lot.

He turned his gaze to the many cells around him.

About his own race.

He walked along the platform, stopped at the door next to his, raised a hand, rapped on the metal.

No one answered. Not a single sound came from within. He moved on to the next one and the next. All the same. He did not tire, he moved around the entire circle of his level, a task that took him all afternoon. By the end his ears echoed with silence.

Back at his own door he stopped, pushed aside its shattered remains, walked back inside, stood over the Goddess.

"Your people have forgotten you," he said to her. He nudged her lifeless body with his toe. A dead deity still did not compute in his brain. "But can you blame them? Indeed," he looked out of the nearby window. It let in only light; no view of the outside world had ever been his. "Who is to blame?" Her black eyes glazed emptily up at him. She did not answer, but then, he had not expected her to. None of them would. Because he knew all about them now.

He bent down and pressed his warm lips to her cold mouth.

"Don't worry," he murmured into her throat. "I will finish what you began."

He slid off her body and climbed to his feet.

The pallet was the first thing he ripped from the wall. It flew through the air with a soundless whine, smashed into half a dozen screens, sent shattered glass whirling everywhere, slashing his skin, skittering across the floor, slicing deep into the Goddess' bloodless corpse.

A chair followed this, took out the console and the main screen, electrical circuits flashing and spitting like a million burst arteries, smoke spiralling blue and choking into the air.

Darbo punched every remaining screen in turn, driving his fist deep into the hollow tube behind the delicate glass, tearing his flesh to ribbons, ribbons that retied in pretty flesh-coloured bows at each and every breath.

His heart continued a normal rhythm, watching emotionlessly while its blank-faced owner kicked in the wardrobe door and ripped the clothes inside to shreds, tossing them over his shoulder to lie with the glass. Cupboards groaned and fell, cracking on the shelves below, ripped free and hurled against walls, gouging great holes wherever they touched.

The pallet leaped into his hands once more and he used it to smash the tiled floor, grinding the metal edge down, twisting it from side to side, sending cracks snaking in every direction.

When the last tile broke Darbo put the pallet down and walked from the room.

The platform trembled beneath his footsteps as he closed purposefully on the pipes at the spire's centre. He caught a handhold and leaped into the web, began swinging down from pipe to pipe with consummate ease, watched each circle of cells appear and disappear, never-changing, constantly rising from beneath him, making him feel as though he travelled nowhere, merely danced the fly's dance of futility.

At one point on his journey downwards he came upon a snarl of vines a little different to the others. These vines glistened an ugly bilious yellow, clutched at the pipes in a strangle embrace, quivered violently at his approach.

Darbo looked at them for a long time before deciding what they were and when he did he tore a piece of cloth from his shirt, wrapped his hand in it and tugged them free. They did not break, but simply reeled out length after length of diseased stalk. He was aware of their poison burning his skin despite his protection because his body was working harder at rejuvenation. With this in mind he quickly continued his journey to the bottom of the spire, vines spreading and growing behind him.

The pipes terminated at the foot of the spire in dry, grainy yellow earth, a vast field of sand in which he sank up to his knees upon letting go of his ladder. He spotted the doorway to what he supposed to be the outside world far away on the other side of the circle. It was sculpted of rock, not metal, as rust red as the ochre that had carried away the Goddess. It was the only door on this, the lowest level, as though no human wanted this final linkage to the earth.

Darbo walked over to it, forging a path through the sand, not noticing when it swelled to his waist and threatened to drag him down, still not letting go of the burning vines, intent solely on his goal.

On reaching it he saw that it stood some twenty feet high, seeming to have been made for giants rather than humans. He reached out his free hand and pushed it. It opened smoothly and easily. He did not open it all the way though, but first bent down and plunged the vines deep into the sand, searching for the solid earth below. Then he rose to his full height and walked outside.

His first view of the city was by moonlight. All about him hundreds of spires converged towards the starry sky, silhouetted in shimmering midnight blue, their blood-hue hidden in the darkness.

He turned in a circle, such a small thing by comparison, dwarfed by these jagged towers, this field of motionless life. They spread in every direction, many of them curved in beautifully slenderous designs, some seeming as though they could only fall over, others narrowing infinitely towards their middle only to swell out again at the top. Wind danced around them, tugged icily at his body, wailed and moaned between the ranks, scoured out small holes that would one day grow perhaps to topple a giant. The ground sloped up before him, leading deeper into the city, winding between behemoths. His gaze turned down to another path, almost invisible now, that led to the edge of the city, the last of the spires, and it was this he ran along as the ground began to shake beneath his feet and the great spires groaned in concern.

Darbo ran for miles, stopped just when the diseased vines completed their circuit with the earth, turned and looked.

A small spark flared in one of the spires, bloomed into a brilliant flower of orange and gold, engulfed that which had created it, shattered it into a million glowing-hot pieces, spread to the next in line.

And now the blood-hue returned and Darbo watched it all, so far away that only the fire reached him, watched the humans die in silence, just as they'd lived.

Chapter Four

The bass boom of Daviki's drum shattered the silence and the dancers raised their voices in a ringing whoop, lifted their arms high and began to stamp their feet in time with the rhythms the old man pounded out. The night sky hung heavy and starless overhead, lights from many fires flickered orange and golden, casting the huts surrounding the ritual circle in mobile relief. Smoke spiralled and spun, alive as the people who danced in its honour, their small, lithe bodies glistening with sweat and bright paints, clattering with beads and bells.

"Yallah, yallah, yallaaaah!" Two women with wild, tangled hair flung themselves from side to side, inching their way towards the motionless form in the midst of the dancers. Men stomped round the outer rim, thickly muscled legs flexing and bending, arms thrashing and whirling, trailing feathers and the aroma of pungent oil.

Daviki upped the tempo, features creased in a smile that covered his entire face with a million wrinkles. The rest of the band followed his lead, their drums and rattles melding to make a cacophonous disharmony that was curiously uplifting. In the circle the dancers hurled themselves into further frenzy, lost in the song. Daviki loved to see his people like this; it made him think that perhaps they were not so far removed from the old times after all. So many people moving as one, so many supple, dark-skinned bodies mingling, calling to the spirits, calling the power for the shaman as Kai-ya had asked. The shaman. Daviki almost faltered then, his stick clattered drunkenly, or so it seemed to him, but no one else noticed. The shaman. His grandchild, Sahla.

He remembered her birth, when the shattered family had gathered close and watched the spirits come to her, stroke her newborn brow, look with grateful eyes upon her exhausted mother. Shamans had once been vitally important to the clan, but over the years spent in this land of dreams where life seemed neither so hard nor so vital anymore they had become less and less so. A family 'blessed' with a talented child was these days more likely to mourn the birth, especially when it was a child as unusual as Sahla. Daviki blamed himself for her misfortune. He had been the closest thing the Dark Ones had to a shaman till Sahla came along. He alone had dreamed the true-seeing dreams; he alone had heard stray voices flicker through his mind. He had been afraid of what people might say, had hidden it, been unable to control it, scared of it, even, and so it had soon left him. Maybe it had chosen his grandchild because of him. Often Daviki tortured himself with this thought late at night when he missed his wife the most. It was the echo of her voice in his mind that had finally driven him over the edge.

He did not envy Sahla her role; he knew all too well what it was like.

"Yallah, yallah, yallaaaah!" The women were closer now, their bodies entwined as they danced the dance of power, ready to awaken the shaman lying so close, so seemingly unaware.

Daviki stilled the drum, the others muffled theirs. The beating continued as an afterthought in a hundred ears.

Oh, Sahla, Daviki thought as the central figure began to stir. *How I wish you had feared it as much as I.* Tears fell from Daviki's eyes. This would be the last time he would ever see his grandchild.

*　　*　　*

Sahla knew when the drums stopped. Knew it with her soul as well as her ears. She knew everyone waited for her now. The whole ritual followed her from this moment forward. Her people, gathered to sing her to her full potential, to bring the ancestors into their hearts and souls, to honour them with their dancing, their fevered breath. Yet she knew that to them it was just a game, that they had no knowledge of what they did and danced only to please the Pale One. A sliver of fear edged into her chest then, a fear she had struggled to keep at bay ever since Kai-ya had told her of his dreams, of how he had seen her and a human man standing amidst the ruins of the spire cities. How she must somehow put it all back together again or both worlds would die. She. Alone. How could she be responsible for so much? And if she failed? If she failed all that she saw about her this night would fade and die, just as it seemed to her it was already doing, blinking out of existence as though it had never been. How could Kai do this to her? She felt two tears trickle down her cheeks as the women knelt before her and touched their foreheads to the moist earth. She wished she had known a time when this honour was real, was felt, was not so rehearsed, when she held all in her hands and was loved for it, not hated.

Tonight, as though understanding a little of her needs, the sacred mountain had dreamed a land just like that the stories said they had once lived in and the swaying, spike-leafed fruit trees of so long ago sheltered and embraced their small gathering. Sahla could feel their presence as a child experienced its mother's arms. Maybe it was a portent.

I hope so, Sahla thought, climbing to her feet and accepting the bowl one of the women offered her. *Oh, how I hope so. It sometimes seems that these dreams are all I have.*

She wondered what she meant as she tipped the bowl to her lips and gulped down the bitter contents. The sacred mountain had also dreamed the *gayata* plant into being beside their camp.

Oh blessed mountain, so generous with your vision-giving brew. This way you have always been.

Sahla half-sobbed, half-laughed and threw the bowl away, the last few drops of the hallucinogenic liquid splashing on the ground and draining quickly away. Whose thoughts were these? Was the trance begun already? Did she care? Was she herself? Had she ever been herself? A life handed over for the good of an uncaring clan since day one. Maybe Daviki had been right; maybe she should have let it go.

And lose us?

"Hah!" She flung back her head, her arms, with the beat of Daviki's drum, shocking, exhilarating in the silence. All about her the clan held its breath, dancers motionless, limbs hovering between moves, feathers the only thing adrift.

The two women quivered at her feet, she drooped with the next beat, arms hanging limp, fingertips caressing their heads. Blood thundered in her veins, filled her chest to bursting, she felt so light, so heavy, swimming, drowning, dreaming, dying, alive.

"Aiii!" She leaped high, birdlike, stabbed her arms to the heavens, inspired the drummers despite themselves, plunged into the reborn beat, the dancers erupted into life again, charged towards her, shrieking high and rushing, touching her, pulling her, dragging her this way and that, swinging her limp form from side to side.

Sahla screamed at them, flung them away, they rolled, came up stamping and chanting, beads and bells a shrill counterpoint. Sahla twisted round and round, the two women attending her, aiding her spin, lifting her up, setting her down. The fires blurred in her eyes, the heat shimmering, overwhelming her, flashing black and red, a kaleidoscope of colours, the drums deafened her, her heart burst, she was thrilled.

Sahla fell to the ground, hands and knees, an animal, all around her bodies circled. Peering through her sweat-tangled hair she thought she saw Kai-ya in the crowd, though that could not be. Pale Ones never attended the Dark Ones' rituals.

She held out a hand to him, voices clamouring in her head. Different than before. Vicious.

Go to him, go to him, he is yours, he is yours. All for you, show him, take him.

But it's Kai, Sahla pleaded, eyes aswim in rainbows. *I can't, he's like a father to me.*

A father no more, they snarled. *You want him, you always have. He is yours. It is the only way.*

Hands slid over her slick skin, inviting, awakening trembling pleasures. She found the body attached to them, made up of scintillant colours and musical water. A mouth met hers, so delicately, so softly it was more like a breath than a kiss. She moaned, cried for more. The teasing continued, fingers lingering in liquid ecstasy. She moulded her body to the heat, thrust her chest high in the air, aching for the touch, back arched and quivering. Faces shimmered above her, she did not know who loved her, who pleasured her. They shifted, struggled, and then she recognised them, something glistened, hard and sharp, pain sliced down into her, blood flowed, she screamed and collapsed, flopping, gasping, thrashing in the mud, choking, choking . . .

*   *   *

"Sahla!" Daviki shot to his feet, the drum falling, booming atonally, from between his thighs. He had known it was all wrong from the moment he had seen Kai-ya's face hovering over her. It seemed his talent was not completely gone after all. A Pale One's presence at a ritual could bode only ill, no matter that it was Kai-ya, their friend since time began.

"Don't just sit there!" he snapped at the rest of the band. "Come on. Help me get to her."

The dancers continued to dance, still hearing the beat of the drum, caught in the shaman's vast power, a part of her vision, her calling, as surely as the horrors that now threatened to kill her.

"Sahla!" Daviki forced his way through their jostling bodies, their chantings now abhorrent to him.

Her body twitched like bloodied glass in a rapidly spreading pool. She seemed only half there and Daviki stared, horrified, at the three ghostly figures fighting over her soul. Two human men struggled with one another, one tall, strongly built, pale of hair and face, waving a dripping knife at another, shorter, darker, in features so similar to Dark Ones Sahla perhaps heralded that for a moment Daviki caught his breath. And was there . . . could he be sure . . . she was so pale . . . a woman standing silently behind all of them?

Daviki, come get her! It was Kai-ya; tall, invulnerable, enveloping the tussling images in a web of gleaming darkness.

Leave her be! the Pale One screamed at them. *Damn you! Leave her be. She will be with you soon enough. Would you kill her so soon?*

Daviki choked on his terror as the knife turned towards the Pale One. He did not look anymore, merely darted forwards, the rest of the band at his heels, and snatched the frothing shaman from the blackness before it closed in a vast rip in front of their very eyes.

*   *   *

Kai-ya woke from his dream of dark-moulding and looked at the blood on his body.

"No," he sobbed. "Hers or mine? I don't know. I don't know." His head sank into his hands. "But it is all my fault. All mine. I'm sorry Dil-ya. I love her too much and there is nothing I can do about it."

Chapter Five

Fainan awoke that morning in a cold sweat. He had never experienced such a thing before, and was mildly intrigued by the feeling of sticky skin and the crawling ice beneath it. These mild intrigues of his were a particular idiosyncrasy on his part, he knew of nothing like them in over five centuries of study. He wondered if he were a faulty human. Perhaps the vine living in him was diseased in some way. Only this would explain why he'd had such a strange time while he slept last night.

He sat up and swung his legs off the pallet, decided to take a shower before dressing to rid his body of the odour of the night. He hummed a single note to himself while he tapped in the appropriate commands on the control panel. It took him a moment to realise what he was doing—unsurprising really, as he had never hummed before in his life.

"What is that?" he murmured. It reminded him of something. A deep, resounding boom. A strange sound. The spires were silent apart from the low-pitched buzz of countless screens, and human ears had become all but oblivious to this background noise. Where then had he heard this? And more importantly why was he—what was the word?—singing?

He shook his head and looked in the mirror above the panel. He didn't look faulty. The same dark blue eyes stared back at him out of the same olive-skinned oval. The same black hair framed his face and the same short, lean body waited to step under the jets.

Busy looking at the eyes in the mirror he didn't notice when he started humming again.

The control panel clicked and unlocked and part of the wall slid aside in front of him, the steam issuing from it announcing that the jets were ready to cleanse his pores.

He stepped over the raised metal rim and into the jet-room. The wall-panel slid back into place, leaving a seamless barrier behind him. Inside, the walls and floor were covered with tiny, pale blue tiles. Emerging from the cracks between these tiles nosed the jets, small, silver, snakelike appendages that would source his body's presence and send a stream of particles through his pores, removing all detritus and refreshing the skin, leaving a healthy pink glow that had been highly sought after back when humans had been mortal.

None of this concerned Fainan, he merely waited, motionless, while the jets did their work, still humming, still trying to remember the strange things that had happened to him last night.

This wasn't the first time Fainan had been aware of something happening in the night. Often he woke before morning and for a moment thought he could hear voices, perhaps see shapes in the darkness. Yet it was not the usual darkness. This darkness seemed to have something else within it, something he could not identify, yet something that perhaps should have been familiar to him. He wondered whether the other people in the spires had similar experiences, and in this, too, he was unusual, though he did not know it, of course. The inhabitants of City Three were just as isolated as those who had once lived in another not so long ago.

It had been something in his head, that was it. The jets finished and slid back into the wall. Fainan did not move and after a minute's pause, they came back and started the procedure all over again.

Something in his head. Pictures no less, like he saw on his screens, but in his head of all things. How could that be? His head had no screen in it as far as he was aware, so where did the pictures come from?

He felt the cold sweat creeping over his body again and the jets whined in anguish as their workload increased.

A picture of a woman entered his mind. She opened her arms to him and he stepped into them. The sensation was alien, that of another body next to his. Bizarre. Unreal. An impossibility.

Fainan's limbs trembled at the sight of her. Her face, indigo-eyed and dark-skinned, a smaller echo of the being he had seen in the mirror just now.

Then an image of another man snapped into his mind and he gasped, stumbled against the wall, confusing the jets, filling the room with a brazen screech as they struggled to locate him. He thrashed on the floor, held his hands over his eyes as though this could keep the picture from him.

"Darbo!" He reeled; the pale man turned on the woman, on him, bright redness spurted. Fainan fell against the wall, the control panel outside registered the pressure and the wall slid aside, depositing him in a quivering bundle on the floor of his living quarters.

Fainan let his hands fall from his eyes.

His room was full of spike-leafed trees.

*　　　*　　　*

Darbo stopped in mid-stride and looked up at the pale blue sky. For a moment he had heard his name called as clearly as though someone stood right next to him. He looked back the way he had come. There was nothing there save for his trail of footsteps etched into the silently shifting sand dunes. And why should there be? All the people lived in the spires and he had just destroyed a third of them.

He remembered wandering through the shattered ruins after the fires had burned out. He had considered the possibility that he might come across bodies, but there had been none. All had been reduced to ash. Spires, humans, Goddess, all. He had sat in the dust for a long time, looking at the scoured hole that had once housed hundreds of thousands of lives. The wind had moaned around him, speckling him with tiny black dots, lifting a sickly sweet stench to his nostrils. But no humans. All were gone, removed, disappeared, destroyed, by a few diseased vines. By him.

Darbo's eyes had swelled in the emptiness; his head had swum with silence. He had not been there for part of the time, so long he was unaware of it, though when he came back to himself his hands had been bloody and a small piece of metal, perhaps from the ruins of his apartment, had lain by his side. Inside his chest he had experienced what he could only describe as a burn. He thought perhaps that this was a little of what the screens had shown him of the downfall of the Gods and the casting into hell of the humans. He had stayed there all that day and on into the night, his shadow falling long across the smoking ground as the sun dipped below the horizon. He had remained awake so that he could greet the next creature to creep from the dark, but none had come and he had experienced a slight shifting of the burn in his chest, a tightening, a constriction in the throat, as though something wanted to burst out.

He had climbed to his feet when the sun rose the next day and started his long walk to the next city. He knew where it was, if he kept the sun to his back he would get there soon enough. There would be many more nights and he could wait through them all. Maybe while he was waiting the thing in his throat would finally loosen. Time would tell.

He took the beautifully sharp piece of metal with him.

Chapter Six

Daviki sat with Sahla when the stress became too much for her birth mother. Sreela had never known what to make of her gifted daughter and Daviki could not blame her too much for it. After all, look what she had for a father.

Sahla moaned and stirred in what could be a trance or merely simple sleep, Daviki had no way of knowing for sure, but something did not feel right to him and that was why he was here. A shaman's body was vulnerable when the spirit journeyed.

He reached for the bowl beside her bed. Sreela had made some herbal calm-water, the cloth on Sahla's forehead was soaked in it, but it seemed to be doing little to ease her dreams this time. Still, Daviki had little else to do but continue what treatment he could and so he dutifully dunked the cloth in the bowl and replaced it on his grandchild's fevered brow.

What had happened during the ritual no one knew. It seemed that only Daviki had seen the figures battling over Sahla's prone body and it was just as well he had for she had lost much blood—a shaman's vision was often as real as life—and if left alone much longer she could easily have died. As it was, Sreela, being the clan medicine woman, had stopped the bleeding, cleaned and dressed her child's numerous wounds and behaved with admirable calm before finally giving in to the tears of helplessness that countless other mothers of gifted ones had no doubt suffered in ages long since past.

Sahla keened and waved an arm at the air above her head, as though fighting off some phantom demon. Daviki reached for the thrashing arm, caught the slender hand in his and held it tight. He could see no sign of the men he had seen before, perhaps it was only her own mind that tortured her this time, or perhaps the dreams had returned. Perhaps she did journey there.

The thought of these dreams sent a cold shiver running through him. He cursed himself for a fool. How could he not have seen it before? And here was Kai-ya planning to send her to the waking world. Surely he would see sense now.

Sahla had told him of the dreams she had been having these past few months. Kai-ya, and Dil-ya before her death, had known something of them, but Daviki was aware that he was the only one who knew them in their entirety. He wasn't sure why Sahla had sought to confide in him instead of her tutors, but he thought that maybe it was because she instinctively knew how he had suffered beneath the shaman's curse before her birth, and that he would understand where no other could. He still didn't know if he had lived up to her expectations, but he hoped that he had. Kai-ya and Dil-ya knew of her true-seeing visions of the spire cities lying ruined but they did not know of the two men she had also seen. She had not told them of the blood and the death these men carried with them.

Her death.

Daviki clutched her hand tighter.

"Sahla," he murmured. "I see it now. I saw those men come for you and I think Kai-ya knows as well for he screamed at them not to kill you so soon. Yet he would still send you to them. Hah. Never fear, child. I will not let him send you away. Not now."

A sound at the hut's entrance made him glance up. Kai-ya stood in the doorway, a tall, featureless shadow in the dying firelight.

"What are you doing here?" Daviki could not hide his hostility.

"Is she well?"

"Well enough, all things considered. I don't think your presence will help, though."

"I know you hate me, Daviki." Kai-ya's voice was hoarse with weariness. It seemed to Daviki, as he looked closer, that the Pale One had not slept in days. His eyes were rimmed with deep pouches and his skin was drawn so tightly that his bones threatened to slice clean through. "But you must know that I do what I must for the greater good."

"The greater good?" Daviki raised an incredulous eyebrow. "Humph! Is that what they're calling it now?" He looked down at his sleeping grand-daughter. "Come on." He loosed her hand and rose to his feet. "Let's go outside. I don't want to wake her when I kick your sorry behind from my camp."

Kai-ya smiled wryly and allowed himself to be ushered from the hut. Once outside Daviki pulled the rough wooden door closed behind them and turned to face the Pale One. It was quiet in the camp. The other Dark Ones slept soundly, exhausted by their ritual and its alarming ending. All about, countless silent huts lay scattered as though by a careless hand. The sky hung grey and ragged with cloud above, the sun would rise in less than an hour and here and there a late-fading star burst into fitful life for a few moments before being swallowed up once more. The air was still, uncomfortably warm, and Daviki felt sweat trickle down his sides, gumming his tunic to his back and his hair to his head.

"Well, Pale One," Daviki studied him with a darkly bright eye, trying to read the man's emotions in his face. He could see pain there, though whether it were for himself or another he could not be sure. "What have you to say for yourself?"

"What would you have me say?" Kai-ya spread his hands. "It seems to me that you've already made up your mind about me and my plans."

"Maybe I have," Daviki said. "But there are many things I don't know.

Sahla has the dreams now. My talents, what few they were, died a long time ago."

"You should not underestimate yourself, Daviki. Sahla holds you in high regard."

"Yes, she does, Pale One. She tells me things, things that make me wonder why you are so set on sending her to the waking world."

Kai-ya's face twisted, mouth a self-tormenting slit, eyes glimmering with a thousand unshed tears. He looked away, to the barren sky, and laughed like a madman, his deranged calls spiralling upward in thin slivers of tortured darkness. Daviki gasped at what he felt in that sudden outpouring of emotion.

"By all the ancestors, you've seen them, too, haven't you?"

Kai-ya looked at him. The old man backed away, subconsciously holding his fingers crossed in the warding gesture. "Yes," the Pale One said simply. "I've seen them, though it aches my heart to admit it."

"Then why? Why send her?"

"I don't know, Daviki." Kai-ya shook his head, silver hair flying like ghosts. "At least in my heart, I don't, but in my head, in my mind, in the true-seeing dreams I know only too well. I see those men as clearly as you saw them at the ritual. I dreamed them earlier and came to Sahla's aid, I thought a dream was all it was then, but now I know that it wasn't. Those men came to her for a reason. They're suffering, Daviki, suffering more than you and I can possibly imagine. That's why they attacked Sahla. They need her, they need her love, her power, her skills with the dark, yet they are afraid of her and that's why they tried to kill her. Because of their fear the land is dying, and so are their minds."

"But what of the visits we make in the night, to teach them of the darkness while they sleep? What of . . ."

"No good, Daviki. Not now. It's been too long, such subtle measures can't work anymore, maybe they never have. The sacred mountain has been drained to keep the humans alive and her dreams are dying as a result. Soon she will breathe her last and the humans will be immortal no longer."

"No . . ." Daviki murmured. His heart clenched inside him, his mind touched on the possibilities and fled gibbering and screaming.

"Yes. You know what will happen when the sacred mountain dies. The dreams cease, forever. We will die and, eventually, so will the humans. There will be nothing left to support them and they are so afraid of the dark that the light will burn them up in the desert they have created."

Daviki looked back at the hut that contained the sleeping Sahla. "No," he murmured again. Why did it have to be her? "No."

"That's why she has to go, Daviki. Even if they kill her, she has to go, she has to try to reach them through the fear or we're all doomed."

"Why her?"

"Because it hurts the most, I think," Kai-ya sighed, and walked away, leaving Daviki alone with the darkness that gave him home. For now.

The old man dropped to his knees and dug his hands deep into the earth, perhaps reassuring himself that it was still there.

Chapter Seven

Sahla came awake to the living moan of winter wind. At least in her mind she did.

A vast panorama of snow-capped mountains opened before her, so many, thousands it seemed, that she could look for a lifetime and never see them all. Not truly. Sahla sighed. When first she had journeyed here—an apprentice then, naive and eager to please—she had been overwhelmed, had felt nothing but the rushing of wind, the exhilarating motion of being thrust out into space, the panic that quickly followed. She had returned to her body in the underground caverns of the clan teba to find Kai-ya and Dil-ya gazing worriedly down at her. They had accepted her feverishly trembling body into their arms with a quiet knowing. They had seen many first flights in their time, and though they could never know for themselves the power of journeying, they knew the terror of a different power and remembered all too well their first dalliance with it. It was then that Sahla had wished for a true shaman to teach her. She had heard that for those shamans chosen for great things the Old Wise One Herself came to train them, yet she had seen nothing on that first trip and Daviki, her only real friend amongst the Dark Ones, knew nothing of these things. His talents were wild, untrained, his dreams invaded against his will, he could teach her nothing of how to fly.

Sahla lifted her arms high and stood for a timeless moment at the world's edge, wondering if this place had ever existed anyplace but her mind. The wind swirled around her, insistent, dangerous, curious, threatened to tug her fascinating form from the rock that cradled it and dash it down, down to the valleys below.

"Yes," Sahla whispered. "You want me, don't you?" She raised her head, threw it back, looked up at the sky above, turned in a circle, sky spiralling as she increased her speed.

The wind picked her up, thrust her high, higher than the sky, she was full of clouds, full of white, struggling to breathe, reigning it in, seeing the thin indigo air above, forcing the flight to level out, then she dove like a hunting bird, time and space unravelling around her, she didn't know whether she was falling or climbing, all was one and the same, her breath left her, she expanded to the smallest thing she had ever been, saw a pin-prick in the lightness, swirled to nausea and crashed.

"You learnt that well, Sahla."

She looked up. Zinni's face broke into a huge smile and the female shaman reached down to haul her to her feet with all the strength of her once physical form.

"And so I should," Sahla said. "You taught me."

"Yes." Zinni flicked her dreadlocks out of her young-old face and shimmered into her wolf form. "I did, didn't I? Run with me, then, pupil of mine."

Sahla changed in the flicker of a thought—it was always so easy here in the world of the dead—and loped off after the shaman who had caught her on her second fall and shown her the way to dream. Zinni was the most powerful shaman who had ever lived, the first ancestor she had ever met, and first loves never died.

Where are we going? the pure white Sahla-wolf asked of its mate.

To see one who would help you, the silver-grey Zinni-wolf replied. *One who wishes to gift you with the power to gift another.*

I don't understand.

You will.

Trees flashed by them in a green-blur haze, thickly wooded valleys a world away from the infinite mountains that guarded all journeys and dreams, both true-seeing or not. The Sahla-Wolf was painfully aware of the pounding red life all around her, the quicker beats of prey, the slower, almost imperceptible shiver of vegetation. Noise careered around her, her own blood and that of all other forest dwellers, the rattling wind and the shifting, rustling growth in the earth. Once her paws faltered, the musk of young deer filled her nostrils, the urge to turn into the chase was strong. The Zinni-wolf lolled its tongue, bared its sharp white teeth, seemed to grin, perhaps feeling the same urge.

No, Sahla. The voice when it came was curiously familiar. *You'll kill me, too.*

Ahead the forest shimmered, a delicate young doe stepped from the mist, slender-legged and wide-eyed, far more wisdom than her tender age could hold in her gaze.

Dil-ya! Sahla gasped and changed in a heartbeat, Zinni close behind her with a moment's regret.

"For shame, Pale One," Zinni drawled. "Tormenting us so. You know Sahla and I always run as wolves."

"I didn't know I ran as a deer." Dil-ya—halfway through her change—hung her head. "I'm sorry."

"Apology accepted," Zinni grinned, wide mouth grossly sensuous. "Be thankful we were not too far gone or you would have run no more."

"Spirits can die?" Dil-ya looked shocked.

"For a while." It was Zinni's turn to shrug.

"Is this who wanted to see me?" Sahla asked, finding it hard to adjust to seeing Dil-ya so young, so uncertain, so lost here in the true-seeing world. The gift of shamanic dream-flight was one the Pale Ones had never had. They could mould the dark, sometimes dream it, but they could not journey to it. That talent had always been for the Dark Ones alone.

"It is," Zinni said. "Though I think me when she has finished with you she and I had best have a little talk. New spirits are so bothersome." She pulled Sahla close and kissed her brow. "Come back to me soon, Sahla-wolf."

Zinni shimmered into a bird and fluttered towards the sky, turned into a bee halfway up and shot off into the forest's depths. Dil-ya stared after her longingly. "I hope she'll teach me how to do that."

"Zinni will teach you a lot of things you never knew," Sahla said with a wry smile. She looked at Dil-ya, wondering how it could be that the spirit of this millennia-old creature was now little more than a child.

"I know what you're thinking." Dil-ya flushed a little, for a while seemed her old self. "But this is all so new to me. I only ever heard of the ancestors in your tales. Now I'm one of them. What do you expect of me?"

"I know." Sahla reached out to her, caught her hand, now so small, in hers. Any bitterness she may have felt at the neglect of the last few years faded to insignificance. Sorrow welled anew that her true-seeing had let her down when it really mattered and she had seen her friend's death too late to help her. "I've spoken to many newly dead, remember. I know how disorienting it is." She raised a finger, concentrated for a moment. A stalk uncurled from her nail, grew straight and strong, flung up a profusion of flowers, fluttered and lost its petals in a summer storm all in a matter of seconds. "But you can still mould the dark here," she murmured. "The dark is everywhere, and so are the seeds it contains."

"I don't understand." Dil-ya sobbed and held up an empty hand.

"Must you?" Sahla turned dark blue eyes her way.

Dil-ya frowned, stared at her hand, watched it shake, shed a tear, turned away, despair in her gaze.

Sahla laughed.

"What?" Dil-ya cried, half-angry.

"Look."

Dil-ya looked back at her hand.

A single rose grew from her fingers.

"Oh!" She closed her hand tight around it. Blood dripped, hung on the thorns, fell to the ground in a small dark pool.

"Why did you want to see me, revered ancestor?" Sahla bowed before her.

Dil-ya looked down at her, child still but growing already, taller now than her still-living charge. It seemed a small and perfect bee hovered near her ear, whispering perhaps of wisdom she had always known. "I wanted to see you to tell you to go to Kai before you leave," she said. "He feels he's doing wrong by sending you away. He has so much sorrow in his soul. You must re-assure him before you go, Sahla."

Sahla jerked as though she had been slapped. Remembered the end of her vision in sudden and violent completeness. Had it been him after all?

Maybe Dil-ya did not know the true reason he sent her away. "What are you saying?" she snapped, not wanting to voice her thoughts. "That I not only have to leave my people but I have to make sure none of them feel guilty for sending me?"

Dil-ya waved a hand and the roses surrounded them both. "Yes, Sahla. Oh, I know it seems harsh to you, and it is, but it will be for the worse if you go and don't do this. Don't let your own pain blind you to that of others."

"The others? You mean my clan or the humans?"

There was no answer and when Sahla looked up Dil-ya's spirit was gone.

Chapter Eight

Roses, Fainan thought. *Roses in my apartment. I wonder if I am dysfunctional?*

He sat very still in his bed, staring with wide eyes at the creeping bushes that surrounded him on each and every side. He had seen them on various screens—the horticultural records were deemed most realistic—but they had not prepared him for this, this thickly cloying scent of wild perfume, this profusion of red and yellow, orange and white, the dark green leaves, the terrifying thorns, the claw-like branches.

Fainan moaned and closed his eyes. The vision of the dark woman flickered in his mind, his eyes rolled beneath closed lids. The roses were still there when he opened them, just like the trees had been, and he knew he would have to get up and deal with them soon or risk sending his vine into malfunction for sure.

He swung his legs out of bed, trying not to let his flesh be touched by this rampant vegetation, but it was no good, it was everywhere, he might as well have tried to halt the sun and moon as they crossed the sky.

"I don't understand," he said, glancing down at the thorns that ripped into his calf, the wound healing before the blood had chance to hit the ground. "Where are these things coming from? They don't exist anymore. How can this be?"

He walked over to a cupboard and removed a large pair of scissors. Armed with these he turned on the rose bushes and made his first hesitant, almost apologetic, snips.

"These visions in my head," he muttered while he worked. "I wonder if they're anything to do with this? But how can they be? How can a vision take on form? How can something in my head, something that shouldn't exist even in there, move out into this physical world?" His snipping grew more frenzied. "My vine," his voice was high. "It must be my vine." He was perhaps approaching panic, and, in this, as in his ability to wonder, he was alone of all human beings. "I am dysfunctional, I am malfunctioning. Maybe soon I will begin to age, my body will need food. What will I do? What will I do? There is no food, if there were I would not know what to do with it. Will my blood begin to flow soon? Will my vine cease to regenerate me? Will I die in here?" His hand slipped, the scissors closed on flesh and he stared at the flap of skin hanging from his palm. It was red, dotted with tiny spheres of blood, soft and disgustingly mobile, staring at him, screaming at him that this was his body and it would no longer be denied.

When the wound did not heal Fainan wobbled for a moment then met the floor with a silent thud.

*   *   *

Many miles away in the only other surviving Spire City a woman rose from her bed and switched on her console.

Kelefeni harboured severe doubts as to the validity of her own vine, though she did not panic, as did Fainan. Just lately she had experienced strange shakings in her body. It was not the most accurate of descriptive words, but she lacked any other and so this would have to do.

She gazed blankly at the screens as they flickered into life one by one, each showing the title page of a different record. She clicked from one to the other until her cursor came to rest on one that held the image of a staff encircled by twin serpents. This one she opened. The screen went blank for a moment, then text flipped into view. A contents page. She scanned down, unsure what she required. Various words sailed past her eyes; tumour, cancer, haemorrhage, stroke, none seemed right, each was too specific, the symptoms meant nothing to one whose body was inviolate. Where was the entry for shakings? It was inconceivable that there was none. Was it possible that primitive humans had not experienced this thing?

Kelefeni continued scanning the record long into the night but nowhere did she find anything to inform her questing mind. Finally, having exhausted all possible avenues of research, she sat back in her chair and considered retiring. Only the knowledge that the shakings would return stayed her decision.

She rose from her seat and walked over to the window. It was dark outside now, but it made little difference to the view, the window's surface was one way only.

Kelefeni stared at it. Was it a viable possibility that something looked back at her from the other side of that featureless hole?

The shakings took her then and she collapsed to the ground, unable to scream for she did not know how.

*   *   *

A shiver ran through Darbo's body, every muscle trembling, though with more than simple exhaustion it seemed. He halted in mid-stride and sat down, almost collapsing in his haste. Sweat fell from his brow in torrential streams. Although his body was immortal it was not immune to the heat of the sun and out here on the mountain's treacherous flanks there was no shelter from its punishing rays.

If ever he had stood at his window and considered the possibility of outside, now he saw it in all its savage glory. The land was dry and barren

33

underfoot, sometimes smooth, polished rock, other times jagged and vicious, yet other times full of drifting sand and shimmering air. It rose forever upwards and forever downwards, a mountain alone and of itself, the biggest thing there ever was and ever needed to be. Grey and more grey ruled it during the day; the dunes were grey, the rock was grey, only the sky, crouched a brilliant, blinding white overhead, offered some small change to the endless uniformity. The sun, though a giant orange orb at sunrise and sunset, transformed into an amorphous circular mist during the day, glowering with impossible heat, sucking at the land like a giant parasite. Nothing grew or moved out here. No sign of greenery, no sound of life. Only the low, almost inaudible moan of the distant star burning its gases interrupted the mountain's lonely stillness.

Darbo sat slumped over, staring at his feet, sinking ever so slowly into the sand. He clenched his teeth against the burning in his throat. It was so tight he considered it would choke him if it did not cease soon. The sensation in his chest had also intensified. Maybe he should not have left the city. At least there the landscape had not been so empty, at least there he could have sat in the ruins and watched the ashes of his people disappear into the ground.

He slipped a hand into his pocket and pulled out the piece of metal he had brought from there. It glinted brightly in the brutal light, shimmered and shifted before his gaze. He touched the tip with his finger; his neck pulsed, the muscles grinding beneath skin.

"Ar," the word struggled out past the obstruction in his throat. He cocked his head, scraped the metal back and forth along his hand, keeping the wound open, watched the blood drip softly to the ground. Something welled up inside him, but it could not get out, and after a while he forgot it and merely sat and stared at the small patch of red sand before rising and continuing once more, waiting for the first of the spires that would signal the second city he must destroy.

Chapter Nine

The first thing Sahla did upon awakening was to ask her clanfolk where Kai-ya was. She had to find him, though not for the reason Dil-ya would have her do so. She remembered well the passion that had ended her trance the other night and it excited her at the same time that it scared her. Yes, Kai-ya had raised her, but he was not her father, he bore no true claim to her body or soul. He was a man, same as any other, and she a woman, such a lonely woman . . . why then should she not be allowed to love him? Who else but he could dare to love a shaman? Fury swelled within her then, fury at Dil-ya for keeping her from him. She wished she had struck her feeble spirit down when she'd had the chance. She shook her head, aching bitterness bringing tears of confusion to her eyes for she knew not whether these thoughts were her own or those of the men in her dreams. Had she not always loved Kai? And he her? What then had become of that love that he chose now to send her away? And what of the woman she also saw in her dreams? The woman she had told no one, not even Daviki, of? What would she have to say on this if only she could speak? But the woman was always silent and the men grew ever louder, Sahla wondered if they were dead or alive for she had never known such insistence, such a complete and utter rape of her mind. This was one more reason why she sought Kai-ya, in the hope that he could tell her which thoughts were her own and if this love was one they could share.

The Pale One spent most of his time with her clan, though he did visit others on occasion, especially when the sacred mountain's dreams performed one of their major flips. This was very rare, happening once every five hundred years or so, usually just when the weather was beginning to turn more wintry. When it happened villages were changed fundamentally, often destroyed, the people drifting as atoms in a formless darkness that sometimes lasted for days before solidifying again in a world vastly different to the one they had known. Kai-ya seemed to understand this best of all, as though he had some secret link with that which dreamed. He spoke of cycles and changes and the last time this had happened, so long ago as to be myth, it was said that he had roamed the clans, soothing shattered nerves and worried minds, a job the shaman had once performed. But, despite clan elders who scoffed at these old tales, it seemed another flip was on its way for the land round about their village had become more and more unpredictable of late, the last few months alone had seen much disruption of the normal way of things with trees and animals appearing and disappearing almost at will. Perhaps this explained why the clan had performed her ritual with little complaint, as though now they wondered if they had been too quick to rid themselves of shamans and all they had to do was dance a little and she would forget all their former suspicions. Perhaps it also explained Kai's absence; perhaps she need not look to more disturbing reasons. The wind rose in rough voice at her thoughts, laughed at her, tugged her off balance so that she almost fell. She moaned and clasped her hand to her aching head, regained her feet and looked up at the sulphurous sun preparing to set on the horizon. It cast the cluster of huts into hunched shadows and a chill took her heart for she knew she was wrong and that this terrible reason was all there was.

To her increasing despair no one had seen him. Or so they said. Perhaps it was all a plan to keep them apart, to deny her this moment as they were denied the true seeing, the dark moulding, the knowledge of the ancestors. Perhaps it was jealousy. They all looked at Sahla with wide, gleefully pitying eyes. Maybe they knew the thoughts that played in her mind and laughed at them like the wind, knowing that in less than an hour, when the moon rose next, she would journey to the world of the others and would never return, never see Kai again, never find anyone to love.

Sahla turned away from the last person she had asked—a young woman of her own age, mated several times, happy with her simple life and bouncing child—and hated her, suddenly and violently, for having what she could never have. "It doesn't matter," she snapped in answer to the woman's helpless expression. "I'll find him myself, you go back to whatever you were doing."

She walked quickly away. Her back felt so stiff that she feared it would snap.

Just like her mind.

*   *   *

Kai-ya stared up at the sky. Blurred clouds swirled high overhead, shunted along by a wind he could not feel down here on the ground.

He couldn't feel his body, didn't think he had moved for quite some time. His legs and arms were, he knew intellectually, still attached, still sprawled by his side, but they felt unreal somehow, as though they were no longer part of him, merely some numbed appendages, useful perhaps to other people but ultimately pointless for one such as he.

He blinked and the clouds snapped back into focus. He wondered whether the crater was still there, behind him. He had come here after speaking with Daviki and had not moved since. This time the land around the crater had been grassy meadows of a green so vibrant as to look more like the paints the old artisans had once used to decorate the spires so long ago. They had stretched far off into the horizon and he had found the crater festooned with flowers and soft leaves, silken tendrils waving gently over the abyss, perfume wafting down into the unknowable depths.

He had laughed for a long time before the flame rose up and the reproach in its flickering gaze had made him stop, had made him cry, had finally made him lay down to die.

Sahla, he thought. *Why am I doing this to you? Is it because I'm angry with you, angry that you let those men have you and not me? Or am I angry with myself? Angry because I killed Dil-ya for this? The dreams that showed me when and how, why she would die, that her death would open the way to a new world. Did they lie? Was I a fool to believe them?*

Maybe I was, but I have wanted it for so long. The sacred mountain to be ours again. Not just in dreams. She would have understood, I know she would, if I had told her. But how could I? How could I have told her she was about to die? Yet how could I dare to take the decision upon myself? Oh, it has been so long since our people walked the true earth. So long.

But Sahla, it is you, you that I always return to. Your face, your body. They appear again and again, transposed so quickly over Dil-ya's that I am ashamed. And yes, I am angry, angry that they dare take you and I dare not! What coward am I? I never told you that part of my dream, did I? But you found it out for yourself and now I'm sending you to them. Who am I punishing here? And why? Why? Why? Why?

Is a reason needed? the flame trilled in his ear, shifting and hovering above him, connected to its crater home by a thin black thread. *And is that fact not all the need there is?*

Need, reason? Kai-ya thought of laughing again. *Why do you always speak in riddles, my friend?*

I have never spoken to you before.

Kai-ya giggled a little at this and closed his eyes. When he opened them again—he knew not how long he had lived in darkness—the flame was gone and the moon hung in its place, huge and full, just risen and luminous on the horizon where endless indigo grass met endless indigo sky.

A small sigh escaped his lips and a thrill swept through his until now forgotten body. He shifted his legs, his arms, cringed as blood tingled and sparked into life, rolled over, as clumsy as a newborn, and struggled to a kneeling position.

The crater circled behind him, its distant edge blending seamlessly in soot-shaded shimmerings while the moon rose slowly higher, reflecting its light in carefully selected places. For a moment Kai-ya thought he saw the flame in one of those favoured spots, then it winked and was gone and he was left staring at the moon, so familiar yet so much larger than the one he had known, hiding every now and then behind wispy purple clouds, deep-etched craters forming muse-like features, stolen light more beautiful now that it silvered everything in dreams.

He felt like crying as he watched it, entranced, hypnotised by this

37

simple, impossible, eternal thing.

How long the voice had been calling to him he did not know but when he finally looked up he saw Sahla standing like a vision limned in jewels, the moon at her back, crowning her, embracing her.

"Kai." She smiled when she saw his head turn her way and that smile made her outshine a million moons. In that moment his heart both leapt and died inside him because he knew now the difference between need and reason and staggered to his feet, desperate to make that vision material in his arms. She reached out, too, moving towards him, love bright in her eyes, body trembling as she waited for him to come to her.

Then the moon shuddered and fell from the sky, the darkness curled around his need and plucked it from his searching hands as though it had never been.

Chapter Ten

It seemed to Darbo that he had been walking forever. The next Spire City was nowhere in sight, each night brought only endless sleeplessness and a dire mulling over the gods that failed now to appear to him. The mountain never ended, merely sloped off above and below his trudging feet, the same dead grey rock, the same sullenly shifting sand, the same jagged outcrops closing him in, thrusting him momentarily upwards, speaking in long-forgotten whispers of a land once full of rivers and trees, now as bare as the gaping hole in his chest.

His breath came a little sluggishly now; his limbs felt curiously heavy and his skin tight, not red and burning, but perhaps struggling to keep things so. He laid a hand over the part of his body that held the wonderful vine, considering the heretofore-ridiculous notion that it was malfunctioning. Yes, those doctors long ago had made it so that humans no longer depended upon the living walls of their apartments, but no one had ever really tested the theory, had they? No one had ever come this far from the spire home of the vine he carried. No one had ever been outside before.

Until now.

Well, it would be a long overdue experiment if nothing else.

Darbo stopped for a moment to rest. His skin was sheened with a glistening layer of sweat and as he turned his head up to the sky a breeze sprang from out of nowhere and sent a welcome shiver running over him.

"What is this?" He held out a hand. The wind picked up, whistled briskly through fingers that could never quite catch it. "Wind? Out here?" He dropped his hand, looked around. All was as it had always been. "There is no such thing anymore. Or so the screens say. Is it a possibility that they are wrong here also?"

The wind, no less for being so denied, hissed in his ears, whispering more loudly than the sinking sand ever had, telling him things he had never wanted to hear, lifting his tattered clothes and twirling his hair, reminding him of what he had done to his home under this same unblinking sun.

"What?" Darbo lifted his hands high. "You judge me?" He turned full circle, watched the sun shiver and slide horrifically quickly towards the horizon. "You judge me?"

He threw back his head and laughed, choking past the flaming hollow in his chest, the constriction in his throat. It was a sound like none the impossible wind had ever heard, for there was no humour in it, no derision, only an echoing lonely madness of dried-out skin and bones, of rocks sliding down endless mountains, of spire cities grumbling and collapsing in vast plumes of dust.

"You judge me, you judge me," Darbo monotoned and turned, slowly spinning, a small dead centre in a miniature cyclone, sand whirling, abrading his delicate eyes, forming futile parodies of tears, turning him into something less and more than human that could dry up and blow away if only it were not so stubborn.

The sun finished its fast forward slide to the horizon and the world glowed psychedelic for a moment before the moon swallowed all in its ebon tide. Darbo's eyes grew large from looking at this vast, craterous expanse that tipped so delicately between land's end and sky's beginning.

"Too big," he remarked to no one in particular. Then it settled above him and split apart in a vast sweeping of lunar arms to smother the mountain in a darkness so violently intense that Darbo fell to his knees and shielded his head with his arms.

Sheer brilliance shimmered over the quaking land, long, gentle fingers of luminous lack of light that reminded him of the velvet blue behind his eyes back when sleep used to claim him.

He lifted his head, he didn't know why, and was just in time to see a small dark woman drop from the moon's centre. She fell to the ground and lay motionless, seemingly unaware of the huge black bird that formed from the strands of her hair and took wing high into the sky with a joyous caw. Nor did she notice the snake that slid down her leg and melted into the ground like some sinuous drop of sentient menstrual blood.

Darbo saw it all, though, and so it was that he knew who she was, or rather what she was, and would be ready for her when she woke. He moved to sit beside her and withdrew his lovely, shiny piece of metal.

The crow cawed again, soaring long and lonely in its new world, a long-feathered shadow cast by its mother moon.

This time Darbo did not hear it.

*   *   *

Something cawed but Fainan ignored it. He had been sitting staring at the bandage that wrapped his hand for a long time now. It seemed almost as though he expected something monstrous to rise from the innocuous white material he had found stuffed far back in a darkened cupboard. Something that would latch onto his face, seek out the life within him and turn his wonderful vine to so much dysfunctional mush.

"I don't understand," he said for perhaps the five thousandth time. He reached out a shaky hand and lifted a corner of the bandage, peeled it back so gingerly it seemed his fingers would snap and looked anxiously within.

"No . . ." he moaned and pulled the material all the way back.

The wound was still there.

Wound. A strange word, but that was what it was. A cut, an abrasion, a gouging of flesh and skin that would not heal, a horrible shifting mass of red and pink that stared him in the face with a mocking leer and chided him for ever having thought to stand immune to such shocking things.

"Why won't it heal?" Fainan wondered. "Was I right, is it my vine after all?" He put a hand to his spine but nothing seemed out of place, no flesh stuck to his hand in great rotting chunks and . . .

"No!" He shook his head violently. Where were these thoughts, these terrible thoughts, coming from?

Something hissed and he shook his head, eyes blurring for some reason. An image flashed through the blur, made his wound seem laughably unimportant.

"Sahla!"

Despair. Despair and a sense of such terrible loss that it wrenched his voice from his throat and tossed it limp and shuddering before him.

He sank to his knees, gasping, choking, looking deep down into the eyes of the scarlet snake that wound slowly about his ankles, looking far up into the gaze of the black bird perched in the rose bushes that grew once more along the walls and floor of his apartment.

Roses that held her face in each and every bloom.

Chapter Eleven

Her face. It was the last thing he saw. Burnished skin, slightly down-turned mouth, wildly curling hair, eyes as deep an indigo ocean as that which opened up and swallowed her away from him.

"Sahla." Kai-ya sank to the ground. The moon closed up and glimmered innocently down on him. "No."

His head drooped, his hands found his silver hair—so close in hue to the treacherous moon—and folded into it.

"No," he moaned again, eyes fixed on the ground. He idly noted the changes as the dreaming mountain shuddered through quick-growing grass, rough-grained rock, filament-fine sand and pounding sea. The sky thundered and boiled, struggling just as he to make sense of this loss, this tearing free of one so precious, one so all-important.

Kai-ya looked around for the crater, the flame he cherished and feared. It was nowhere to be seen. The sacred mountain's dreams whirled in agony around him, all form gone, time and matter flipping in darting pinpricks of whining music and chiming harmonics, he a speck of multiple atomic attraction adrift in endless space, waiting for the new, the old, reformation and reclamation, what will be will be.

"My friend," the glowing mass of electrons that was Kai-ya thought to the non-present, omnipresent flame. "What have I done? This flip, it seems, will kill all. How do the Dark Ones fare? Have I killed all in trying to save all? Ah, no, this is all my doing yet I never meant for it to be this way. She was supposed to go in glory, not disaster, not turmoil. She was supposed to go to heal the Others, to go with the blessings of her clanfolk, her ancestors, my ancestors. With me. Always and never with me."

Electrons clashed and annihilated in globular tears, new sparks were formed from destruction, Kai-ya took on fresh responsibility.

"Flame eternal. My friend, my foe, whatever you are. I am yours now, for better or worse."

Fire billowed in the formless dreams of a once vibrant land, raging with the loss of a billion billion memories. It consumed this lonely thought and in so doing birthed it once more.

It was a birth best left unfulfilled for one.

Yet not so for all.

*   *   *

A man lay curled foetally on a dark beach. Up above purple-edged clouds spun sable cobwebs and millions of tiny glimmering star spiders waited impatiently for the white-hot explosion that signalled an end of life. Below, black water lapped silently for a while, softly edged onto silk-sodden land to taste of this creature it had never seen before retreating back carrying wondering murmurs of this delight it would soon fully know.

A breeze lifted, perhaps born in one of those faraway spiders' webs, and the man groaned and shifted, raised his body up from the clutching sand and coughed long and loud, his voice finally trailing away into a throaty sob.

Kai-ya lifted long-fingered hands before black eyes, turned them this way and that, seeking but not finding any imperfections. All skin was smooth and silver, soft and young, despite the many years of life from which it had sheltered the inner workings of this body.

"I knew it would be too much to ask," he muttered sardonically. "I suppose it would be too easy for me to die, wouldn't it?"

The ocean sighed behind him, in sympathy or reproach he could not tell, and he began to walk along the far-stretching beach.

He wondered if the Dark Ones had been so similarly, blessedly cursed.

*　　　*　　　*

"Be still, people," Daviki stood before his frightened, bedraggled clan, cloth-capped stick poised over the skin of his drum. "The Pale One will soon be here and the rebuilding will begin." *At least I hope he will,* the musician thought. *If I did not drive him completely from us this last day.*

He pounded out a calming rhythm on his drum, took some small measure of comfort from the fact that his people settled, pulled family and loved ones close and gathered round, casting wide-eyed but no longer quite so terrified glances at the sand and sea that had replaced their village home after this latest and greatest dream flip.

When the land had reformed about them he had found that all were changed, those that were old had become young again, those few children had grown to adulthood, some had even disappeared altogether, gone to dream with the ancestors now. It scared Daviki, more so than he would ever admit to those around him, and he struggled to smile reassuringly at Sreela when her strangely youthful eyes turned on him. Did she even remember the daughter who had only so recently left them?

It was too much, the flips were said not to change things so greatly, ever, they were disturbing, but never mortally so. Never this, never this sea of faces he barely recognised. And why was he alone untouched? Why was he still old, still wrinkled and wizened, still full of the knowledge of what had previously been?

Kai-ya, he thought. *Please forgive an old man his foolish words. I cannot deal with this alone.*

"Daviki."

Daviki turned at the sound of the voice. Kai-ya stood motionless some little way down the beach. He, too, was unchanged and Daviki gave voice a joyful, childlike sob that here at least was one familiar thing in a world gone madder than even dreams should ever be.

Kai-ya did not move, merely stared, his eyes so black that all matter seemed to disappear within. Daviki stepped back, afraid where once he had been so sure. Perhaps all was not the same. Kai-ya was indeed different somehow. Changed. Hurting. More so than a previous incarnation could have wished for.

Then movement blurred silver before the old man's eyes, his nose snapped beneath a delicately hard hand and he toppled forever backwards, the shivering gasps of his people doing little to cushion a fall of booming, snapping drum skins and splattering blood.

"You kept Sahla from me, old fool." Kai-ya stood over him, Daviki whimpered, bled, scuttled away, the Pale One followed, pinning him with contemptuous black gaze. "You kept her from me when we needed one another. Now all this," he waved a hand, "all this is yours. Your creation, old fool. Made from unfinished perfection, lost love, drifting passion, a dark gone mad." He turned away. "Enjoy it."

"Wait!" Daviki scrabbled for his feet and pride both, red-stained sand slick and slippery against his palms. He felt anger and shame in equal measures. He had done what was best for his granddaughter, hadn't he? He loved her, didn't he? "Kai-ya, damn you, you can't go. What of the clan? How will we rebuild without you?"

Kai-ya stopped. Did not turn. "You can't. You never will. That which binds us is gone."

"What?" Daviki stared after the Pale One's retreating form. His hands hung limp at his sides; blood trickled slowly from his broken nose. Behind him the clan stood in a forlorn and broken circle, too many pieces to put back together again.

*   *   *

Kai-ya passed a multitude of broken circles that night, a hundred clans all crying out to him and he ignored them all—he could fix none when the circle of his own heart lay shattered and seeping into cold air. As dawn broke on this new dream land of endless sand and ocean he laid himself down to sleep and dreamt in time with the flame he sought, the crater at the heart of the sacred mountain that could tell him and only him how to heal the ultimate wound.

Chapter Twelve

Kelefeni stared at the blood-soaked bodies for a long time, finger poised over her mouse, eyes riveted to the images on the many screens, back stiff and rigid. It seemed perhaps that a memory of distress or horror, maybe a primitive function left over from a long dead ancestor, stirred for a single, brief moment behind her pale green eyes and then it was gone and there was merely calm contemplation once more.

Many days' study of the console's medical records had somehow led her to this. She did not understand how, perchance a link had become corrupted and had taken her to an unknown site. There were an infinite number of information pages locked within the computerised records that each and every apartment dweller had access to, indeed many minds had mused long ago, before immortality became reality, that a human being would need to live forever to read them all. But however she had arrived here the site itself was of little use to her, there were no entries on shakings here either.

The shakings. They had grown worse just lately. Marks appeared now on her skin, waving burgundy lines as though her veins sought exit from her flesh, pulsing and trembling with unnatural life, making her whole body crawl and itch. One twitched now, sending her finger into a jerking spasm. She frowned at it and forced it to be still—this control was getting harder she absently noted. Shakings over for the moment she moved the pointer to take her back the way she had come.

Yet just for a moment she hesitated. The bodies of the small dark demons—for that was what the text labelled them—burned deep into her retinas, they were not so unlike her, were they?

*   *   *

Sahla blinked lashes gummed thickly together, aware of a bright yet diffuse light shining upon her. It was not like the warmly hued sunlight of her dreamland and fear tugged at her heart, made her close her eyes tight again for one craven moment before opening them wide to greet the new world. The world of the Others.

The knife flashed towards her. She reacted instinctively, hand snapping up, catching the wielding arm just behind the wrist, twisting sharply. She heard the knife clatter to the ground but not a murmur from her attacker.

Blinking her eyes quickly she lifted a hand to rub them, spun, light on her heels, alert with each and every sense for further aggression, but none came. Able to see clearly now she looked around, saw her attacker sitting motionless before her, knife back in his hand, face blank, eyes fixed on her every move.

She returned his scrutiny with equal composure. He did not seem to offer any further threat to her, yet she had the feeling that beneath that glassy exterior lurked a soul more than capable of killing her in cold blood if it had to.

Glass. It was a good way to describe him. His eyes were an icy grey-blue, his hair palest blonde, almost white, his skin so colourless that she thought he could not have been out here long, for the heat from the glare in the sky was intense and would surely reduce such a fair-skinned individual to ashes in a few days. Yet, curiously, the dishevelled state of his clothing, a simple blue shirt and black trousers, indicated that he had been here for many weeks.

"I have waited a long time for you to come. You are one of the others." His voice took her by surprise, so smooth and free of inflection that it could have come not from a living being but rather a robot in organic form.

"Others?" Why did the human use this word? Surely he knew that *he* was one of the Others? "What do you mean, others?"

"Demons," he said, still making no move to attack. "You are stronger than the pale one. She died very easily."

"The pale one?" Sahla struggled with this for a moment, then realisation struck her and she shot to her feet, lunged for him, screaming her pain and loss to this horribly empty world. "You! You killed Dil-ya!"

He moved like lightning when aroused and the spear of darkness she sent at him shattered the rock he had been sitting on to a million shards before she noticed he was gone. The knife appeared at her throat a second later.

"Dil-ya. The Goddess' name." His breath was a flutter against her skin, his hand a nauseating caress along the curve of her neck. "How intriguing. You have names. It is possible you could be the demon the console says you are, or one of them, burnt from years of sin. That you started out all the same. It is viable that you created us to atone. That flash of darkness, I consider, was a power of the demon-gods. These computations may be correct, demon of mine."

Sahla's mind raced. What was this human talking about? Demons, gods, consoles? Yet the tales, Kai-ya's tales, was it not possible that the humans had come to think of those they had feared and murdered as gods and demons?

"Too late. I consider it best you join your Goddess. I have many more of you and your creations to destroy, time with you is limited."

His grip tightened, the knife dented her skin. "Wait," she gasped. "You said you have many more of us to kill, but you don't. I'm the last, kill me and you'll never know my secrets."

"What?" The knife stopped, but did not back off.

"You want it, don't you?" She could not let up now, spoke quickly, feverishly; her life depended on it. It seemed the humans were indeed as mad as Dil-ya had always said. "The power of these things you call demon and god? Don't you know we're a dying breed? The pale one you killed was the last of her kind; I'm the last of mine. Kill me if you want, but think what you'll lose if you do."

"The last?"

"Yes."

"How do I know this is correct?"

"You said you had waited a long time for me. Why do you think that was?"

"Yes." His hold loosened. The knife's edge shifted. "You are correct. How inconvenient." He let her go. She moved quickly away, watched him warily.

For a long time he remained still, head down, yet she did not dare move. The land round about was steep and smooth; there was nowhere to run, nowhere to hide.

"You are the last." He looked up at her, gripping the knife—which was merely a shard of metal she saw now—so tightly that blood ran in little runnels to the ground. She opened her mouth to say something, then he put the metal away and she saw that his hand was clean and unmarked.

"You are the last," he said, unaware of her shock. "Demon or god, there is a viable possibility of both. Out here," he waved his arm at the grey sky and land, "I have . . . learnt this. The console never told the whole truth. But you are here and you did make us and you did cast us out into this hell to suffer and for that you will watch while I finish things." He dropped his head again. She caught her breath. She had been right, the humans had somehow managed to twist things so that they were not to blame for the devastation they had wrought. Something akin to anger billowed within her and she raged and cried at Kai-ya for sending her here to help such as these, these who did not deserve her help. Her help. Where had been the help for her through all those lonely childhood years? She bit her lip in shame. Kai-ya and Dil-ya had always been there for her, hadn't they? But what of this last year? And what of her real mother, her own people who treated her as little more than a leper? A child needed more than fearful tolerance and considered lessons to grow. She choked back a sob. To think such things, how could she? She a shaman, keeper of a race's soul, helper of the weak, succourer of the dead and dying. How could she dare to have a thought for herself?

She raised her gaze from the ground to find him studying her again. A cold shiver ran through her. Who was the monster here?

"My name is Darbo." He lifted a hand, took hers. "And you are. . . ?"

"Sahla." She laughed, a high, manic little laugh, overcome by the ridiculousness of it all. Somewhere overhead a crow's lonely caw echoed her trembling soul.

"Sahla. Good. Teach me your power. I would use it to kill your creations."

It was so reasonable a request that she laughed again.

The caw, when next it came, seemed farther away.

Chapter Thirteen

Fainan giggled tentatively. He felt a little strange. The plants were growing all around him. Masses of them. The roses had been fine, he supposed, and even the spiky trees, but now there were millions of them, others too, so many colours and varieties that he sat, lost and cocooned, within a curling bower of green and purple tendrils, gently nodding buds and fatly bursting seed pods.

Sssssssssssssssssss, the little snake hissed at his feet and his giggle turned into a chortle, a great, yelping guffaw full of irony and self-directed humour.

"Oh yes," he muttered to himself. "Oh yes, indeed. My vine is definitely dysfunctional." *Ssssssssssssssssssss.* "Snakes. Good. Good." He rocked backwards and forwards, hands wrapped around knees, fingers drumming. "Snakes in my brain, in the screen in my brain, escaping, all the images escaping, like the woman, the woman in the flower." *Sssssssssssssssssss.* "The woman!" He leaped to his feet, thorns tearing at his hair and skin, shredding his shirt and trousers so that he was half unclothed. "She came with the bird and the snake, but now only the snake is here. Where's the bird? What has happened to it, to her? Oh no . . ." He buried his head in his hands, bramble-snared limbs bleeding unheeded. "What's happening to me? I'm becoming like they used to be, the others, before we learned to live. What was it? Madness . . . that was it, they went mad through fear of death. But we've conquered that now, surely. So what is there to fear? What is this in my head? Is any of it real?"

He looked up at the jungle creeping ever farther up the walls of his apartment, noticed the droplets of water begin to fall from the misty air, groaned a little, debated whether or not to start laughing again.

"It looks real." He reached out a hand, felt the shiny smoothness of flowering cactus leaves, a green so deep he felt he could swim in it. "It feels real." He plucked a satin-cerise flower, sniffed its upthrust petals, cradled its attention-seeking head in gentle hands.

The first human to hold a flower for six centuries.

A tear ran down Fainan's cheek, the flower shuddered and soaked it up.

"So beautiful," Fainan murmured. "You're so beautiful. So much in a perfectly tiny form. Why did I never see you before? How could I have missed you?"

Another tear watered his long-lost love.

"How did I live without you?"

A tiny pool gathered in the flower's heart, a face swam into view. Hers. This time he was not afraid, this time he looked long and hard, studied the intricacies of a face that seemed only the female, softer version of his, so that in the end he knew not whom he looked upon.

Sssssssssssssssssss.

Fainan tore his gaze away from his perfect flower to see the scarlet snake approaching him across the moss-covered floor. Its forked tongue flickered softly in and out and its bright black eyes watched him with a brilliant intelligence.

Fainan looked back at the flower, then down at the snake. He knelt before it and lay down the flower with all due reverence. He stepped away from his offering, watched as the snake grew in size till its coils could have wrapped him thrice around the waist. Glowing a red so radiant it seemed to hold the blood of the world in its smooth-scaled body the snake eased up to the flower, gazed hypnotically within, nodded its flattened head and circled around it, encircling but never crushing the fragile petals and their female pool.

Finally it stopped, rested, hissed and curled, looked up at Fainan out of liquid eyes, reflected his face back to him in endless shiny shadows.

You search for her?

It took Fainan several minutes to realise the snake spoke to him in thoughts not words. When he did it did not seem at all unusual.

"Yes," he said. "I think I do, though I didn't know it until now."

Good, the snake said. *So do I. So do we all.*

"I don't understand. What do you mean, we're all looking for her? And who is she? I see her in my head, but I don't know how."

The images you see in your head are dreams. All humans have them, but they have become lost, just as I, just as she.

"But you're not lost now. I see you here, before me. Or are you a 'dream' too?"

Dream or no, I am no less real whatever you choose to believe. Yet it is the beliefs that damage me. This is why I have been lost for so long.

"Belief? You mean that no one can see you unless they believe in you?"

It is the way they see me that changes.

"And is that why you're lost? Why she's lost? Because no one sees you properly anymore?"

Yes, Fainan. You see me truly. But you are alone, so alone. Even she forgets me, the true me. Ah, I fear for her, out there with him and my wisdom so far from her. The bird went with her, the ever-faithful bird, but even that she finds hard to heed.

"She's in danger?" Fainan felt something run through him then, a true emotion. Fear. It must always come first, he thought. "Please, who is she? Tell me, I have to know."

She is part of you, part of us all and she must be loved, finally, for once and all, or all is doomed. The snake's eyes closed for a moment and, incredibly, it seemed to be mourning. *If you want her you must spread me through this city of yours. You must bring back life so that when she comes here she will come to her home.*

"But I want to go to her now, tell me where . . ."

No! The snake rose up, hissed, snapped its tongue; a single drop of water spilled from the flower and Fainan felt an almost uncontrollable urge to lick it up. *You must stay. This city alone can be saved, the other I fear will die, as will you if you meet them now. No, take this, these plants, all of me, take them to those who dwell alongside you, make them live again and, if you must, sweet-talk her in your dreams, tell her what I cannot till she sees me again.*

"Tell her? Tell her what? I don't even know her name. What would you have me do? Do you know how big this city is? How many people live here?"

Do you?

The snake smiled and dived into the pool, water roared, lifted the flower on a scintillant tsunami, caught up plants and human alike, smashed them against the door and out into an echoing wilderness of metal pipes and weary silver vines where the wave fell in endless waterfalls and Fainan clung for dear life to the bars across his city.

Chapter Fourteen

Sahla's head flicked up, her eyes brightened momentarily. Was that water she heard? For countless hours she had been walking along so deeply lost in thoughtful misery that she was scarcely aware of the ground beneath her. Darbo had said nothing more, just led her on towards an unknown destination, and this unnerved her, especially after his earlier request and her own reaction to it. His silence, teamed with the colourless devastation of the sacred mountain that, in its dreams she knew, was so rich and vibrant, brought her almost to her knees. She longed only to return to her home, to taste and feel and smell once more. Out here in the land the Others had destroyed there was nothing and she wondered how they could live, how they could want to live, in a world so dead. The sound of running water awoke something desperate within her and she pulled away from Darbo's guiding hand, instinct, intuition, leading her over the wasteland they traversed.

Darbo did nothing to stop her, merely followed in her tracks to see what was of such interest to her.

Sand shimmied beneath her frantically questing feet, seeming pitifully glad of a chance to move at last, a chance to prove its life to the world. Sahla could understand that, though she wondered if she would ever know such fulfilment.

The land dropped quickly away beneath her feet and she would have fallen had not Darbo suddenly been there to haul her back. It seemed he did not wish to lose his prize quite so pointlessly and for a moment the urge to wrench herself from his hands and throw herself into the gap that yawned beneath was strong.

She did not. Life, however derided, was still too sweet to relinquish. Perhaps a fear of leaving before she had fully experienced she knew not what held her back. Perhaps the view that greeted her gaze spoke of promises she had never been made. Perhaps she heard a faraway caw. Who knows how the strands of fate are woven?

"Oh," she murmured as she looked, fed upon that which she saw, felt the memory of a precious wind blow through her. Darbo looked at her askance as her hair shivered and lifted, then he, too, looked at the scene before them.

A gorge so wide and deep it seemed cleft from the body of a universe sheered away far below. Deep red rock sank in jagged troughs and swells for thousands of feet, striated with boundary lines of ages so long lost that only dreams remembered them. Its foot could not be seen, lost in blue-tinged shadows. Here and there solitary teeters and overhangs clung to a tentative life, etched in waves, spirals and meanders from the raging waters that had once kissed their flanks, the mischievously destructive hands of nature that respected none save the spirits of change.

Lost in a private whirl of biting air Sahla saw only the mountains that bordered the land of journeys she had visited so often in her life. She fancied that maybe somewhere down there raced the river she only thought she'd heard, that Dil-ya and Zinni, Hi-ya and all the others she had known, ran wild and free, feasting on the succulent delights of the dream dead, shying from the darkest of all nights at the forest's centre, the dark that held the ultimate knowledge, the dark that shattered you, tore you apart by the flesh and the bones and threw you roughly back together again, wiser, stronger, yet curiously vulnerable, out into a world that may or may not be more real than this. The death she had so tentatively visited to earn her rights as a dream travelling shaman.

"An experiment." Darbo's voice chilled her wandering thoughts, did not yet break them into shards of this reality. "Your dark powers. I am intrigued. I ponder the viability that they will save you should I push you over the edge."

The wind dropped, it perchance never was. Sahla turned, a whirl of curling hair and gaping mouth, fell from the ledge in a beautiful continuation, scream of betrayal skirling the heights of the spot she had occupied, flailing the cheeks of the one that leaned over, raced from view, watching her, watching her die-fly.

"No!" Arms snapped out, scrabbled and lashed at rock that wailed past her at an alarming rate, those achingly lovely views of ages past now mocking her feeble attempts to save a life that could never match even a fraction of theirs.

"No!" Images flickered through the dark of her mind, she settled on one, the crow, changed in her mind, her body shrieking its protestation, a shapechange in this reality, what nonsense! what whimsical sense! and yet the bloodied fingers, the torn nails, the battering speed, all told it that yes, whimsical it may be, but so it would have to be, or it would never be again.

"No . . ."

Black wings filled her vision, she did not know whether they were hers, or another's. For a single timeless moment she hung in the air, then her feelings, her thoughtforms, changed and she soared for a while, free and delighting, before simply alighting and ducking her head to clean a niggling feather.

The change back, when it came, brought the recognition of the road a moment before the shock set in.

Far below it curved, ribbon-like from up so high, yet she could still see the winking of the gleaming stones set all along its centre. Just like the roads her people had built all those millennia ago. To find one here, in a land beyond saving, made her want to cry.

"Good." The voice made her jump, sent a black-feathered presence skittering for the safety of the sky. "You've found the path. Something informed me that you would."

"Darbo." The name was half a sigh, half a curse. Could she push him as he had pushed her? And yet she needed him, didn't she? To find the Others, in more ways than one. And who amongst the dead would welcome her again if she sent this one to them? Did the Others dream even when dead? An experiment, perchance . . . Her hands itched. He looked at her, climbing quickly, impossibly lithe, ridiculously out of place with his pale skin and hair in this place of dried and crusted blood-rock. Did her face betray her emotions? Did he see the wish for death in her eyes? Whose death did he see?

His hand closed over hers with infinite unfeeling care. Inspected it.

"No feathers." He turned it over, dropped it, reached for the other. "So quickly come. So quickly gone. A shape summoned from nowhere. Sent to nowhere? Possible. A new experiment for later, when I find the city you have found the path to."

"City?" Too late, the chance was gone. Had probably never been. Somehow she felt that they two were meant to be together. What a poisonously sweet fairy tale ending. "What city?"

"Clever demon. You're testing me. If any should know it's you." He pulled on her hand, almost dragged her from her tiny ledge. A whole world swam for a moment and the glance downward cost her much courage, more than she had to spare. "Now come with me. The climb will last as long as it does and once the bottom is reached the end begins." He tilted his head, considered his speech. "Yes, I like that. This play with words is most intriguing, it eases the . . . eases the . . . "

"What? Eases what?" Her turn for the tilt of the head now, a hope for something human in this one that pretended to the title.

His gaze snapped to her for a shocking instant and she saw a hatred more violent for its unknowing briefness rear before her. "Nothing," he said, turned away from her. "There is nothing. Nothing at all." He turned away. His next words were clear and toneless, heartbreakingly so. "That's why we're climbing. Climbing, climbing, climbing. To begin the end. Come on." He pulled her free of her precarious hold and out screaming into a gap that filled her next few days with a constant terror that next time she fell the crow would not come.

Chapter Fifteen

"Have you seen him?" Daviki felt like screaming. His face seemed to grow a new line for each and every time he was met with a negative response. "Have you seen the Pale One? Have you seen where he goes?"

Hundreds of familiar/unfamiliar faces shook numbed incomprehension for answer. Daviki had tried not to notice when their faces shimmered and changed before him, playing through a myriad of features, his wife's, his father's, his brother's, all long, long dead, before settling on those that pained him most.

Sahla's.

At first, as he led his oh so disturbingly changed clan along the restless beach, he had tried to convince himself that he was imagining things. That those features were not there, that they did not slip from face to face, that they did not ultimately seem to slide from flesh and skitter off into the air, frolicking like so many transient ghosts, teasing him with his uncertainty, tormenting him with the thought that this world was populated only by the viragos of his own imagination. Indeed, when he asked the others what they saw they reaffirmed his views that he was hallucinating from lack of food, water, sleep, peace of mind . . . whatever. For the first few days their bland smiles and ingratiating platitudes soothed him, he walked each night, alone amidst a vast spread of whispering people, and smoothed the shattered skins of his drum, fought hard to find solace in the symbols of his life etched around the ancient frame. Symbols of his life and how many other musicians? He thought perhaps he saw some of their faces flicker momentarily across those who came to bring him what meagre food they found. It was a strange world, this new one the sacred mountain's dreams had birthed. All night long could be heard the cries of birds and the roars of beasts, drifting on an unchangeable wind. The sea echoed to the splish-splash of remembered fishing boats, the creak of heavy nets. Sounds, tormenting sounds, breeze-blown leaves, scents drifting, formed from a thousand wishful minds. Nothing was there. No life stirred, just the hollow spectres of a world long gone. It was almost as though this was all the sacred mountain could manage now, too tired of it all to continue any longer. What food that was found may well have been image alone for the sustenance it gave. Daviki knew it was only the sodden footsteps they followed, the living essence of the Pale One, that brought brief life to this place. Whilever they followed him they would not starve, but neither would they live. Yet what else could they do? What else could he do? The only leadership he could offer this faceless people was to follow the one who rejected them. He wondered many a time why they came so meekly. Did they know what he did not? Why did they not tell him? Why such pretence?

It was after the twelfth night, when his group of miserable Dark Ones had swelled to nearly five thousand, that he began to realise they lied to him. Each of them purposefully carried Sahla's features on their treacherously mobile faces and the world would soon be full of nothing else. Even though there be a million visions of her they would never ever be enough, they were his punishment for loving too jealously and soon they would be mobile no more, soon they would watch him constantly.

He thought then that this was hell and buried his face in skinny brown arms, moistening old withered skin with the tears of a misty, long-forgotten youth spent in a land that, for him and so many like him, had never been.

*   *   *

Kai-ya saw too much while he walked and so kept his gaze pinned to the ground, to the memory of earth he had once truly walked, trusted it as he had then to keep him safe.

For a while it did. He managed nearly a fortnight's travel of endless one foot in front of another, of wraith-haunted nights spent thrashing and sobbing at the scene of countless deaths. The true-seeing dreams that had told him Dil-ya's sacrifice was worth something were shown as hollow lies and the bitterness he felt, the hatred of self, sometimes threatened to overwhelm him. He could handle it when it was only in his mind—at least he thought he could—it was when it began to leak out into the struggling dreamland that it all became too much. When it started to make its mark on sand and sea, lifting tornadoes of grain and foam into shudderingly recognisable shapes, when the wind began to sound like the voices nightly heard, then he began to worry and quicken his pace, desperate for the end of a journey he knew in his heart of hearts he had only just begun.

Which path shall I take? he mused when the sand threw up those long ago bright-starred roads. He did not even question from whence they came, merely took it for granted that a mountain too exhausted to dream for itself was now creeping into his own mind and taking up what it found there.

The left hand, he chuckled to himself. There was a first time for every-thing. Zinni had always teased him about his lack of balance.

He walked slowly forwards. The glowing stones gleamed and winked at him, the sun's bright light captured in their depths and transformed into something tearfully different. Entrancing.

They wound off over the sand, these three paths, and he could almost fancy that he saw the spires at their end. Maybe these paths were the old pilgrim's ways; maybe they would take him to the camps that lay at the foot of the great machines. The machines that so enhanced the sacred mountain's life. For they did not live in the spires, they never had, had never been meant to. They tended them, worshipped them, fed them with their love of life. Living next to them, travelling amongst them, was a joy both Dark and Pale had once experienced so many thousands of years ago.

Back, he thought. *It's what you want, isn't it?* He did not know to whom he spoke, maybe the land, maybe the flame. He missed both. *The future is born of the past, my friend, but you have no past now, do you? There are too few of us to remember it for you. The Dark Ones have no memory of you, all they know are the tales, the wistful images held in heads that see only a pale shadow of your former glory. Dreams can never make up for reality, though reality cannot exist without them.*

He smiled. Overhead the sun hissed and flared brightly for a moment. A violent streamer of orange-gold light stretched down from the heavens and touched him on the head, blessed him with a corona of his own.

Effulgent, he took a step forward. The left hand path bowed in the middle, sinking inwards to a dazzling darkness that welcomed the light and the one it brought, melded the two into one, encouraged his step down into the underworld and closed seamlessly above him with a soft sigh.

*   *   *

No time and all time later a wash of skirling Sahla's danced on Kai-ya's living grave, weaving the day and night into a silken cloak, waiting to lay it down once more.

Chapter Sixteen

Kelefeni's veins danced. It was the only word she could summon to describe it. Her single sheet lay like a pale cloak atop her, shaking in time to the sensations quaking through her body. Indeed it seemed as though a thousand grave worms roiled across her belly and she stared with fixed, unblinking eyes away from the shrouded form she no longer dared to notice.

Her body.

Unusual, she thought. *That before it was merely a tool to me, something to cleanse and exercise, to consign to the automated vine, but now ... now ...*

She had awoken an hour ago, drifting slowly from the empty darkness of sleep to the carefully controlled daylight her apartment window allowed to fall in perfect diffusion across her white-tiled floor. She had not risen, however, merely remained in bed assessing her surroundings.

How was it that she had lived here for so long and not noticed how colourless it was? The walls, the floor, the ceiling, the bed she lay upon. The console and chair across the room. Even the screens were white. Her eyes shifted slightly, irises disappearing so that only the whites remained. So much white, so sparkling. How then could it be so dull?

Her legs juddered madly and she was helpless to stop them. She had been all morning. She had not dared to peel back her cover to witness the veins waltz defiantly before her gaze, had considered it, but had not found a legitimate reason to do so. She did not want to look upon her body's protest and so instead remained safely locked in her head where she could stare out at nothing in particular and so remain immune to this and everything else.

Again her gaze shifted, eyes lifting up in her head, farther then was, perhaps, possible. A tendril of nausea overcame her, a wave of aching pain, like a band encircling her head. Zigzag lines flashed at her peripheral vision and she tried to catch them but could not for they tap-danced out of her way with mocking alacrity.

Colours came to replace the virgin plain of her existence, exploded with shocking violence, made her cry out as the newest shakings invaded her body, snapped her in half and threw her from bed to floor where she curled in a childlike ball, wrapped her hands around her eyes and stared at the veins that waved at her and drifted from fingers to brain and filled it with blinding, flashing colours.

"Aaaaaaaaaaaaaahhhh!" Kelefeni scream-moaned, shook her head, fell on her side, limbs out of control. She tried to bring them back, caught one, then two, her legs, forced them beneath her, struggled to a standing position, staggered towards her console, horribly heavy head supported by a hand, another appendage won back.

She reached the console, entered her password, watched with almost worshipping eyes as the screens hummed to life and the colours, thankfully, seemed to stop their dance and return ownership of her mind once more.

Sighing, she sank into her seat, wary of limbs that had so recently betrayed her. Was it over now? Finally over?

The main screen hissed, the console whirred, clacked angrily, as though a million beetles battered armoured legs at prison walls. Kelefeni looked up, hand poised to click her console to better temper.

Demons leered at her, a hundred of them, thickly muscled, dark skinned, black horns upon their heads, blood smeared across their maws, too-bright light in their smoking eyes.

"No!" She flung the mouse as though it had burned her, pulled away. Her chair toppled; she fell in a vast whipcrack snapping of plastics, bruised her forgotten back on the hard tiles, felt numbing pain only briefly, uncomprehendingly, but not for much longer.

Flat on the floor, head canted gratingly upward, she saw the other screens blink into life. A thousand demons now, all wrapped about in vines. She stared, aghast. No human should see this, the vine inside their bodies, stripped bare and flailing, viscously thick and red, knobbed and curling around skin, hair, eyes, demons caressing and sucking, blood dribbling from life-giving machine to eager, devilish mouth.

"No." She climbed to her feet, hand sneaking unconsciously to her spine. "No." This was not happening. She refused to entertain it. Stared stubbornly at the vile screens, willing them back to inertness.

The demons were one. No black skin, no horns, merely one human face, as pale and colourless as the room that enclosed her.

She gasped. The scene shot away from her, background rushing, dizzying. His face stayed the same, growing bigger, grey-blue ice eyes staring straight into hers as though they could see her. A city of towering red spires appeared behind him, she wondered what and where in the instant before the vines sliced from the ground that encased those spires and tore them down in huge jagged shards of black-edged rock and spiralling whiteness and still the face, the solitary human face stared back at her, seemed to mouth her name.

"Kelefeni." It filled the room, vibrated it and her bones both. "Sweet Kelefeni, so sweet. I'm coming for you. Coming precious one. You can teach me so much, so much suffering, so much pain, denied for so long. Do you not love it, Kelefeni? Do you not want it? Open up for me, sweet one, I am coming, coming for you. Not so long now."

Kelefeni's jaw dropped, she backed away, shaking her head. The screens grew bigger, crude colours filling the whiteness she had earlier questioned. His face fattened and bulged, tongue licking parched, cracked lips, breaking through the fragile curvature of glass and entering her domain, opening his mouth wide for her.

"No!" Kelefeni turned away, thrust up a hand, the demon's jaws closed on it, she screamed, her veins wailed and flapped, trailed off into the space her hand had once occupied, spraying her blood out onto the floor in a vicious dance of joy.

She fell to her knees, holding her mutilated arm close to her body, soaking her pristine gown steadily scarlet.

"Oh god," she murmured and the metal band around her head returned, clamped about her and sent her vibrantly shaking body spinning to the floor and oblivion.

*   *   *

The head nodded at remembrance of its name and sank back into the screen with a satisfied smile.

Chapter Seventeen

Sahla wondered why Darbo smiled when she caught the gauzily spinning seed in outstretched and wondering hand. It was only a momentary flicker upon his lips, but so unusual that she could never have missed it. For just that single instant it transformed him, made his face light up and his eyes sparkle. In that solitary second she felt such love for him that she almost dropped the seed. Then it was gone and the cold blank mask was back. She wondered if she had in actual fact seen it or whether it was just a remembrance of someone else, far, far away.

"This thing you have caught." He approached her, caught up her hand, peeled the fingers back. "I have not seen its like out here before today. What is it?"

She looked up at him, unable to believe he did not know. When she did not answer he lifted his gaze to meet hers. Glaciers they may be but they drew her in all the same and she pulled her hand away, closed the seed in safety and dropped it into her pocket.

"It's a seed," she snapped, angry for some reason. Perhaps because of the fact that they had been travelling this same road at the bottom of the gorge for several days now and still she had not managed to spark a single conversation with him. Indeed, this question was the first he had spoken to her since they had awoken that morning. *How can I save them?* she thought, turning away from him. *They have forgotten even the joy of speech.*

"Seed." He tried the unfamiliar word for size, pulled her roughly back when she would have walked away.

"Don't!" She slapped his hand away, turned, glared at him. She was tall for a Dark One, stood nearly eye to eye with him. Above them bloody cliffs slit to infinity, made them seem all too young and half-grown by comparison. "Don't do that again."

"This seed," he said, unconcerned by her threatening tone, her stance. She wondered if he even noticed. "This seed is part of the dark power you wield. Now you will tell me of it. The second city is close. The spires. I would use it to destroy them."

"No." Sahla grew tired of his ordering her about like a child. She had gone so far, but no more. "No, I will not tell you. Why should I? You've told me nothing. Every time I ask you where we're going you ignore me. Every time I ask you where the rest of your kind are you ignore me. In fact, Darbo, you have barely acknowledged my existence save when you feel an experiment coming on. Your lack of interest in me is quite astounding to say I am one of your goddesses."

Darbo stood quietly till she finished then raised a hand and lay it on her chest. She looked down, almost backed away, realised he did no harm, merely . . . felt?

"Curious." He pulled his hand away, touched it to his own chest. "Such a thunder within. My own heart is so much more placid."

"That's your problem," Sahla struggled with her anger. He was such a curious paradox.

"My problem." He looked up. "Created by you, demon-goddess. I already know of you, why need I ask more?"

"Because what you know is wrong, you idiot!" She stabbed her arms at the air with all the violence of a lifetime's frustration. A strand of sweat-soaked hair fell into her eyes and she tossed it away with an exasperated flick of her head. "I don't know how such a supposedly intelligent race could have come up with such a ridiculous idea. Gods and demons! Your ego is so over-inflated you can't be simply born of flesh and blood, can you? Oh no, you have to invent a whole mythology of divine intervention to explain your sorry little lives. Well, you're wrong! You were born of us, like any other creature, in blood and sweat and tears and then you turned on us and wiped us out. If any deserve to die it's you, and here I am trying to save you! Hah, save you! Save what? There's nothing left to save, for all I know you're the only fool left alive and here I am following you all the way across the desert. Damn it, what am I doing here?" She laughed and twirled madly, stumbling drunkenly, almost falling. "What am I doing? What am I doing? They sent me away, they sent me away. Oh but I'm not surprised, not surprised, never surprised. I'm always the expendable one, aren't I? Always the one to be left alone. Always feared, always hated, but never loved, oh no, never loved."

"Who told you that?"

"Told me what?" She stopped, unaware of the tears running freely down her cheeks.

"This tale."

"Tale?"

"Yes. Tale. As much a one as mine."

"What?"

"I, too, have a tale. It belongs to the history of these humans you so casually created. Blood, tears, divine intervention. It matters not. You made us, but you did not think. Who ever asks to be born? We cannot, it remains to the parent to decide the right or wrong. And did you?" He laughed hollowly and twirled in emotionless mimicry of her. "Oh I am not the only one left. There are many many more. Two cities of high spires, full of humans who can never die, full of your children who cannot live, full of pointlessness. You created a life, you who lurk in the darkness, you brought us into being and abandoned us, you never taught us what to do with the gift you so thoughtlessly gave and that is where we go, to the cities to wipe out the mistake you made and ease the . . . " He stopped, looked at her with something approaching slyness. "Have I told you enough now, demon? Have I given you food for thought? A veritable feast? Celebrations of how facts can twist and turn like the seed you caught and hide now from my worthless eyes. Oh, yes, I do so like this play of words, this dance of symbols. What games we can enjoy you and I while we watch the ashes of a million bones float by overhead." He pulled her close, pressed her bewildered head against his steadily beating chest. "You will help me, won't you?" He stroked her hair; awkward gestures, as stiff as his words. "Your mistake, Sahla, your mistake. I'm only rectifying your mistake. You'd like that, wouldn't you? I know you would, you hate them as much as I. See what they've done to the world. Your little seed is oh so lonely, Sahla. It doesn't have to be. They sent you away, Sahla, but they sent you to me. Sweet one, precious one, you belong to me now."

"No," Sahla sobbed her misery into his chest.

"Tell me, Sahla." He picked up her hands, kissed them like a suitor of old. She had to fight hard to still that mad laughter again. "When the moon rises high this night, tell me. For the sake of our children, tell me."

Sahla laughed in his face and he crowed hollow, empty delight to the sky and held her in the sudden shadow cast by the gliding wings of a lone and melancholy bird.

Chapter Eighteen

Birds. There were birds in here. Fainan looked on them with wonder from where he crouched in the heart of the spire's metal network. Their cries were by turns mournful and sweet, their wings a constant rush of half-heard air. For each colour of the rainbow there seemed a living representation, a flurry of whisper-soft feathers and moist, gleaming eyes. They spun and whirled amongst the tubes and pipes, diving and curling playfully, momentarily alighting on innumerable trees before taking off again with loud squawks, sometimes flashing so close that he could feel their wings touch his face.

More remarkable than this was the jungle, the waterfall that poured down the middle of the spire in an endless jewel-blue tumult and disappeared into echoing emptiness, casting great clouds of fine fragrant mist into the air, drenching him to the skin in moments. The water flowed from his room. He could see fecund darkness beyond, had a feeling that console and screen no longer existed in there. Every so often startling chitters and chirrups would sound from within and he would jump and rethink his plan to venture in.

Farther up a different world grew. He could just see it if he climbed to his feet and swung out into the gap, hanging grimly on to the piping, for if he should fall there would be a long time to scream before he hit the bottom. He knew this instinctively, even though he had never been out here and did not even know for sure where here was.

The world above him was dry, crackling, yet damply moist in places. The trees were tall and spreading, gentle boughs that one could perchance sit in on a sunny afternoon an age away. Their leaves were green, dark or pale, silvery in places, the limbs that held these pliant and swaying. He thought he saw a glimmer of water snake through rich dark earth and wondered how this could be, how a land could grow in mid-air, how water could run straight and true when it should fall like that before him.

Tired of sitting and staring, this world drew him on, he reached out to a pipe with a beautiful silver vine twined about it, a vine that seemed, until recently, to have hovered long over the chasm of death.

Up, up, he clambered, tattered remains of clothes plastered to his skin, hair limp and dripping, skin slick, fingers fighting for grip. This world, this world, he had to see it, had to be it. The waterfall raged beside him and he could see directly into his room now. No sign of his earlier life existed and he saw the vines and branches grow inch by inch before him, filling the void, blooming with flowers, nudging their way oh so slowly out and along, sniffing at the next door in the great round, concealing grey metal beneath virile leaves, hoping for welcome and a new home.

Fainan knew that he would have many doors to open for this new life, but that would come later, right now he had to see the land above, had to sit with it for a while, in contemplation, meditation, learn a purpose in what he did.

He eased into this new world with a small sigh, head breaking through a tumble of ancient leaves and scuttling insects. He planted his hands to either side, felt solid ground beneath and heaved himself up to fall face first into a land of deliciously busy smells and dappled light.

Life here was quieter, but it was there. All around him the trees wavered branches, the ground rustled, water lapped, light peered occasionally. He thought he caught a glimpse of something moving in a tree and looked up just in time to see a small furry creature with a long brushy tail bound sinuously among the branches and freeze so suddenly that he could almost believe he'd never seen a thing.

Birdsong drifted down from the trees' tops and his thoughts turned to the bird he had seen back in his apartment. He had seen it only that once and this made him fear again, for he knew that its fate and that of the woman were intertwined like the vines that mingled with the small and beautiful wood.

He wandered slowly, leaves kissing his skin, feet sinking deep into pliant ground, seeing her face in his mind's eye once more. What was it the snake had called such things? Dreams. Could you have waking dreams, then? Daydreams?

His steps brought him to the glittering stream he had seen from below. Branches dipped to taste of the water while dust twirled incandescently in hazy streamers of light and tiny insects careered madly, snapped from life by sudden-leaping fish. Silver grey rocks covered with moss that was surprisingly soft and dry to his touch peered up out of the water, so clear he could see the bed below, strewn with smooth round pebbles and endless sticks and leaves, maybe even a coin here and there.

Coins? Ancient means of acquiring goods, long ago become redundant.

"But you grant wishes, too, don't you?" he mused to himself and kneeled down, plunged his hand into water so cold it reminded him he was alive and pulled one out.

"Whose were you, I wonder? Did you come true?"

He looked at the face, all noble female features and regal bearing, then brought back his arm and flung it far far out where it twirled in the air, caught in a shaft of golden light and fell with the smallest of splashes to begin the ripples that snared him in a web of sleep and pulled him down to the ground to dream more deeply for a while.

The wood was the same but not the same. Darker, deeper, more intense, full of large, prowling golden felines that a whisper told him were lions, but only cubs, still so much to grow, to learn. That they were out of time, out of place, out of bounds, no humour spoilt the perfect jest. They came to him and sniffed, gazed with wide unblinking eyes, accepted him. He felt joy rise in his chest, quickly mounting to fear when she appeared and they bounded towards her.

"Sahla!"

The name. A name he'd heard—spoken?—so many times.

She saw him, closer now, walking with the beasts, smiling, calm, safe.

And beautiful.

Oh not in the way that countless books he had never read betold, but in a way that made him want to be awake instead of dreaming. A way that made the slight downturn of her mouth, her too-strong nose, her unruly, tangled hair and lanky limbs seem only the sweetest of sights to him. A bundle of imperfections that made being human seem the best and only thing in the world.

And yet not. For she was a mixture of all things and he saw in those impossibly indigo eyes a knowledge of a land and life he could never know, and in the umber skin a cast that was not entirely his, though he was only slightly paler. And those limbs, too awkward for a being that should naturally be this way.

"Sahla." At home in neverland she came to him and he pulled her close, kissed her in desperation, held her glorious hair in his hands as though it were a net he could cast to keep her forever.

Kisses grew and grew and he did not want to free her, felt a pain burn hot and furious in his chest, felt that they were partners, cousins, brother, sister, had always been together, had been too long apart.

"You know me," he murmured. "Don't you?"

"Yes," she said and he wanted to peel her head away from his shoulder where it momentarily lay. Kiss her once more. "I do. But you've been gone so long I only ever saw you once before and I didn't know it was you."

"I'm sorry." And he was, because here and only here he knew what that meant. Here he knew and felt everything and it was wonderful.

"You'll go away again."

"No, I . . . "

She pulled away, looked up at him out of eyes too strong to ever have to bear tears. "Yes, you will. You'll have to."

Paths stretched away into the forest, each and every one a dark bare layering of earth, trees stepped back on crook-bowed roots to make way for them.

"Chhhoooosssssse," they hushed and Fainan caught her up, desperate to be alone with her, but every way he turned the path was blocked by people, people with a single face, a face of glass and ice and he knew this one, too. It laughed at him, at them, as they turned and darted, always caught, always pushed back, never alone, always with the hateful him and he screamed when he knew she was right and he had to go away. Had to leave her.

*   *   *

He woke and scared the animals with his grief.

Chapter Nineteen

Sahla woke abruptly with a cry on her lips that was shocking in its shrillness. Wondering, she raised a hand to her cheek, touched the tears that coursed from her eyes, remembered the cause of them. The strangely beautiful man with the twilight gaze and the hair so dark she saw countless images in its depths. How could a man like this remind her so strongly of Kai?

She heard a low mutter and looked up to see Darbo awake, too, sitting with his back toward her not so far away. He rocked gently backwards and forwards, seemed to be humming to himself. She felt a little shiver run through her that she had lain asleep and helpless while he was awake. She still found it strange to sleep through the night as he so vehemently insisted.

She climbed to her feet and approached him, drawn against her will, fighting against the terrible fascination he held for her.

He heard her, she knew by the sudden, almost imperceptible tensing of his shoulders, but he did not move, merely carried on with whatever he was doing, although the rocking seemed to gain in momentum slightly.

"Darbo." She whispered, it seemed the right thing to do, the nights were so quiet here, the air heavy, motionless, the moon luminescing nothing save emptiness and scattered rocks, countless shadowed holes like scars on a diseased face. "What are you doing?"

He didn't answer, merely held up a hand which was sliced nearly clean through from the delicate webbing between his middle fingers to his wrist, displayed it for a moment then took it back down to complete his job.

"Dammit! No!" She caught him by the shoulder, spun him round, stared aghast at the clotted blood pooling in his lap, the metal in his uninjured hand slick and black in the moonlight. "What the hell are you doing?" She snatched the knife from him, terrified and, bizarrely, ashamed, at the expression of complete detachment on his face. "What the hell are you doing?" she repeated, staring down at the knife, seeing the shreds of flesh it held and casting it away with a shudder of revulsion.

He made no attempt to staunch the bleeding and she kneeled before him, picked up his limp and unresisting hand, tore a rag from her shirt and wrapped the terrible wound with careless, clumsy haste, not wanting to see what he had done to himself again. The picture of the tendons and bones so horribly exposed was still too clear in her mind, she felt it always would be and cursed him even as that wave of shame overcame her again.

"Darbo." She looked into his face, lifted his chin, tried to force some response. "What did you think you were doing? Don't you even feel it? You almost cut your hand in half."

"No." His eyes refocused, shockingly, suddenly. His injured hand tightened around hers and she yelped, tried to pull away, fell backwards, he came with her, still holding on, straddled her like an unwelcome lover.

"No." He released her hand, thrust his own mangled appendage before her face, pulled at the bandages.

"Oh no," Sahla moaned, turned her head this way and that. He followed her with hand and eyes both, grabbed her chin and moulded his forehead to hers, pushed her down so hard that her neck shrieked.

"No, Sahla." His breath sighed across her lips, mouth grazing hers, touching, dancing along too-sensitive edges. "Not true. Look."

Her eyes flickered. She looked. The hand was whole.

"Impossible," she hissed through clenched teeth.

"No," he stroked her face with his uninjured hand. "Not impossible. Do you deny the evidence of your own eyes, Goddess?"

"Eyes can deceive."

He slid the hand along her body. She shuddered, quivered. Fear sparked within her.

And desire.

"Can this?" He touched her breast, squeezed the nipple tightly, painfully, exerting a force too powerful for one so shattered.

The hand moved, sliding downwards, she caught her breath, fingers parted her violently . . .

"No!" Sahla yelled, convulsed, threw him from her, sent him rolling over the rocks to fetch up against a jagged boulder where he rose to a crouch and remained, dust-covered and bloody. But whole. Looking at her. Watching, making her scream inside . . .

"You stay away from me! Just stay away, or so help me I'll make you wish you *had* cut your hand off!"

"Threats, precious one? Oh the games you play." He climbed to his feet, approached her again.

"Stay away," she warned him, searching the dark for an image to kill.

"You don't mean that, demon-Sahla. You have always desired your creations. Isn't that why you made them?"

"You sick bastard!"

"Sick? Sick?" He raised his arms to the air as though asking for some divine witness. "Who is the sick one here? Who desires whom?" His eyes narrowed. "I have no emotions, remember?"

The image shivered in her mind and Sahla grasped it greedily, slashed the air with hand and thought, cast a javelin of perfect ebony wood speeding towards him.

"Uh!" It took him high in the chest, knocked him from his feet, sent him staggering, falling, arms pinwheeling, legs kicking up clouds of dust.

He looked at the spear in his chest, laughed and settled to the ground abruptly.

Sahla stared at him for a moment, painfully aware of how alone she was.

She took a tentative step forwards.

The corpse moved.

"Shit!" She backed away. It moved again, or was she just imagining it?

The javelin stuttered and jiggled, working its way out of Darbo's body as though a swarm of tiny burrowing creatures scurried beneath it.

"Shit," she said again when the javelin fell with a soft clatter and the corpse stood up.

"You're going to have to do better than that, my dear," he said politely.

"How?" She kept her hands high in front of her chest, ready to . . . to do something . . . should he approach her again.

"How? Another test, demon dear? Very well. It is the vines. Or rather what we made of them. One of your inventions I assume. We took them from the walls of the spires and now we live forever. Nothing can kill us. Well . . ." he lifted his gaze as though remembering something. "One thing can." He looked back at her. "You look pale, Sahla. What is wrong?"

"Nothing." Sahla shook her head. *Kai*, she thought. *They took the vines; they tore them from their roots. No wonder the sacred mountain is dying. They've destroyed her, raped her, murdered her.* Then another thought. *You knew, didn't you? You knew and you never told me. Damn you! And damn them; And I am to save them? You sent me away for that? Hah! Think again, father who is no father of mine! I would rather kill them. All of them, for what they've done.*

"Is this all you can do?"

She looked up, saw him pointing at the javelin. Sickeningly, blood gleamed along its length.

"No." She wondered why she had been so afraid of the blood before. She remembered his earlier plea. "No, it isn't. That's the least of it, Darbo. I can do much more, so much more."

"Good." Darbo said. "I am glad." He picked the javelin up and tested the strength with his hands before snapping it with terrible ease. "Tell me more."

Sahla smiled and told him.

*   *   *

High above the sacred mountain, in a sky that belonged to many worlds, a lone crow circled once and parted its beak in silent cry. It banked over a cloud that had almost formed and flapped away to a land that blinked into existence before it, soaring down to find the one, the only one now, who could help them all.

Chapter Twenty

A small dark woman with an age-lined face and ragged dreadlocks lay sleep-waking in a bower of vines and bright coloured, velvet-scented flowers watching the crow fly in ever decreasing circles above her. It seemed the only shadow in a sky so blue as to be a child's idealistic drawing and the woman sighed in remembrance of smiling stars and closed her eyes again. The next time she opened them the sun had risen for one of the moments it so often aspired to in the land of the dreaming dead and cast its scintillant rays over the blue-black feathers of the bird that sat patiently on a swinging branch, waiting for her to acknowledge its existence.

"Well hello there." Zinni stretched lazily, welcoming the sun from her long ago pictures. One did not usually feel such intense warmth here; she would have to paint more often. She reached out an arm to the giant bird. It cocked its head at her, regarding her out of coal-glinting eyes before hopping onto the proffered perch.

"I haven't seen you in a long time, darling," she crooned to the bird, gently smoothing its flight feathers. "What brings you to me now, here in the land of the dead?"

The bird's head sank, it gazed deep into her eyes and Zinni returned the gaze in all seriousness. The two remained locked in silent communion for nearly an hour before Zinni shuddered and shook her head, reached up a finger to wipe away the tears she had not been aware she was crying.

"Oh dear," she murmured. "I must be getting old. This would never have affected me so before. Or mayhap I am too young. Who knows?"

The crow merely regarded her patiently and she laughed.

"Hah! No time for foolish old spirits such as I, darling. You'll have to forgive me; I've been away so long you see. Many generations have passed since I left. In fact, I think me you had best go there for your help, my beauty. You'll find another there seeking much the same."

The crow hopped from foot to foot and cawed harshly.

"Now don't give me that," Zinni scowled in amusement. "You know one is much the same as another. Besides, they'll all be expecting you, I'll make sure of that."

The crow stopped hopping and gave her a long calculating look before quickly taking wing.

"Damn bird," Zinni sighed. "I knew I should have listened to it back then. Oh well," she shrugged her shoulders and set to dreaming a new pattern into being, "there's a first time for everything."

* * *

Kai-ya walked a long time in the dark, moving through the earth that had swallowed him up, blind yet not groping, led along by the memory of a light he had once thought to understand. Images from his dreams overtook his mind. Sahla and the two men, the one pale the other dark, yet both human. They seemed too real to be merely part of his tortured imagination and more than once he thought he heard the echoes of conversations, saw and felt emotions that were not his own though he wished they were, and yes the violent ones, too. It had felt good to strike out at Daviki, good to walk away, to see the despair on their faces, to know he had it within his power to make someone feel, experience that. It had been too long since he had felt those shattering sensations, those instinctive urges of wanton lust and mindless rage that he and his people had so long fought to control. To still feel, yes, but to let it out only when and where required. And the requirements seemed to lessen with the years, didn't they? Did it start before or after they fled to the dreamland? He couldn't remember now—why was that? He had always prided himself on his memory, was he wrong to do so? Had he lied to himself and others? Sahla? It scared him sometimes, shocked him in moments of unwanted discovery. That they were so like the Others and maybe, just maybe, they were responsible for all that had happened, that they had, unknowing in their search for perfection, influenced the uncomprehending humans for the worst. Perhaps the urge for control had grown to mean too much to them; perhaps that was why they had dwindled where the simple, natural Dark Ones had continued on. Perhaps a love for life could not survive without a little loss of self once in a while. Perhaps the impossible lust, love, adoration? that he and these men had for Sahla was trying to tell him this, that they had been held back too long. Perhaps it was because of this that he no longer dared to sleep for he knew that if he did these waking thoughts, these tempting mirages, would be little compared to the horrors his true unconscious would unfold.

And so he continued on.

Down here there was no light to tease clever retinal windows, yet what he sensed was, perchance, more true because of this. He could smell the age in the rock, feel the immense weight of a world above, the entombed pools and falls, the imaginative statues of other times. But he could not see it, could not pierce the dark, could only wonder that his feet never stumbled, that his limbs never bruised, his head never bled.

Water slithered moistly everywhere and the unchanging icy drip, the steady calciferous splash, the slow forming vales and mountains, comforted him, beat in time with the blood in his head, the pulse in his heart, the endless revolving of the universe around him, gave him comfort, a deception of permanence, an ultimate truth that could never be completely proven.

I wonder . . . The thoughts would not be stopped for long . . . *If I stayed here forever, in this place of changeless change, would time cease to be? Would I cease to be? Would I walk forever yet never ever be? Would all my cares, all my guilt and shame, all my longing and my confusion never take form? Am I actually moving now? I have no way of knowing. All around me is dark, all sounds the same. Perchance I merely drift in the centre of a cave with no boundaries, or perhaps I am at this non-existent boundary and have not yet learnt how to turn back. Are these the thoughts of a sane man, or a creature cut off from all and everything? A creature that must be so cast away, a creature that must float for a while until he finds a place to fit again?*

He laughed, but the sound did not arrive, the silence of the cave swallowed it stillborn and he knew now how felt the babe in the womb. It was terribly pleasant to feel that your madness did not matter any more and he sank farther back, continuing onwards into the same place as before and repented a while of his mortal, meaningless sins.

*   *   *

When next he became aware of his thoughts it was amidst a kaleidoscope vision of Hi-ya, tiny child Hi-ya, playing with his wife. They were in the centre of the dark cave, a perfect egg, and he could not see them running and chasing, hiding behind rocks that he had no way of knowing were there. He did not hear them laugh and squeal, he did not see his wife bring down the squirming bundle of scrawny limbs and begin a tickling to end all ticklings. He did not see this, it was too dark, yet he looked on them and thought for a while how different they seemed, that this was not his wife, that something in her face was slightly slanted, that a new light burned in her liquid black gaze and that Hi-ya, tiny child Hi-ya, laughing and bouncing in his wife/not-wife's lap, was blessedly free of the death that would eventually steal him away.

"Spirits?" Kai-ya's voice when he spoke was shocking to him, he had gone so long without hearing it that it seemed some stranger pondered thoughts aloud, invading this personal space in which he divined. "Ancestors?" He lifted his head from his eternal cradle, thought of a movement once more. "Are you those who came before my beloved?"

She who was perhaps Dil-ya looked up, child held to her breast, tired and exhausted from their manic motion, and smiled at him. He smiled back; he could not help it. The smile, the smile was the same and he had not seen it in so long that it broke his heart and he cried, tears sliding from his cheek to the floor where a crow broke from the pool in a gentle explosion of streaming feathers and alighted on his shoulder. It spoke softly in his ear and he thought he saw a familiar flame in its eyes before he held it lovingly in place and took a step—his first—out of this place and into the next.

*　　　*　　　*

The first thing he saw was his long-lost flame-friend burning before him. In its fiery gaze he saw beyond and into a world the elements had long since ceased to care for. Here sat two figures from his dream and their voices were so clear to him that he groaned and sank to his knees, buried his head in his hands to block out the betrayal and did not notice when the crow flew away once more.

Chapter Twenty-One

"What?" Darbo studied her closely. For a moment, halfway through her explanation of dark-moulding, her face had paled, drained of all blood as though she saw some terrible vision over his shoulder. He turned to look but saw nothing there that should cause such an expression. The land merely rolled on covered in the shadows of night, unmolested by either wind or rain. The moon sank sullenly towards the ground and stars hung miserably overhead, too disenchanted with it all to twinkle. The sun would not struggle over the horizon to replace them for another three hours yet.

"What?" he repeated, grabbing hold of her arm simply because he knew it disturbed her. "What do you see? A spirit?" She had told him this much. How she spoke with the dead, saw them in her dreams, sometimes even journeyed to their land.

"No." She looked meaningfully down at his hand and he removed it, but slowly. Time enough later to finish what he had begun here tonight. Goddess, demon, or both, he had meant to kill her the moment he saw her, but she had proved so intriguing with her garbled tales and strange powers that he had decided instead to observe her. She was so easy to read, her thoughts and emotions lay bare upon a face completely incapable of dissemblance. Easy to read, yes. Also easy to provoke. He could see the passion of her demon nature burning behind her eyes, knew that to play on this was his gateway to her heart and soul, that he could take all that he wanted from her by appealing to these passions and that she would be helpless before him. It provided a viable experiment to while away the interminable journey to the next city—the waiting between kills. It appealed to the hollow in his chest to play in this way. Made it expand and contract in ways that often brought him close to piercing her with his many weapons just to see what would happen next.

"No. No spirits, Darbo. Just my own playing tricks on me." He looked up to see her eyes on his and knew that she could not see him, not as he saw her, and the thought only exacerbated the burning in his chest. Those eyes. So blue. Why did they make his throat want to strangle him so?

He turned his head away and played with the metal blade. He felt her eyes settle on his hand. The smile he gave was a mechanical twitch of muscles, calculated purely to unsettle her. And him. He bid her continue her tale before he gave way to his visions and plunged the metal into her to satisfy something deep and screaming within him.

"You told me of the spirits. Ancestors, you call them. Where is this land of the dead of which you speak?"

Sahla sighed and settled farther back against the rock that supported her. "What you're asking, Darbo, is a question that has puzzled some of the greatest thinkers for thousands of years. Time, worlds, death, life. Who can know the truth of it? Who can ever know how it all fits together?"

"The dark-moulding." Darbo forced himself to lay the knife down. "That is the secret, I think."

"Yes." Sahla looked at him with slightly widened eyes. "You're right. Oh, how can I explain this to you? I barely understand it myself."

"Try."

"Try." She laughed dryly. "If only you knew what you were asking. But of course, you can't can you? That's all a part of it. Why I'm here. Why you're here." She laughed again. "Zinni," she decided. "Zinni had the best explanation for it."

"Who or what is Zinni?"

"Zinni is a woman. She lives in the land of the dead now, but she was a great, perhaps the greatest, shaman who ever lived. She told me what I am going to tell you on one of my first visits there. It was hard for her, too, to put it into words. I think when you describe something you lessen it somehow. Only a mind unbound by thoughts and words can begin to see the whole of anything. That's why people can only approach the truth in dreams. How would you describe a dream, Darbo? You don't dream, or so you say. But I think you do, I think you'll recognise what I say somewhere deep inside. Oh, in dreams things happen that are completely illogical. Time is not linear, places and people change in an instant, ridiculous things happen, conversations are nonsensical, colours are different, the sun rises at night, the grass is blue, the sky green. Madness, yet all possible, all touched on by a wandering mind. That's the land of the dead, Darbo. It's the wandering spirits of all who have ever lived, cast adrift in the endlessly changing universe. That's why they can be and do anything, because they are free as we are not, for what we think of as time, our reality, this all around us right now, is really only one instant, one possibility out of an infinite number. The universe is a huge pattern, full of smaller patterns, yet we only ever see such a small part of it while we're alive. All is constantly changing, everything that can be is and has been, will be again and always, is present forever, somewhere out there. We see these patterns as moments of our life, parts of our world, hop from one to another, experience something different in each one and so believe we understand time and the world, but we're wrong. The dead know, the dead see. All is open to them. They exist everywhere. In all patterns. That's why I dream true things, why I journey. By letting them come to me, or by going to them, I see more of the pattern. Dark-moulding is the ability to reach out into the endless web, into the darkness that forms between each momentary pause in the patterns' motion, and pull forth something from that pattern into this one. When I sent that spear at you I pulled its possibility from the endless web, I saw between the dark, looked to the many pictures. And that is the land of the dead, the realm of the ancestors, the unreality that hurts the mind. Don't ever try to understand it. Don't try to explain it any more than that. Many have tried, it drove them mad." She finished with a wry smile but Darbo was not looking.

"Who is to say their universe is the land of the dead?" Darbo murmured. "This world of mine would seem more worthy of the title."

"Yes," Sahla said softly. "It would, wouldn't it? It could be so. Anything is possible. But you see now, don't you? How many worlds and times and realities there are? Now you see where I came from?"

"Another possible world? A different pattern to this?" He tried to comprehend what she had just told him. That time was an illusion. That they merely hopped from possibility to possibility. What then if he were to stab her? Could he reach out and pull down a possibility wherein she was alive once more? Did this mean that death was not immutable? Did it mean that somewhere all those people he had killed back at the first spire city were still alive? That somewhere there was a world in which humans knew an ease to the sensation that daily threatened to stop his heart and close his throat? It was too much to comprehend. Surely she must be lying. Why would she be here if it were true? Why not somewhere where her creations thrived and welcomed her? Was this one possibility that was an impossibility? If he were already mad as he suspected would this understanding drive him sane? Which was the worst possibility? Could he hop to the pattern that contained his sane self and see? "Oh yes," he said. "I see. I see, Sahla-demon. I see that you are just as lost as I. How fine."

He looked at her. Studied her. He enjoyed this expression. One she wore with increasing regularity now. One in which her whole body seemed to cry and the scent that rose from her was perfume to his nostrils. It was the same way she smelled when he touched her. The same gleam in her eyes when he had lain face to face with her.

"I see there are possibilities even you cannot comprehend."

"What do you mean?"

She backed away now. How intriguing. Should he let her? Should he get her?

"I mean that when we arrive at the city together you and I will reach out to that web in a way you never thought possible."

He stood and pointed into the distance. The mountain dipped gently before them and somewhere far below the shadowed leviathans of the second city fluttered in the fleeting light that came before dawn.

"Who called them?" He dropped his arm and turned back to her. "You or I?"

It seemed for a moment that she would run, the muscles beneath the delicate skin of her face twitched and flexed, her hands clenched till the knuckles stood bare and white, a thousand words hung unspoken on her lips. Then she smiled, dropped her head and for once he could not read her.

Chapter Twenty-Two

Fainan clenched his hands, fingers digging deep into the moist black soil, dislodging countless stones, leaves and tiny, glistening insects. He thought perhaps that he would stay in this forest forever. That if he did he would dream again and she would come to him and this time he would not wake up, he would stay with her in that other world where beasts and people walked together and there was no fear.

If not for him.

The iceman.

The birds continued to sing above him, uncaring of the dilemma he held in his mind. The sun still peered through swaying leaves in diamond drops of light, the trees still spoke in whispered, breathless hush, the river still rushed past him, the flies still flew, the fish still leapt. It seemed unfair, in a way, that the world was so immune to his suffering, that he, a human and therefore so terribly important, should mean so little to the land around him.

"Surely there should be some silence," he mused. "Some change in the scheme of things to show how bereaved I am?"

Something scuffled in a nearby bush, branches shook and shivered wildly. A speckled bird burst forth with an indignant shriek, scratched Fainan's cheek with its clawed feet and wheeled to safety high in the trees.

A triangular head lifted from the hastily exited bush and Fainan gasped and scuttled away, acting as much on instinct as the bird.

Then he realised his mistake. It was the snake that had spoken to him back in his apartment and, ecstatic, he fell to his knees before it.

"Please," he begged. "Please help me. I'm so confused. You told me to go to her but I seem to have done more harm than good. Who was that man with her? I feel I've seen him before, but that's impossible, I haven't seen another human since I was a child."

The snake looked up at him out of slow-blinking eyes and he saw that it was not his snake but merely a smaller cousin, the scales the same bright red hue but that was all.

Yet he fancied he could hear it speaking in his mind, and the words it spoke made no sense and all the sense in the world.

Keep dreaming, Fainan, it said. *For every time you do you create me anew.*

The snake slid towards him, coiled around his legs, cool and comforting, ancient and frightening, flickered its tongue lovingly over bare skin and then continued on through the undergrowth, finally disappearing smoothly between the slick and mossy stones of the river.

Panic flared in Fainan's brain. He shot to his feet, raced to the river's edge, almost falling in his urgency. He thought to save the snake, that it would drown, but when he looked into the crystal water he saw it swimming quickly, purposefully, away from him. And the more he looked the more he saw.

The river was full of snakes, their undulating scarlet scales a new path, a forgotten underground spring, the beginning of a city of old for those of the new and he staggered back and cried aloud, wondered how long he had lain dreaming and if he were dreaming still.

*   *   *

In a dream or not he wandered down that red-scaled road, his friends the snakes fleeting round his ankles, the water shimmering in corridors beside him, mirroring him a thousand times over. Each reflection was slightly different. Taller, shorter, darker, paler, clothed and unclothed, sometimes armed with leather case, others with wooden spear. He wondered vaguely which he was right now and if it really mattered.

Up ahead the water turned, lifted, falling vastly upwards, and through this roaring curtain he saw the bird he had so worried for. It flew from, or towards—again he wasn't quite sure—a man who was like no other man he had ever seen.

This man was tall, far taller than any of the other Fainans he had seen. His skin and hair were of moonbeams and wishes and his eyes as black as night. His limbs were long and slender, facial features delicate, sensitive, hands and fingers pointed and tapering. A work of art.

Welcome here. Help here.

"Hey!" Fainan cried as he came to a halt in a sweeping rock pool of turquoise water that also hung above his head where a beautiful woman with long dark hair and a fishtail for legs sat on a rock combing her hair and giggling sweetly at his fearful delight. "Hey!"

The perfect man showed no sign of hearing, merely looked straight through him as though seeing something entirely different.

The mermaid laughed again and reached for Fainan's hair, touching him oh so softly.

Fainan looked up into her limpid upside down eyes, saw the familiarity and cried again.

The mermaid nodded at his tears and held a willow-thin finger to her rosebud lips.

"Help." She spoke the words for him. "Help!" Sang them, made them into a million choirs. "Can you hear me? Who are you? My name is Fainan and I don't know why I'm here."

79

The fall of water thickened for a moment, the tingling mist closing and swirling like a live thing. Sunlight lit on it and Fainan and the mermaid lifted their hands, blinded, eyes flashing with reds and greens, quick-burnt after-images of a million scintillant prisms.

"Help! Are you still there?" They turned, still blind, stumbled and splashed through quickly warming water, the sun's rays growing hotter, steam beginning to rise in coiling twirls and wisps, blinding them yet more, sheening their face with moisture.

The heat was immense now, grabbed at them, threatened them. Afraid, they forced their eyes to open against the light and saw that the fall of water was now a fall of flame and the man stepped through it, his silver limbs melting like mercury till he was a fall of his own.

Those drops, that liquid silver, raced through a million configurations before their eyes. The choirs lifted their voice, half-screaming, crackling like lightning, unearthly and worshipping. The world flicked to darkness forever and an eyeblink and Fainan felt the mermaid drift from him, her arms flailing desperately for him, her eyes wide and childishly sad, her wail of misery scaling new heights. He felt pity for her and tried to catch her but his body spun away from her, turning and mutating, shifting and juggling, finding perfect and imperfect form before settling once more.

The snakes shivered before him, biting their own tails, leading him inwards. The silver man saw him then, as they recombined in their own personal instant. His eyes widened in recognition, he screamed in rage and flew at Fainan.

"Aah!" Fainan flung up his hands, fell backwards, into the water, the flames, the night, the light.

He saw what the other man saw, tortured visions of a forbidden love, a dark man, Fainan, entwined with Sahla. She was beautiful, held close to his heart, close to his body, her eyes seeing deep into his soul, her lips a sweet promise on his, her touch a tantalising delight.

He threw back his head. Fire roared through him, he felt hands around his throat, knew love and its cousin hate just as he had in his other dream and screamed along with his attacker. Full of compassion and rage he plucked those hands from his neck and cast the bearer away, deep into a hell of burning land and shattered bodies, dead people whom he recognised for a single bonded moment. Then the man was falling from him and the crow appeared, touched his cheek with its wing and dropped down into a maelstrom of twirling shapes. The land within flickered for an instant before Fainan's eyes and then faded to black, locking him away from both man and crow and he knew something terrible was going to happen.

Chapter Twenty-Three

The man he had seen for just an instant blinked out of being and Kai-ya fell to the ground and pounded at it, sobbed that he had so little time with him, sobbed that he had no beating heart in his hands to make up for lack of his own. When the crow came to him he swung his arm at it, sent it flapping and cawing back into the sky.

"Get away from me!" he screamed. "Traitor! Traitor flame and bird both! Showing me such things. Two betrayals now. Is that why you were sent? Do you think I do not suffer enough at the thought of her with them?"

The crow pealed sorrowfully and for a moment Kai-ya regretted what he had said, almost held out a hand for it, then he looked for the first time at the place it had brought him to and the hand fell as though the life that had given it motion had never been.

"Oh no."

Not one but a million crows circled above a field of total destruction, their wings the still and muffled flutter of death's cloak. The sky hung heavy with cloud, the sun a sulphurous glower within. Dead people littered what had once been green and fertile land, the burnt-out remains of their tents sullenly smoking even now. The stench of corrupt flesh was nauseating, would have brought him to his knees if the sight of the children had not.

For they had not escaped the attention of those who had come, seen and conquered. They lay in a small and pathetic heap, cut down where they had been herded like so many sheep. Some still held tight to the hand of the friend whose comfort they had sought in their final moment of life. Some no longer had hands with which to hold. Flesh hung in pale and rotting tatters, gashes lent the curious a glimpse of what should never be seen, heads hung limp, connected only by a few tendonous strands and flies feasted and bred in vile frenzies, creeping and insinuating into the bodies of Pale and Dark alike.

"Oh no."

The adults had not fared so well. The women had been tied to stakes, their breasts and sexual organs mutilated, in some cases removed completely, the gaping holes in their chests and bellies and the agony on their faces silent testimony to the pain and indignity they had suffered before succumbing. One woman lay across his stumbling path. She was face down. He rolled her over. Her belly was a ragged, glutinous hole; her bloody, unborn foetus had been rammed down her throat. It was human. She was Dark.

"Oh no."

The men had been dealt with quickly and brutally. Thick-shafted cross-bow bolts bristled from countless bodies like pinecones. The trauma from just one of these giant missiles would have been enough to kill. These men had up to fifty lodged in their bodies. Each and every one had been mutilated after death. Eyes had been gouged out and genitals hacked from between legs, the blood thick and crusted, black and congealed, so that it seemed they lay in a sea of bitter wine. Here the flies feasted with abandon and tiny white eggs pulsed with busy life.

"Oh no."

Halting steps took him towards the only tent that remained erect. It was large, would have belonged to the shaman of this particular wandering tribe. The feather-staff leaned slightly but remained thrust into the ground beside the entrance. Blood coated the delicate ornamentations and he thought that was why they had left it. The final insult, that even the holy were not safe from the fury of a maddened race. His hand faltered on the tent flap. He knew what would be inside, had seen it too many times, more times than anyone should have to, but he took a deep breath and continued on, the screeching of the carrion feasters overhead urging him laughingly to his fate.

"Oh no."

Inside the tent were all those body parts that had once belonged to living, breathing people. Purple, gore streaked sexual organs in horrible congress reached to the ceiling. Around this unnatural orgy hundreds of eyes kept perverted watch, speared on the end of slender stakes, a punishment for a sin only the humans could see, to continue in death what they had done so innocently in life.

"No." Kai-ya shook his head. Had it really been this bad? Had he forgotten so much over the many, many years? Did he really want to save those who were responsible for such atrocities? And yet what choice did he have? They were still killing his people even now. What hideous irony that he must save those he hated to save those he loved.

"No, no, no." He shook his head more violently, his whole body trembling, electrically alive in the face of death.

"No!" His hand swept out and a wave of black fire plunged into the dreadful pyre and set it alight, flames leaping high and invisible, no less deadly, and for a moment he did not move, felt the fury touch upon him, fancied he saw the faces of those who had done this dancing in the shadows and then he screamed, tortured frustration of one who cannot afford the luxury of death, turned and fled, flinging himself to the ground outside as the tent erupted behind him.

He lay face down in the dead earth for a long time, listening to the patter of sparks and burning canvas falling around him. He heard the flames consume and fade, knew that all was gone, yet still he could not lift himself up. He did not want to walk back through this ruined camp, did not want to see the feasting continue and with that thought the crow alighted on his shuddering back and the flames leapt back into life, rippled along the ground like lava in the night and ignited on each and every child, woman and man with a soft hiss and pop, made them flare like torches, a sublime starfield on the sacred mountain's shattered womb.

The world became one of living, moving fire, seeping and bubbling, shifting rock and cinder-bodies alike. A million faces formed and reformed within, mouths open and beseeching, begging, screaming, crying.

A single black flame rose from this mass, hovered and fluttered like a breeze-driven candle. Spoke to him in a voice he had only so recently come to know.

Who are you to think you alone know pain?

Kai-ya's tears stopped and he looked up at his long time friend and foe.

"So," he murmured. "Even here. Are you the only constant in my many lands?"

You have so many to bring back now.

He smiled at the irony of it all, forged his determination from its castigation and climbed slowly to his feet, alone now, inviolate amid it all. The lava parted around him and continued its purposeful flow onwards. Straight and proud he stood, the crow perched on one shoulder, the flame at the other. A searing breeze lifted his hair into a silver halo wherein the eyes seemed windows to more than one soul.

The clouds overhead shifted to scarlet and black and a bloodied moon hung in ecliptic attendance, a hue echoed in the roiling land below. Thousands of crows slashed the sky with dark-hued wings and voice.

Kai-ya raised his gaze upward and thought he saw eyes.

"Where will you take me next, I wonder?" he asked of them.

The eyes blinked and so did he.

*   *   *

Zinni's eyes fluttered slightly in her sleep. Spirit Dil-ya, so sweet and young, hovered nervously nearby and waited for her time to come.

Chapter Twenty-Four

Kelefeni did not sleep anymore. She sat awake, curled up on the ground beneath her console and stared at the hissing static screens, tried hard not to notice that her hand had not grown back and that blood seeped steadily from it, a single trickle, like tears. Tears that filled her apartment, scarlet salt water that rose a tiny amount each and every day, lapping at her body, staining her clothes, touching lightly on the door that led to another way she did not know.

In her mind logic told her that this was impossible, that her vine should have healed her, but then a human had never suffered such a trauma to her knowledge so maybe the needed repair was beyond it. Her mind also told her that to lose so much blood would lead to the vine's demise for surely it could not keep creating such quantities forever.

She hugged her wounded limb closer to her chest, felt the unnatural shape of the stump against her soft and yielding flesh, felt the spreading warmth as it soaked into her breast.

Her veins had become excited at the sight of so much blood, dancing into a frenzy at the thought of viewing the substance they had so long carried, standing out on her skin in naked wireworks of purple and red, straining to be free of her body, to waltz with those few companions that had found freedom when the hand was lost. Kelefeni had decided that they talked to one another, these veins, that while she watched the screens for the man's return they sang and whispered and muttered together, conspiring of the time when they would need her no longer, laughing when her helpless body trembled and jerked in their grasp. Occasionally she tried talking to them, asking their names and what they did here, but they merely laughed at her transparent attempts and returned to their tap-dancing on hot nerves.

Kelefeni shuddered a little when the red water marked a new tidal line on her clothes. She looked down, saw her face reflected in garish visceral hues, bleeding from mouth and nose and eyes, hair no longer golden but red and red and red.

"Oh no," Kelefeni murmured. "Oh no, no, no." She smashed her lone remaining hand down into the water, shattered her image of self into a hundred ripples that spread out across the room, growing as they raced, carrying cackling, freedom seeking dancers on their crests. They crashed into the door with enough force to crack it into a million hairline splinters, enough force to make her bring down her hand again, urged on by endless voices, and this time the wave shattered everything into a whirl of screams and flying metal.

*   *   *

Faces, faces everywhere. The same one all the time. The one he loved and hated.

His people grew around him, he came across clans he had never known, and Daviki feared the land, the land that even now fell away beneath his feet, blocks of rock spinning away into eternal darkness and brilliant spearing light, he feared that they would soon have nowhere left to stand.

He led them on, put one foot in front of the other, steering a way through the nothingness, hoping to come at last to a way to a land he dreamt of.

The dancing Sahlas made him want to scream all the time.

*   *   *

Red water screamed, surged and bubbled, frothed and roared, fled the imprisoning room in one vast heartfelt flurry, echoed down the darkness beyond in a choir of murmuring wonder.

Kelefeni sat very still on the floor and stared at the shattered door.

"Oh God." She hushed a remembered phrase and looked at her hand that was no more.

"To go or to stay?" she interrogated her maimed wrist. "Do you suppose that either proposal is viable?"

Oh the veins wanted to go, those that hadn't already, vanished on a flume of her life fluid, but she hesitated to follow, held back by a new trembling, and not even their derisive laughter could make her get to her feet and walk towards that gaping hole.

Freedom frightens life-long captives. A cage is never ever quite gone.

"Bother," Kelefeni sighed and climbed to her feet, began her long walk. The veins cackled and writhed within her.

"Oh shut up, all of you!" she snapped, slapped her jigging arm, and the veins, shocked and outraged, subsided into silence for a while.

Tentatively she reached her hand out into the space beyond the door. Nothing but cool, motionless air greeted her and she considered what else she should have expected.

"Foolish," she muttered. "I have grown foolish. How long has it been? How long since I was not so foolish?"

The veins murmured at her and she remembered the time, not so long ago, when they had acted as veins should and not spoken back and shown more life than she ever had.

Encouraged, though she knew not why, she inched farther forwards, made her way out onto a deceptively delicate meshing that was all and alone the only thing separating her from a fall of many endless moments.

"Oh!" She lashed out at the nearest thing, wrapped her fingers around cold metal that was in turn wrapped around with desiccated vines and screamed when they crumbled and fell away beneath her frantic hand. She leaped back into her room, gasping and gurgling for breath and sense.

"The vines!" she moaned, her blood trickling out the door even if she would not. "The vines, they're free. How can it be? And yet they're dying. Are dead. This is not viable, can't be viable. Impossibility."

"Ho-ho-ho," the veins tittered at her, reminded her of the impossibility of her dripping blood.

"I told you to shut up!" She clamped her hand over the stump of her right arm but the blood merely pumped through her fingers and continued its break for the great outdoors.

"Kelefeni."

She whirled.

"No."

The screens were coming for her, reaching their way from the console on long, pliant stalks of twisted knotted flesh. Each bore a picture of the man who had mutilated her, his tongue lapping grotesquely from his mouth, tasting those few drops of blood that had not yet become free.

"Oh, Kelefeni, sweet Kelefeni, precious one, you are waiting for me, waiting for me, waiting for your love."

"No." She backed away. The faces grew legs, dropped to the floor and skittered towards her.

"Come to me, sweet one, come let me drink of your blood, come let me feel your life. Feel your flesh. Feel you."

"No." Her foot slipped from under her, she fell in a pool of her own blood.

"Anoint yourself for me, sweet one, await me appropriately red, appropriately dead."

Tongues and claw-legs reached for her. She curled away into herself. Helpless against the truth.

"You belong to me, Kelefeni."

"No!"

Galvanisation, shrieking veins, she shot to her feet, screamed, smashed inviolate hand into screen, sent flesh and metal spinning.

"Arrrrrr!" The many heads reared up, thrashed from side to side, raged as one, she turned, fled, threw herself out into space, caught metal piping, swung herself down and down, quicker than he could follow.

Down to safety.

*   *   *

86

The first drop of Kelefeni's blood hit the dust at the bottom of the spire and the great doors to outside opened a crack.

Chapter Twenty-Five

The sun sank between a crack in the gorge wall when Darbo and Sahla finally reached the end of the path to the Spire City. It lit the sky in bright cold gold for a perfect moment, silhouetting single boulder towers far above in bold unbroken black, then it dropped suddenly and irrevocably and their world descended into early dusk once more.

They had become used to walking in the dark and the cold that the night brought with it—in this, at least, Sahla had finally had her way—their eyes growing large and colourless, Sahla's magic keeping the elements at bay, their bodies in seamless tune to a world that had quickly become not a home, but a recognised hunting ground for both of them.

They had not spoken again since Sahla had explained the dark-moulding. There had been no need to. Each knew what they expected of the future and themselves; each knew where this path they trod would ultimately take them. What cause was there to fight it anymore? Darbo had called the dark to him at various unrelated intervals, reaching out with a skill and sureness that should have frightened Sahla had she been in a mood to be frightened. Instead she merely watched the plants curl from his fingers and die in the flames he pulled from other patterns. She took the food he gave her and ate it, knowing he would not poison her, not now. For they were indivisible now, entwined now, entangled in a way that would cause immediate collapse for one or the other if they were broken.

And now here they were, face to face with that which they had sought for so long. It lived up to their expectations. A pity really.

Thousands of sand red spires, dark and brooding in the encroaching night. Unlit and bewitching, cutting the gorge-slit sky into countless branching stripes of speckled indigo. They were a field of child-gods waiting for the return of greater minds, too sublime to cry, silent in their misery and solitude. They were a collection of limbs, spears struck into the ground for some long ago victory, petrified hair from some giant princess, frozen in waves and curls. They were . . .

"Beautiful," Sahla murmured. "They're beautiful."

Darbo turned to look at her. In the dying light she was lit only by the shadows they moulded and he thought that the words could be used to describe her too. Her face carven in milk-dark sculptures, troughs and curves, lashes long and spiderous, lips a moist and mobile gash. He thought, too, that this burning would consume him whole and he must see inside her one way or another before the night was out.

"So beautiful," she repeated and walked on down the pathway that led deep into the heart of the slumbering giants, twining worshipfully around mile-wide bases, wonderful denouement awaiting somewhere within.

"You live in these?" She spun to face him and he quickly stilled the urge to grab her, throw her to the ground.

"Yes," he said calmly, keeping pace behind her twisting and turning, wondering form. "We did."

"Did?" She stopped, looked at him. "I thought you said you still did. That's why we're here."

"Live is such an ambiguous word, Sahla."

"Yes." Her head dropped, tangled curls hiding her away from him. "I suppose you're right."

She moved along, thoughts, feet and voice trailing.

"Kai said they were sacred to us. We never lived in them. I suppose that's why it began. Maybe they planned it all along. Maybe that's why they drove us away, they wanted our spires. And the vines. The vines. I wonder how many are left alive? By all the ancestors, there must have been so many, once. How did the Pale Ones ever do it? Or did they? There seems so much he never told me. Maybe it was all us, after all. We built the roads, maybe we also built the spires . . . "

Darbo listened intently. How curious her tales were. Not at all like those on the console. Its tales were logical, with beginning, middle and end, there was no confusion, no meandering back and forth, no doubt, no untruth, only facts. He considered telling her this, putting an end to her pointless diatribe, but he found it agreeable to listen. The sound of another voice eased the constriction in his throat somewhat and he decided that talking was useful and they should have done it more often, it helped free his words—and whatever they concealed.

"Sahla, you find this intriguing? So do I. It is much larger than my city and I consider the possibility that the last one will also increase in size. Perhaps it is to test us. Our strength, our ability to think it out of being. Look around you. Look well. Do you think an alternative exists out there? Somewhere where all this is just so much dust? Have we already been and seen and conquered and merely have to look back to what has already happened? And what did we do before we did that? Look to yet another happening? Happenings within happenings within happenings. So many layers, Sahla, so many, more than the spires that sleep here, more than the humans who do not live within."

Clouds dropped over the sky so far above and Sahla looked up into their shower-blossoming mass. Ahead the centre of the city loomed. The roads met in a single crossing of points, a circle of land, and all around stood the tallest of the tall, the most perfect, most slender, most delicate, as though all that had gone before were merely artist's cast-offs, broken moulds, shattered sculptures, and here, here were the final, finished articles. Here amidst the deepest field of spires were the remains of the long-ago camps, so many vanished people, small and large circles of stones arranged by loving, intelligent hands, a ditch around them, spirals etched into the stone, the ground, the spires. Dots, lines and meanders, thousands of them, like grains of sand, like the stars above. They seemed to cover all that could be reached by mortal hands.

Nothing new had been added for a long time. Age settled in between stones and etchings. Particles from a land that had grown old alone.

"They don't live." Sahla looked away from sky and spires both, sighed in an impossible pattering of rain. Her skin tingled. "But they slumber still. I can feel them. I can feel them all. It's how we used to come to them, when there were more of us. We wanted to remind them, but they forgot us too well."

"Yes, Sahla. Yes." He stepped up behind her, slid his hands down her slick clothes, feeling the shape of her body beneath, pulling her close. "They forgot you, sweet one. Your people forgot you. They don't care about you. They never did. But you are so powerful. So powerful. You can have vengeance."

"Yes." Her voice was small; her body trembled next to his. The rain fell harder, faster. "They forgot me." Remembrances of a mother and father. "They all forgot me." Remembrances of being given away. "It is the gift's curse." Feared. "I have always being alone." Abandoned. "They never loved me."

Tears and rain were equal.

"So much more powerful than I, Sahla." He turned her in his arms, lifted her face to his, touched the tears with a fingertip. "You can see it. A world without them."

The sky rumbled, the clouds lit from within by a light of their own.

"Yes." She looked up, straight into his eyes and the light that lanced from the sky was little compared to that which shot between them. "Yes I can." She pulled his head down and kissed him. For a moment he simply stared at her, forgotten heart in his eyes. The world hung motionless in a second of electric-white arc-light, forks of destructive energy skittered and skirled over the surface of each and every spire, the sky awash with a million clouds and the possibilities within them.

Images fluttered through a mind. Black on red on black on green on black . . .

Kai-ya stood frozen in mid-step on a journey towards the towers of a city so beautiful it had to be new. Rock shimmered in a sun stock-still in the sky; clouds hung white and pure, trees were flush with spring growth. He was so determined.

Black on . . .

Feathers, rushing towards her, a bird, a crow, delivering her.

Black on . . .

"Sahla." A word, just one, gaze turned on her, crying for her, for what she did. Tears perfect spheres in which she could see her face, and it was too beautiful, seen through his eyes. She wished she could take the hand he held out to her.

Black on . . .

"Caw!" High in the sky. Seeing everything. The snake so far away on the ground below. Scarlet.

Black on . . .

Zinni sleeping, smiling, surrounded by leaves and flowers at the centre of it all. Dil-ya hovering close by. A million worlds revolve around her, a child's toy of spinning pictures and she must help to choose, to stop it in the right place.

Black on . . .

Daviki, crouched, still, like a statue, hands over head, a child in the throes of a nightmare, not wanting to see, not wanting to see the many shes caught mid-leap, mid-twirl around him. Behind each dancing figure a face she thought she knew. One. Mother.

Black on . . .

Spires crackled and hissed, flashed, blinding her. Cracked and teetered. Thunder deafened. The world faded to . . .

Black on . . .

The man before her, holding her, the pain and despair in his eyes . . .

Black on . . .

The bleeding woman falling, falling from the spire that shatters and folds behind her, disappears in a plume of dust.

Black on . . .

And the spires are a field of dust and Sahla dances and leaps among it.

"Mine, mine. The power is mine. I can create and I can kill. I am capable of murder and hate, death and destruction!"

Screams into the storm still raging, the storm that takes all.

"Yes! Yes! Yeeeeees! Aaaaaaaaaaaaaaah!"

Hands held high, head thrown back, exhilaration, pounding heart, fly into the night, the light that cracks at the heart of it.

Fade to black.

Knife held high, appearing from a cloud of dust and destruction.

"No!" Sahla screamed, flung out her arms, broke Darbo's grip, smashed the knife from his confusedly loving hand, stumbled, staggered away.

"No."

All around her the Spire City was no more. Thunder and lightning flickered and murmured softly in a sky now returned to gentle purple. Each spire consisted of no more than a fold of dust upon the ground. A field of smoke curled endlessly into the acridly vibrant air, a faded whisper of what once had been. The only dots and spirals were those caused by the rain picking tracks in the sand.

A single woman walked out of the smoke. Her hair was gold streaked with scarlet, her face a perfect oval, her eyes pure and gleaming green, her lips a pale and gentle bow. She was slender, like a young doe, yet womanly, too, long-legged and full-breasted.

She held her right arm close to her chest. It ended in a ragged stump from which hung waving veins. Blood coloured her dress and her eyes were wide with fright as she looked upon these people who had destroyed her home.

Chapter Twenty-six

"You!" Sahla staggered and fell to her knees as she recognised the silent woman from her dreams. The woman answered with a soft moan and collapsed in a sweetly small pool of her own blood.

"No!" Sahla sobbed, scrabbled over to the fallen woman, hung over her in a sweat-soaked tangle of limbs and hair. That she should find her only to lose her so soon. Not fair. Oh, not fair. "What's wrong?" Her voice was shrill, she couldn't help it, the woman's face was so pale, her wound so terrible. "What's wrong with you?"

Darbo pushed her aside, picked up the woman's arm. It shivered and trembled in his hand. Veins bulged obscenely; one broke through the skin and reared up at him, filament end flickering like a scorpion's sting.

"Oh!" Sahla shrieked and jumped back, Darbo merely sliced the vein free with his knife and watched impassively as it pumped its blood into the denuded earth.

"Is she...?" Sahla ventured, watched as the ground grew moist and red around them.

"What?" He looked up and now she was afraid of him. Afraid because she remembered the feel of his lips on hers. Afraid because she remembered the look in his eyes. "One of us?" He climbed to his feet. "No, not one of us." He looked out into the thick and choking air. "Not one of us." He lifted the knife high. As though in answer the moon drifted briefly into view behind an unnatural cloud. "Not one of us."

"But . . . "

He turned on her, smiled too widely, teeth white and sharp.

"She's dying, demon. Not one of us. We do not die. Hah! How ironic. How amusing. We have one survivor, one sole, impossible, wretched life from so much wonderful destruction and she is dying." He began to jig on the spot, kicking up plumes of dust, making Sahla back away, hand held to mouth, coughing, eyes streaming.

"Dying! How very fitting! Yes, indeed. Saved only to die. Worthy of any great mind, any great saviour. Ahoooo!" He screeched and whooped, caught her arms, swung her around and around, threw her away, loped off into the shattered city, running fast, faster, too fast for anyone not possessed by madness.

She saw his dust for a long time.

"What have I done?" She fell forward and sobbed into the ground. "What have I done?"

Then she heard the voices of the dead and screamed as she never had before.

*   *   *

They clamoured and clutched at her with a million and one cold and vaporous hands. *Where are we?* they asked. *We were asleep and alive, then we were awake and dead. We are in pain. Suffering. Where is the peace promised us? We are so confused, so alone. Where are we to go? What are we to do? There are others here, they lurk at our edges, but we are afraid, so afraid. They are not like us. They want to take us to places that twist and turn. Nothing makes sense, it appears and disappears, flashes and blinks, is dark, too dark, we can't see, we can see too much. Oh we are dust, we are dust, how can this be? We cannot die, we cannot, we are immortal, where are our vines? We do not want to go, we do not know how to, we are not wanted. Ah, some of us are caught, they are hurting us, they blame us, blame us for their own deaths. Oh how can we have killed this child or that child, burned wives, murdered fathers, we did not know, we do not know. So much blood, so much fear, help us, help us . . .*

"Leave me alone!" Sahla beat at them, spun between a multitude. Tears ran down her face for their pain, pain she had caused—how could she?—pain she could do nothing for. There were too many of them. "Please, leave me alone. I can't help you. You're too much for me."

No, no, no. We can't go away. Can't.

Hands fastened on her. Pinched her. Tight. Choking.

Won't.

"Please," she was sobbing now. Powerful shaman, broken and bewildered by the dead.

No. You did this to us. You don't deserve to live. We are taking you, too. Out into the dark awaiting us. You will change it for us. You will help us. We will keep you as our own. Our pet.

Faces now, faces devoid of flesh, scoured bone, seared from existence, chattering in her face, clattering, falling into forever, pulling her apart, taking her flesh and eating it to fill their hollow rib-bone bellies, pawing at her, ripping great chunks from her shuddering, heaving body, and then her own bones, pulled apart, thrown out into space, to divine a future, a future for those who had none.

"No!" A disembodied jawbone talking, she was aware of her lack, her no more flesh, her bones so far apart that worlds separated them. "Not again."

Flames came up and mingled with the hands that carried each and every part of her. Torched her to see if she were worthy and laughed at the weakness that had brought her this far.

You think you are strong, they hissed. *But we are stronger. We will have you, have your death and you will never fly again. This is all you are. Bones.*

Nothing more, no clothes do you wear, no flesh do you deserve. This is all and yours for eternity. Knowing who you are, who you can never be. This is death, this is hell. Nothing can prepare you for this.

"I won't run," Sahla's bones chanted, vibrated in the hands of the dead. "This time I won't run."

And the bones fell still and watched their ripping apart a million times without a word. They watched their blood torn away, the pretty skin, the delicate flesh and though they quaked and feared they did not shed a tear nor turn away. They faced it and the taunting of all the dead could no longer harm them.

They knew then what death was and they looked farther and saw that there was more. An old and beneficent face smiled upon them, worn and gnarled hands gathered them up and a voice sprung deep from within sang over them and rearranged them, spewed them out once more into a sacred land.

*   *   *

Sahla woke to the face of a beautiful woman with cracked skin who touched her cheek in mindless concern.

"I'm all right." She caught the hand in her own, moved it gently aside, recognised the woman who alone had survived the death of the city, her head cocked slightly to one side like a startled cat.

"Shit!" Recognised the cuts and slashes all over the woman's poor body. Recognised the mark of the knife that had made them. Recognised the man who sat so close by and watched the woman's battered vine struggle to heal the many wounds.

Recognised herself in him.

Chapter Twenty-seven

"You bastard!" Sahla pushed the woman aside—she fell like a wooden doll—flung herself at Darbo and knocked him to the ground where they went thrashing and rolling in swarms of suffocating ash. "You bastard." She smashed her fist into his face, felt blood burst warmly. "Why did you do it? Why did you do that to her? What harm did she ever do you?"

"No more than those people in those spires did you, Sahla." His words were muffled, bubbling, his mouth full of blood, his eyes clear, mocking her with a straight and serious glance through hyper violence and twitching, pounding of arms. "Will you kill me now demon?" He fell limp, unresisting, beneath her. "Will you finish what you began so long ago? Will you destroy your bastard creation?"

"Nyaaah!" She hated him, brought back her arm for the killing blow.

"Come on, Sahla. Let it all out." He encouraged her, spread his arms wide. Behind them the broken doll watched in silence while a city fluttered and drifted all around on so much disturbed air.

Sahla's arm shook, caught in agonised indecision. She blinked wildly, sweat poured from her so recently enfleshed body; she saw the spirits skirl at the edges of her vision, a maddening rainbow confusion of monochrome and red, skeleton fingers and creeping dead.

Oh yes, send us another, they grated in glee. *Another who will wait for you when your turn comes. How many more will you take, shaman? How many more? Do you dare to come among us again so soon?*

"Come, Sahla. Creation is so bland, so boring. Is not destruction something to aspire to?"

Flesh fell from Darbo's face in curling streamer strips and she saw the skull that made him what he was, dark, hollow sockets reflecting her own. He looked so like her, so like them all, reduced to this.

Send us another.

"No!" Her arm dropped, she shoved him away. "No, I won't. I won't give you another."

He sat up, looked at her with what should have been contempt. She didn't know whether he was capable of it. Didn't know what he was capable of.

"Such mercy, demon-Sahla." He rubbed the blood from his mouth, looked at it intently. Murmured. "Such sweet and tender mercy. How would you show others that when you incinerate their sleeping bones?"

"Not me." She slumped, arms limp, mind reeling. As fascinated with all the blood as he. The broken doll-woman was full of blood at the edge of restraint; it fell from her mangled wrist, just like Darbo's. She looked at her own hand. She alone did not bleed. "Not just me," she begged, wished her limbs would show that life still coursed within her. She needed proof right now. Her soul felt so new and raw, old and fresh from the land of the dead. "You as well, Darbo. Please, you as well. I couldn't have done it without you . . . Wouldn't have done it without you." She looked up at the woman. She sat fearfully still nearby, staring into nothing, breathing so slightly she might as well have been dead, blood streaming from a body cross-hatched with a hundred replicas of those sacred symbols that had once graced other beautiful constructions. Her clothes were so drenched in blood that they moulded to her body, making her into a statuette of slaughterhouses and battlefields. A perfect Goddess of War, missing only her carrion cavalcade to assist her choosing of the dead. Yet who would want these dead?

Sahla lifted her face to the sky. Behind the woman night had fallen and the sky was a black so inky that she wondered how it was that she could see so clearly. She worried that she had not emerged from the last darkness before the city's fall, that maybe she still travelled, a spirit cut off from her body, in some terrible void where she would pay over and over again for her crimes.

The blood lapped at her ankles, black in this lack of light land, this mountain that was sacred no longer. She felt like crying for this was all that was left of a city that had held hundreds of thousands and not even this would bring it back.

"Why?" She didn't look at him. Didn't expect an answer. "Why did you have to hurt her? After all this. Couldn't you just let her be?"

"Why does it matter?" He climbed gracefully to his feet, pirouetted, entranced and majestic amid all the blood, stalked the broken woman. "She can't feel it." He raised his knife and looked at her for a while. She did not move. He brought it down across her chest.

Sahla whimpered, the woman merely took a deeper breath and returned to her silent contemplation of nothing. The wound bled for a while, the veins beneath her skin writhed furiously, then, slowly, the wound began to close up.

"See?" Darbo cut her again, again, again. "She can't feel a thing. She's already dead, Sahla. Already dead, all of us, we all are dead, dead, dead, dead. Dead to it all."

He was crying now, tears pouring down his cheeks and Sahla stared, aghast. He didn't know. He didn't know he was crying. How could he be so blind?

"Dead, dead, dead, dead. All this, all this and it's still no good, still no good. We have killed a world and it's still no good. Still no good!" Tears and blood mingled, his arm became a blur of metronomic motion and Sahla groaned, staggered to her feet, wrenched the knife from his hand and tossed it away.

"Stop it, for pity's sake, stop it!" she shrieked into his face and he turned on her and struck her, sent her head snapping back. She did not resist, could not resist, felt that she deserved it, and then he was done, snatched up his knife and ran off into the night.

"Darbo!" She called after him, not knowing whose pain was greatest, not knowing if she could ever do anything to change it. She turned to the woman at her side and wanted to cry again when she saw the terrible scars, a beauty ruined by an eternity of loss and fear. She had to leave, she had to leave Darbo and take this woman with her. This was all she had now. It seemed that those who had been human could not rest even in death; this she had learned while she died the million deaths a shaman must, and so she would save this one, this last one, at least

"I'm sorry." She climbed to her knees, tottered forwards, touched the pale and tortured cheek. "Can you ever heal the scars? Poor woman. I don't even know your name. Can you forgive him? Can you forgive me? I came here to heal but I'm so wounded myself." She let her fingers trail along white, raised tissue, thrilled and bereft at the touch of another living being. "So wounded." Her head drooped and she cried without a sound, no emotion, no precious waters of life left to her. "What can I do to change it? What can I do? I'm only one woman. Only one." She flung herself at the silent woman, clutched her close and moaned into her breast. "I'm only one, I'm only one. I'm so sorry, so sorry that I failed you, I failed everyone and now there's nothing left to me but to save you and hope this one thing will be enough." And she did cry then for now she was strong enough to know what to do, the Old Woman of the Bones had seen to that, and it scared her more than anything else in the world.

*   *   *

Unknown to Sahla her silent confessor shifted her head slightly and looked down at the small, dark woman sobbing at her breast. An eternity of confusion creased her face and then a single drop of moisture welled from her eye, dropped from her lashes and fell to the ground where it began . . . something.

*   *   *

Far away in the distance, on a cliff overlooking a crying, unaware man, a single pure emotion came into being, took animal and holy form and filled the until now voiceless night with an unearthly howl of sadness for a long and lonely second.

Chapter Twenty-eight

There was a wolf in these woods. Fainan had heard it all night as he wandered in the dark, too desperate for knowledge to be afraid when he really should. Nothing in his life had ever prepared him for this. The complete lack of light, the sensation of being cut off from the world you know, of standing in the middle of nowhere at the boundaries of everywhere, to know that space opens up all around you yet you are as trapped as the bear at the bottom of the pit.

The forest changed at night. It was quiet yet full of sound. Everything seemed multiplied a million times over now that his sight was shaded and he heard the rustle of soft wings and the high-pitched, short-lived squeal of a hunted animal. He heard water running and trickling far, far away. He could smell the scent of distant flowers on the breeze, feel the dampness in the air, hear leaves falling and branches creaking, ants scurrying and cutting, the rustling of a myriad forms of nocturnal life and the most amazing thing was that he had a name for it all.

"I wonder if I'm still dreaming?" he murmured as he continued on into the night, circling and wandering, seeing trees with an inner eye and slinking between them like any one of the night creatures he heard. "I wonder if the wolf only began to howl because I couldn't catch hold of the vision I saw in the darkest part of this wood? Is it my fault that Sahla and the city suffered? My fault for what she did? Should I have tried harder? If only she had taken my hand, if only I had loved her more. But for me the spires would still stand. Oh, I have never seen them from the outside, but they are so beautiful and she destroyed them. I saw her do it with my own eyes and yet I did not question, I did not hate her, for I knew she truly regretted it, and only one who truly regrets deserves forgiveness and who can forgive her if not I? I who love her so but not enough it seems. And what if I knew how to? What if she had taken my hand? Would she have come through the veil to me, like the man I saw in the flames? Would she have welcomed me any more than he? What do I see in these moments? Something I never considered could be. Too many different places and possibilities for me. Too many dreams of reality. Oh what am I doing here? Someone at least tell me that?"

As though in answer to his last question the wolf howled again and for a moment he caught a glimpse of it against the backdrop of shadow-slit trees. A flash of pure white fur, a spark of fleeting, moving light, questing as much as he in the forests of eternity.

"Wait!" he called after it and though it was already half-gone it stopped, turned and looked at him. He saw another's eyes within those pin-prick coals that alone stood out from the virgin snow of its sleek and muscular form.

Hardly daring to breathe he approached with light and worshipful foot. This beast had responded to him, had recognised him, watched him with a curious and welcoming gaze. He felt a sensation close to that which he had known when he held Sahla in his arms and the more he remembered the more he felt. He knew he must be dreaming still and if he wasn't then he must be in that ancient legend known as heaven.

"Sahla, is that you?" He stretched out a hand, fingers hovering butterfly-like above a moist and sensitive nose. Would touch shatter this dream, this heaven? He felt that what he did right here and now was the most important thing he would ever do and he began to cry with fear and frustration that so much should be laid upon him. He wished the snake were here so that he could scream and shout at it and blame it some more.

The wolf's head reared a little. Its lips curled to show strong white teeth and he almost drew back his hand, almost turned and ran when a little hiss sounded at his feet, irony touched his mind and he saw the wolf for what she truly was and fell to his knees before her.

"I once was pure," the woman spoke to him from her snow-white, wolf-fur cloak. She looked so much like Sahla, but there was something in her features that told of many lives. Something that said here is one who has seen all and still desires to live. "But purity can never last. It is too lacking in contrast. With only purity a life can know nothing of boundaries, nothing of darkness, nothing of what it means to truly be. Purity must be tried on the racks of pain and suffering, it must sit long decades in the dark, it must fly high into the sun, it must realise that no one may dig too deep or soar so far that they forget where they belong."

"I don't know if I understand." Fainan realised he was still kneeling a moment before her cool hands closed around his in a moment's delight, lifted him to his feet and face to face with a woman so radiant and so terrible that he wanted her and only her for the rest of his life.

Her lips parted in a gentle smile and he heard the many harsh words they had spoken, the many whispers of love.

"How can it be?" he murmured, folding his fingers more tightly around hers.

"How indeed? And yet it is so, is it not?"

The white fur cloak rose in a whip of frigid wind and the wolf stood there once more.

Come run with me, it said with a toss of its great, proud head and loped off into the invisible trees.

Fainan hesitated for just a moment and then he was like the stag, speeding naked and free through the forest, feet pounding, head down, charging for the sheer thrill of it.

I hunt such as you, the white wolf said and Fainan fled before her. Trees flashed past him, brittle limbs tearing at his skin and raising hot, hard weals on his all too human body. Wind burst around him, tugging and tasting of him, freezing his sweat in glimmering streaks and crystal drops. His legs bunched and thrust him up and down, over and around, darting and diving, seeing with eyes other than those in his head, seeing with something less confining, less real, more purposeful than anything he had ever known.

"Ah!" He gulped and panted, struggled for breath, felt hers hot against him and struggled no more, now he was the terrified animal, the pounding blood his ally, the only thing between him and death, an instant of life of such blistering intensity that to die now would be the capstone of all.

His fleet foot caught in grasping brush and he tumbled and rolled to the ground, scrabbled to be up with neither a thought nor a fear in his head. The white wolf leaped above his head and landed in a smooth and perfect fluid mass before him.

He met her black eyes with a clear and steady gaze. He realised now that life was beautiful and death was beautiful, that she was both and he wanted her with all his body and soul. She was all he had ever wanted. All he ever needed.

She circled him slowly, regarded him out of brilliant eyes before leaping in a great and sinuous coil.

He closed his eyes.

Not yet, she touched him with her breath and a wisp of hot and powerful fur.

He opened his eyes and saw a sliver of white disappear into the night.

*   *   *

Wisps of dust rose and floated off into the night, carrying the tale of the spires they had once been to any that might be interested.

Two women rose in their wake and hurried off into the night before the man came back.

The wolf ceased its howling and looked to the broken man at its side.

It too carried tales for those who might listen.

Chapter Twenty-Nine

Kai-ya was listening for the caw of the returning crow and so it did not unduly alarm him when it settled with a vast flurry of quick-folding wings on his shoulder. He did not know where it had been, but some days ago it had turned its head as though it saw something vitally important and had flown away, leaving him alone with the now invisible flame, wishing for its return in a way he never thought he would until just now.

He had changed much in these days spent traversing the ancient pilgrims' ways. Those eyes he had seen in the burning clouds had deposited him here in the past, a past when these pathways still shone bright and unworn, when the towers of the Pale Ones' ancient cities flickered like a million welcoming candles on an eternal horizon, where he travelled to the first of these for a reason he did not yet understand but knew was as vital as that which had taken the crow from his shoulder all those days ago.

Yes, he had changed. He had emerged from an ocean he had not consciously realised he drowned in. An ocean of guilt and self-pity, an ocean that tugged him down with thoughts and deeds that had once seemed so terrible to him. These waves had been dashed on the rocks of raw horror and now he understood all too well true suffering and could waste no more time on pointless emotions. Now he must journey to the very beginning and seek some way of stopping it before it began. Then he could return to his own land, his own time and he would have no reason for guilt and shame, no reason to fight against his own nature, no need to fight against others. All the answers lay in the past, that time when they had lived in harmony, that time before the Others were born. And this time, if he succeeded, they never would be.

As he walked he took a simple delight in his surroundings. The sacred mountain was young, full and flush with life. Great rivers rushed in valleys studded with rich green trees and brightly coloured flowers. The rocks were alive with the many shades of a land fresh born, the path beneath his feet shone with a million stars and the birds wheeled high overhead and sang to their many reflections.

The first city was close now. He had seen it for many days and always it seemed just over the next rise, yet this did not dishearten him, no such beautiful sight could ever do that, and he lifted his hand to shield his eyes from the glaring blue sky, shielded away one beauty to see another.

The towers were just as he remembered them. Though he had not been alive at this early stage in his peoples' history he had heard many tales from his grandparents and he recognised them both from these and the fact that they seemed barely to have changed in the intervening centuries.

The Dark Ones lived in tents then, unwilling to give up their nomadic lifestyle, but the Pale Ones had decided early on that they desired cities. There was something deep within their group soul that needed a home, and thus they had built the slender towers of shimmering silver pearl and rose crystal he saw before him now. Small versions of the wondrous rock spires that gave the land life, they sparkled in the sunlight like a thousand shards of broken glass, melted and coaxed into shapes so wonderful they defied the eye. Windows curved in graceful circles everywhere, so that it seemed the towers were made more from empty space than actual matter. The sun shone through these many openings, struck off reflective walls inside and exploded into scintillant scatterings of light that made all glow from within as well as without. Fragile bridges spun from silver wire crossed the gaps between houses, linked all together, provided a framework from which the customary quarter days could be celebrated. Days when the sun stood still in the sky, or matched its shadows equally at noon and night and all came out onto the trellised catwalks to sing and dance and simply look. It was from here that the Pale Ones worked on new ideas to keep the vines in the spires healthy. It was from here that they observed the sun, stars and distant galaxies that were their gods. From here that they spread their terraces and grew their food. From here that they had journeyed to their friends the Dark Ones to share the knowledge of the ancestors and the dark-moulding and give in turn their own magic and learning.

How did it all go wrong? Kai-ya wondered to himself before lowering his hand and setting foot back to the trail that would lead him down into the centre of the city.

From this far away he could see no people but when he reached the final path and passed between the gates that never closed he saw them in their multitudes and for a long time he merely stood and watched them, crying soft and silent tears for the people he knew were dead.

They were perfect, it was the only way to describe them. Tall and slender, skin shining like the towers they inhabited, eyes of liquid night, hair so long and curling that they barely needed the clothes they wore. They moved with languorous ease. No voices were raised, no hustle and bustle marred the gentle heat of the early spring day. No pushing, no shoving, no hatred and dissent. How could these people have spawned the Others?

"I will stop this," Kai-ya vowed and brushed away his tears. He moved into the flow of his people, bowed to a young woman who carried a wide-eyed child in her arms, a child who reached out a small and pudgy hand to him, as though knowing he was something special even in a world of such delights. He held the arm of an elder who stumbled in his step, receiving a radiant smile of gratitude in return, he looked upon the many wares for sale and thought how clever was the weaving, how intricate the jewellery, how succulent the food. People looked down from thrown open windows with trailing leaves descending below and smiled and waved at him, the blossom on the trees shook and shivered in greeting, all knew him, all loved him. The past was so wonderful. Why should he not stay?

He felt the crow shudder in its place on his shoulder, suddenly realised that it was the only dark spot in this city of light, that it must feel so out of place, so lonely, and with this thought the invisible flame at his shoulder leaped blackly into life, rippled out in a whirlpool of night, burning and maiming as it went. People fell and were consumed, others screamed, fled, scattered in all directions, could never escape and Kai-ya sobbed and called for mercy but it would have none. None at all.

Out of that pool of darkness fell a vision of a dozen Pale Ones, flogged and bleeding, their gossamer thin clothes opaque now with blood. The voices of damnation rang out for all to hear.

They had sinned in treating the Dark Ones as their equal, sinned in lying with their women, sinned in bringing back a cult of death and evil and these sins could not and would not go unpunished.

Children would be born to them and they would hate their parents, those who disapproved would see to that. These sinners, these wretched betrayers of the light, these seekers of the flesh, would die at the hands of those their sin had created, their names would be wiped from the face of the sacred mountain and their wickedness used as a warning to all others who strayed from the pure path.

Kai-ya cried as he saw this, created this. Fell to his knees in an eddy of seeping black mud. "Lies," he pleaded. "Lies. Oh let it be lies. We would not do that to our own, we would not condemn our own. We did not teach the humans to hate. We are not responsible." He lifted his hands to heaven, the crow flew upwards and those Pale Ones who still lived turned accusing gazes upon him.

"Please." He fell backwards, too weak to hold himself up anymore. Fresh ripples ran through the pool of flame and the people, his people, raised their voices and their hands and came for him.

"Please," he appealed to the crow. It saw, turned on ebon wing and came to him. The pool flared up as it dived, the waves rose, took his people, swallowed them and their sinners both. The crow folded its wings and disappeared after them.

For a while.

Chapter Thirty

Daviki had stopped walking a long time ago. It took him nowhere. So now he merely sat and watched the last piece of land slip-slide away beneath him and wondered how it was that he alone remained to see his home cease to be.

The sky sheered above him in a great, twilight dome; he had forgotten the shape of the moon's face it had been so long since it last rose. Stars flickered in their aerial rivers but their cold light was no comfort to the musician who had never dared to be a shaman. Occasionally a wisp, as of some ghost, would cross the heavenly map and he thought that perhaps they were the spirits of his people journeying onwards. He turned his gaze earthward, to the other place that spirits go. Yet there was no earth here, all had gone, all had fallen and spun away beneath the feet of his clans, into the formless black, each spiralling block taking those people that stood upon it, swallowing them silently, the last he saw of any of them Sahla's sad and accusing face. He wondered if the foaming white horses that rode at the cap of the ocean's waves were yet more spirits cast into the great eternal mix that only the ancestors and brave magicians knew.

The ocean. It was all that remained to him now. The beach had long since gone, all that could be seen in every direction was indigo water, soaking up the darkness in the sky, strengthening it, enhancing it, making new and frightening life from it.

Daviki hovered cross-legged above the restless mass of water. He could hear its endless sigh, like a woman mourning. He thought he knew what she mourned and he unslung his broken drum and tapped out a slow and awkward tune, felt some small response from the world he would soon leave behind.

Boom, boom, boom. The waves beat against the invisible beach his memory-seeking hands sounded out. He smiled and increased the rhythm, rocked gently from side to side, a small wave himself; a breeze blustered from nowhere and lifted his thin grey hair in a shimmering cloud.

The drum went on.

He would conjure a new world with his song, refused to give in even when he felt his eyelids drooping, his head nodding. Then he became aware of another presence out there, floating at the ends of his ocean dome, hearing the beat, the pounding heart, that moved within the waves. Recognising it and adding its own sweet notes.

His smile grew.

He played on.

And began to dream.

*   *   *

Zinni opened her eyes in one of the many places she was. She felt a shallow echo of movement in another and hummed a little tune to herself, high as a bird. She had always had a beautiful voice. She wondered to herself if Dil-ya was ready. She had taught the young spirit much over the timeless time they had been together but one could never know if it were enough, one could only encourage and allow to grow. Perhaps the wisdom of the woman's life would provide the last part of the puzzle, perhaps it would show her the way where Zinni could not, for she would never wake in that land again and she thought how funny it was that the dead could die. It made her think again on the mysteries of life and death, waking and dreaming and if one could ever truly be sure which was which.

She laughed softly and looked up into the dark circle above. For just that one moment she hung between instants. Anything was possible.

She heard a familiar caw and the circle exploded into rushing movement around her. For a moment she was drowning, lungs and nostrils burning.

Then she chose and flew upwards.

*   *   *

Dil-ya keened sorrow into the air, took her friend's limp hand in hers and laid it on her chest. She raised her head high in search of why and the circling crow looked down on her rapidly diminishing face and wondered that they always cried.

*   *   *

Kai-ya stared deep into the pool, unaware that he cried for the loss of bird and flame both, aware only that he was held, caught, helpless, transfixed by this liquid darkness that bubbled and pulsed with hideous life, surrounding him on each and every side yet never touching him, viscous tendrils recoiling mere inches away from his body as though some invisible barrier stood between them.

In this pool he saw too many visions. He saw those who had been cast out, he saw them beaten and whipped by their own people, he heard the accusations hurled their way and none of them made any sense, for how could it be wrong to love and learn, and yet how long had he run from just these things? How could he dare to know what was right and wrong? Whose thoughts were these he carried in his head?

106

The pool fell away at its centre with a suddenness that snatched away his breath. He knew not whether he fell or flew as a woman burst from the morass in an explosion of glittering black, carrying both bird and flame on her back.

"Zinni!" He flung up his hands so he would not have to see. "It can't be." He sobbed, all determination so fleeting now. "You're dead. You died when I was a child." He peeked through his fingers. "You can't be alive now."

"Can I not?" Zinni smiled and wiped away the darkness that veiled her eyes to reveal the darkness burning even deeper in her soul. The crow clacked its beak in gentle amusement and the flame flared at the snapping of her fingers.

Kai-ya dropped his disbelieving hands.

The pool was gone and a distant land of shifting mist hung in its place, he and his impossible guide standing over it like gods peering down from heaven.

Zinni took his arm, stepped out into the abyss and pulled his screaming form with her.

"Come see what else cannot be, Kai-ya," she murmured.

Chapter Thirty-One

Dil-ya sat in the bower holding Zinni's hand for a long and lonely time. Leaves and flowers hung around her in rapt and poignant attention. Their colours seemed a little faded now that the one who tended them was no more; they curled and shivered at the tears of the one who sat alone among them.

And Dil-ya was alone, for no other spirits dared approach such sorrow; no other ancestors cared to face the fact that even they could not escape death.

"Zinni," Dil-ya moaned, clutched the limp and lifeless hand a little closer to her chest. "Zinni, Zinni, Zinni. Why? Why now, why this? You can't be dead, Zinni. You can't be."

A tiny bird fluttered round her head and landed with a hop and a trill on the body of her dead friend.

"You can't be dead, Zinni. Please. Please don't be."

A neck drooped, a mop of white curls sagged, descended into the lap of one who had cradled her through countless years of confused wandering as a new and unfocused spirit.

"Please don't be dead."

The tiny bird chirruped softly at such sadness. It fluffed out its feathers so that it became a small and comforting ball and nuzzled up to the sobbing white head, singing gently into its ear.

Now others did come, a tide of hurting, frightened ancestors that stood and watched in respectful silence. A thousand thoughts blended into one as they pondered what it bode for them that their most powerful one was gone and death, it seemed, was not so unlimited after all, could reach them still in their wonderful land of blessed peace.

Dil-ya raised her head and the tiny bird looked at her with bright, wise eyes. She lifted a hand and stroked the feathers on its brow, thought to herself of all the things left to her now.

She rose to her full height and lifted her hands over her friend's body. Already Zinni seemed hardly to be there and it took but a moment of searching the boundless dark to find a place that seemed eager to take her. With a clap of her hands and a tug of her heart Dil-ya sent her teacher's body out into the universe that none, not even the dead, could know and turned to those who held so many questions.

Circles within circles they stood, and she the hub of this dysfunctional wheel. They regarded her with unwavering eyes and she thought she recognised many of them, some from lives she was unaware she had ever even

lived. She knew with a suddenness that shocked her that she could never answer them, that what had seemed so simple was proved too hard and so she
returned their gaze as frankly as she could and they understood her loss, in
all ways, nodded slowly and turned away, resigned to wait for their own trip
into what they had once thought to know.

Dil-ya turned away from the bower that had held her friend and looked
out at the land that had sustained them all for so long. The memories she
had of this place . . . were they hers at all? How long had she really been here
when the dead could die and faces from a past she had not lived could look
her straight in the eye?

A fragrant breeze shimmered by her, sent on a streamer of scintillant
sun, and on its breath she smelled the ice that capped the mountains far out
on the rim of the world. She let her eyes travel to that distant plane, over the
dark green forests, over the foothills, on to the jagged peaks that countless
saw in dreams but never ever climbed. Were these truly the limits? If she
were to scale their cold grey heights up to where the air was so thin and blue
her breath became her death and not her life, would she see the answers that
the others yearned to know? Would she be able to return with a knowledge to
help them grow, to help them move from life to life and world to world in full
and complete understanding? Blind no longer? Or were they born to be
blind? Was this the only way it could be? Would a mind go too insane if it
knew the enormity of it all?

She moaned a soft and lonely sigh and held out a hand that the until
now forgotten bird was only too happy to hop onto.

"I suppose I have to go there," she said to her tiny companion. "Up there
where my death awaits a second time. I suppose this is why Zinni spent so
long with me, explaining. I suppose this is why she told me I would meet a
past I would not recognise. I wonder if it can be any worse than the one I do?"

She stepped down from Zinni's bower. The ground beneath her bare
soles was soft and rose to encompass her feet in comforting moistness. All
around her animal and human shapes flitted by, darting through the drifting undergrowth, dancing through thickly growing birch and ash, setting
rag-tipped wildflowers and slender boughs to rocking and swaying with
their eternal play. She wondered who was the bird who rode on her hand and
whether the sunlight that spun through the high-laced branches above had
also had a face or an awareness in a previous life. If it still did.

"Do you mind, little friend," she spoke to her bird at the same time as it
vanished for an instant and returned an eternity later with a new and subtle
cast to its iridescent-feathered sheen. "Do you mind," she repeated as
though nothing had happened. "Do you mind if I travel as a doe? I think I'll
travel much faster this way and I know I'll welcome some time where my
thinking does not weigh me down so much."

The bird did not reply and she nodded and began the change. When it
came she welcomed the dark and primitive pulse of an animal's mind.

The doe that had been Dil-ya tossed its head and moved off into the forest. Shapes and shadows of other worlds danced at her rear and the bird that twittered in her ear seemed the only one of them all that understood.

* * *

Somewhere between worlds two shadow-selves sang on and the patterns shifted in the dreams of one land and all.

Thirty-Two

Sahla and her silent woman had been walking for five days now. The shattered city of spires lay far behind them and they had seen no sign of Darbo or any other living being in all that time. The mountain stretched on before them, always up now, though there was no sign of its peak and no indication that it had once been home to two entire races. It scared Sahla during the time she allowed herself to think—a thing she tried not to do so much just lately for it was too painful and confusing. It scared her that people could disappear so completely from a place, it scared her to think that maybe the mountain had forgotten them, forgotten itself, and they could never come back. She risked a glance at the woman whose name she did not know and wondered what she hoped to achieve by saving this one person. Could a disaster be put to rights by picking up one tiny building block? How alone would it look standing uncertainly amidst the ruins of all its friends? Sahla shook the tears away. She hadn't enough left to weep out all the misery she felt. Once started they would never stop.

The air, which had until then hung heavy and still, lifted suddenly, blew with increasing strength and she turned her head sharply, lifted a finger into the air, trying to get a feel for which direction this unbidden wind came from. Out here she was inclined to treat everything as a threat. She had not forgotten that Darbo knew how to mould the dark, thanks to her own foolishness, and she did not believe for a moment that he would allow the two of them to get away so easily. They were his prizes, after all.

The silent woman gazed at her, childishly accepting of this abrupt halt. She seemed to take everything for granted, even the veins that extruded more and more from her once pristine skin with every day that passed. Sahla knew why. Terror could only go so far before it reached a point at which nothing else would register. When that point was reached all descended into vague detachment where the world seemed too bizarre and nonsensical to bother with. The silent woman had reached that point; Sahla envied her for it.

"That wind," she said, more to hear the sound of her own voice than out of any wish or expectance of conversation. "Do you feel it? There's been no wind out here since I arrived, so now there is it must mean something important is going to happen." She turned slowly on her heel, revolving at the centre of the world, the silent woman's eyes still transfixed upon her. "Something . . ." the sky melted into a red-grey whirligig as she turned, she did not comprehend the meaning of the scudding clouds, "is about to happen.

I feel it in my bones."

The red clouds shuddered and pulsed as though they were alive and she strained her neck in staring at the sky. The setting sun laughed and jeered at her, disappeared behind sultry shrouds of imminent danger. The silent woman whimpered like a wounded animal then the sky cracked apart in a flash of blinding violent light and the ground shook in answer, flung them to the ground with bone-snapping force, sent them rolling and spinning down the mountain's now so steep flank.

Sahla screamed, or at least she thought she did, it was hard to hear through the thunder in the sky, the rumbling, cracking, falling, tumbling, as the world collapsed about her and everything sheered into darkness broken only by vicious slashes of jagged-edged light and pelting rain that sent a nightmare of leaping black shadows straight for her throat.

"Aaaaaahhhhh!" She scrabbled and clutched at mud that had once been sand, despaired of ever gaining a hold, shrieked again when it reached out and caught at her, held her down, tugged at her legs. For a moment she was full of panic, wanted only to escape and continue her fall to oblivion. A fear of the dark took her—she who could command it at will—then she felt a hand close around hers and looked into a face of wide eyes and writhing veins illuminated by a flicker flash of deafening intensity.

"Storm," she gasped into that face, as though by naming something she had never before seen she could somehow fear it less. "Storm. That's what it is, that's what it is. Nothing to be afraid of. Nothing at all."

The face broke into a smile of imbecilic incomprehension and the hand closed more tightly around hers. Pulled at her.

Pulled her down.

"What are you doing?" Sahla screamed, prised at the fingers, struggled to peel them back, veins lashed up through translucent skin and snapped around her hands, skittered up her arms, wended their way up to her face. She screamed as they began a delicate caress and the hands pulled her ever inwards. She saw the bones and flesh of the earth, touched the dusty dry moist hot cold heart of the sacred mountain then all faded to seamless black and the laughing old woman of the bones appeared once more with a grating song of destructive creation to add to the other.

*   *   *

"Oh!" Sahla jerked back to consciousness and flailed frantically at her throat. The choking veins were gone and the silent woman sat at her side, watching her with patient eyes.

"You!" Sahla struggled to verbalise her turbulent thoughts. All seemed well now. Had she dreamt it all, then? "What happened? Did we . . . ? Are we . . . ?"

The silent woman shook her head and thrust out an arm to indicate their surroundings.

If the land they had once traversed was considered a desert what then was this? This land of pure white sand and pure white sky where a mind could be convinced that nothing existed at all. A land where nothing save they two did exist for as far as the eye could see. Each direction leading only to flat and featureless plains. Not even a single dune to break the monotony.

Sahla sat up and dipped a hand into the sand, brought it up to her gaze in desperate hope of finding some meaning to this. The more she looked the more it seemed that each grain she held shimmered like the glass it could one day be and she fancied she could see within a single life that was all the more intense for its battle to survive. A single flower redder than the blood of her most painful days, a flower that knew the meaning of sorrow and hardship, a flower that knew how cruel and warped life could be, a flower that grew to spite it all, watered out here in the desert of a soul allowed only so much room to breathe.

She shed a single tear for its struggle, its loneliness, and let the sand slip through her fingers, feeling as though her own life went with it.

She looked up at the silent woman and saw that her gaze was fixed on a spot just ahead. When she turned to look she saw that a door now stood where before had been just bare desert.

It was a curious door for it was alone and no part of a hut or tower, merely built of solid and natural wood without polish or working, handle or decoration, a flat and vertical expanse, a brown-grain barrier from one part of the desert to another.

"Where did that come from?" Sahla climbed to her feet and approached it, the silent woman following obediently behind.

She came to a halt in front of it and noticed how the sand seemed to curl and rise where she had walked, forming steep dunes in her wake as though her footsteps awakened something deep within the land.

She raised a hand and touched the wood, felt the roughness, the slightly sticky moistness of sap just recently wept.

"What are you?" she asked of this still breathing door and thought for a moment she heard the wind that had once blown through its boughs. Then it gave a tiny, inviting creak and opened just a little way to give her a glimpse of what lay beyond.

She hesitated for a moment and then stepped through, the silent woman close behind.

Chapter Thirty-Three

Darbo did not know why the four-legged creature had decided to follow him. All he did know was that ever since he had left the city it had been his constant companion. He thought he knew its name, but it wouldn't come to him. He had seen a picture of it on one of the many screens back in his other life and he knew that it was a predator, a pack animal, so maybe that was why it had chosen to travel with him. Maybe it, too, sought the two women, maybe it, too, longed to bring them down and have them for its own.

He supposed in a way that he had only himself to blame for their leaving. He had left them unattended for too long, had indulged his need to see and understand the destruction for too long. Had wandered silently through the ashes for too long. Perhaps his attack on the dying woman had not been so wise after all. He had only wanted to understand her, to see if she could bleed. Yet it had upset Sahla; he had not expected that. He had thought she saw things his way. He had thought she helped him because she wanted to, because she . . .

He hung his head.

Because she what? What had all that water on his cheeks been for? What had he meant when he screamed, when he said they were all dead? It had all seemed so clear then, just for that one moment. And what of that moment, that wondrous moment, when Sahla had shattered the towers, summoned a dark he could never hope to see? When she had pressed her mouth to his. The feeling in his chest had slipped aside and out . . . out had come something he barely recognised, something he . . .

The four-legged creature whined and Darbo stopped and sank to the ground. He put his head in his hands and cried, cried for something he wanted so badly but feared he would never have. Something he did not know, did not understand, for how can one who has never known love know what it is that he lacks? And yet he did know, deep inside where the feelings of pain and loss—feelings, oh yes, feelings—clutched at his heart and his soul and locked them away, choked off their breath, kept him a prisoner from the only thing that could save him. For yes, he knew love, knew it on a level so deep that no amount of immortality, no amount of segregation or loneliness, brainwashing or misery could keep it from him. It was an instinct as strong as life itself and what was life without it? What was his life without it?

"No!" He threw back his head and wailed into the air, brought out his knife and lashed it down into his arm, sent bright blood splashing everywhere, made the wolf dance back, its coat beribboned with scarlet. "No!" Pain, pain was all he had, if he could feel nothing then he would feel this, be this. The knife rose and fell, he cut such pretty designs, such perfect agony upon his skin, upon this body that had never been his and was now his in the only way he could make it.

"No," he hushed as he cut for his vine, cut for the thing that had given him life at the cost of another. When he found it he severed it from the veins that had so long fed upon it and fell face first into the red sand. He did not move for a long time.

* * *

It seemed to Darbo that while he lay there with his life slowly bleeding out of him the four-legged creature infiltrated his dreams, infiltrated him, so that he became the creature in thought and body. And so it was that he came to see a human from an animal's point of view. He felt the fear and resignation of a species reduced to a mere handful of its former numbers, saw through the eyes of the last female the men who came to destroy her. He turned away with her to run for one final time before the bullet ripped through flesh and thudded into bone with a dead and thudding ring, before life flashed in brilliant scents and visions for one final time, before breath escaped at last and a body went spinning into earth that could do nothing to save one it had loved and nourished, challenged and starved for so few years.

As he died he became man again and knew that he did this to himself and others always and forever and wept bitter hopeless tears because he could see no other way.

* * *

He awoke to find his body whole, save in one small place where the vine had once upon a time been, and the four-legged creature's breath hot against his cheek. For a moment he thought he saw familiar features ripple over that lupine face and sat up suddenly, Sahla's name tumbling from his lips. But it was not her, not the one he had lost, and he pulled the shaggy head close in recompense, whispered her name into its ear, wound his hands in thick fur and shed a few more tears for it seemed he had not yet wept nearly enough.

The two stayed like that for a long time, entwined in danger, two predators together, yet both capable of a love so strong and so vicious that the wonder was they had ever managed to share a world at all. Above them dark clouds shimmered. Red and murderous gloom filled the air and the sky rumbled in long-pent fury, eager to roar forth again.

Darbo let go of the creature's head and the two of them looked up just as the first spots of rain fell from the sky and spattered against skin and fur, sparkling on one, silken on the other.

A wind began to moan around them and Darbo smiled, the first genuine smile of his long life. He remembered the first wind he had encountered on this mountain.

He was not surprised when the sun slid quickly from the sky and darkness took the land amidst a crashing of thunder and a shaking of the ground beneath him. He was not surprised when the darkness cleared to show a desert of dazzling whiteness wherein he and his animal companion stood alone. He was not surprised to find a small red flower growing at his feet and he bent down to cup its delicate petals in his hand, barely flinching when a sinuous head rose from the watery pool within and stared him straight in the eyes.

Darbo, the red snake hissed. *You have come at last. I knew you would. We all did. Soon the last of the many parts will be ready. Come then, take me with you and together we will find she who made us all.*

Darbo offered his hand and the snake slid slowly up his arm and wound about his body until it came upon that tiny, almost-healed wound and found its home at last.

The four-legged creature looked at him for a long time and he returned the stare unblinkingly. It seemed for a moment that an age-old mistrust would rear its head and then the creature's jaw dropped, its tongue lolled out and Darbo thought how strangely right it was that animals should laugh, too.

They stepped through the door that appeared at their right and the wood eased closed with a small and grateful sigh behind them.

Chapter Thirty-Four

When the forest began to thin out Fainan was not surprised. Ever since his meeting with the wolf he had thought of little else but finding Sahla and somehow he knew that he would not find her in here, at least not yet.

During the days it had taken him to reach the forest's edge he had thought of many things, including what had happened to the world he knew. Where was the spire he had left behind, what of his commitment to the rest of his kind and what or who was this woman he had transformed his whole life for? Was she wolf or human, or something in between? These thoughts were much to have on any mind and he amused himself daily with remembrances of men that disappeared into worlds beyond his ken and snakes that swam and flew and talked in voices he was sure he never heard. Occasionally he would laugh out loud and some tree dwelling creature would chatter and shower him with leaves in its haste to escape this seeming madman.

Fainan was not mad, though. He was just seeing a lot of things he had never really noticed before.

These things have always been with me, he thought, remembering the images in his head—the dreams—that had flickered through his many nights of sleep. Was it here he had first met her? Was it here he had first seen the darkness come alive, where it had given birth to as many lands as he dared think of? Was the only barrier his mind, after all?

And then he had thought that he would like to see the end of this forest for a while, much as he had come to love it with a passion he once would have considered with idle puzzlement. He thought that it would be nice to visit that city he had seen before and then he had thought 'what city?' and it had appeared before him and he had thought no more.

So here it was, the city he had dreamed of remembering and it was very fine and very sad. Like nothing he had ever seen before and everything he had thought it would be.

The change between forest and not-forest was viciously sudden. At one point trees and softly rustling ground were all, at the next the land became stark and grey, made of a hard material that Fainan was not accustomed to. It caused a shiver to etch its way down his spine and for a moment he considered turning around and returning the way he had come.

A river ran from the forest's depths and cut a channel through the hard grey matter down into the city. Wide and rushing at its source it narrowed as it closed on the town and disappeared into the massive arching tunnel built of large pale stones wherein lay all of this unusual city's buildings. Though the sky was clear blue overhead and the day was bright and sticky-hot the light barely penetrated the tenebrous depths, barely lit upon the first of who knew how many houses within.

These houses were built of the same large stones as the tunnel that concealed them. Each and every one seated on a terrace that dropped lower and lower with every level, perhaps meeting somewhere at an unseen centre. Fainan could not tell where the tunnel that shielded all this ended, to his eyes it seemed that it continued forever, its stony back stretching far off into a distance without limit where the sun kissed the colourless horizon in a shimmering glare of glassy heat. He wondered what kind of people would build their homes underground in such a way, what kind of people would choose to lock themselves away from the sun. Then he realised that his own kin had done the same and he thought perhaps that he knew these people after all. All had to live like this at some point or other. Some things could not and should not be laid bare to the light. Did not so many things grow in the dark?

He nodded to himself at this thought and with it the shiver along his spine melted away in understanding, his back unbent and allowed him to stand tall and walk away from the woods and into the heart of a new jungle.

He followed the river's course all the way down. After a few minutes of silent travel—all life seemed to have been left behind in the forest, not a single birdcall or breath of wind shifted out here—he noticed a flight of steps cut into the grey stuff, which led down to the water's edge. He followed it down, wondering how it could be that even the water made no sound lapping against its confining edges. He crouched down and dipped his hand in the water, sending ripples careening out from his fingers, yet not a single splash could be heard, it were as though the very air caught and devoured all noise before it reached his ears.

"So this is what it's like to be deaf," he said silently to himself and mused at how different a voice sounded when sound was not allowed.

He opened his mouth wide and screamed as loud as he could, marvelled at how his ears thudded with the memory of a voice, how the mind could create anew from nothing. He thought he heard a gentle creak, as of rocking chairs and breeze driven boughs. He decided he liked it and so it sounded again but it did not but he heard it anyway.

He climbed to his feet, turned around and blinked in surprise at the door that had appeared in the middle of the river, floating above the slowly settling ripples like another heat mirage.

"Well, well," said the goldenly silent Fainan. "I think this was not here a moment ago. I wonder if my silent scream called it up? Maybe sound that's taken away can be made into something else . . . "

For a moment he reached out a hand to push upon this freshly created door but then he stopped, hand hovering in mid-air.

"No," he said and the door creaked again. "No, this door is for someone else. But I think it's good for it to be here. I think now, at last, I can find Sahla."

He smiled at this thought and his skin flushed at remembrance of her in his arms, of a being warm and loving just for him. Then a frown flickered across his face with the arrival of the thought of a man he knew all too well and a barrier set between them once more, yet weaker now . . . maybe . . .

His hand dropped.

"Stay there and be a good doorway, my friend," he said. "Many are those who will come through you."

Strangely, he felt no fear at all now, as does one who has suddenly received word that all will be well, and he turned away and walked with light step into the darkening tunnel as the sun slid from the sky in readiness.

"Sahla," he sighed. "I went away, but now I'm coming back." He started to cry and the tears made waves. The sounds they left behind joined with others far away and a song went on and grew stronger.

Chapter Thirty-Five

Kai-ya screamed like a baby during his journey through the mist and felt no shame at all for doing so. For how could he stay sane when the very universe he thought he knew disintegrated completely around him and showed him a multitude of variations that made the flips of his dream land seem just that, as dreams, to him?

Through it all he was aware of Zinni as only a far distant presence. The arm she held onto seemed no part of his own self but more a part of all that spun around him.

And it did spin, twirling in a multitude of colours, red and green and blue and white. He wondered how a simple mist could hold so much and then laughed amidst his crying for this was no ordinary mist, though simplicity may lie behind it all. He watched with wide and streaming eyes as shapes shifted before him and endless parades of numbers vied with patterns and bounding animal forms. Planets revolved and stars flared and died without a breath of movement, all seeming so strung together that he thought he could see a million histories but whenever he focused on a single one everything collapsed and he lost so much that eventually he closed his eyes and merely sobbed softly to himself.

Then he felt ground beneath his feet once more and fell towards it as one who welcomes a mother, kissed it with trembling lips and looked up into the face of she who had brought him here.

"Zinni." He had no pride left and was not afraid that she saw him cry. "Zinni, what is this? What have you done to me? Where have you taken me?"

She smiled at him, just like that long ago mother, and he felt his tears dry miraculously.

"Why, I've brought you to see what you wanted to see, dear Kai-ya," she said with a laugh in her voice. "What you came in search of."

"I don't understand," he moaned. "I came in search of nothing, didn't I?"

She stared at him oh so patiently and he put his head in his hands, still unable to look about him at this new land.

"Think, Kai-ya. Did you not? Are you so sure? You had a reason for visiting the past, didn't you? Something brought you where you had to go, it always does."

"Am I helpless before fate, then?" he appealed through concealing fingers. "Does my life have no direction save that given me by a higher being, a greater cause? Do I exist only to serve one I will never know?"

Zinni threw back her head and laughed out loud. For a moment he wanted nothing more than to rise to his feet and seize her by the throat, wring out the life in her for daring to mock. Then he recognised the laughter as that which played through his own head when certain forbidden thoughts arose and so he stayed this urge, climbed to his feet and looked around for the first time since he had arrived here.

He stood in the middle of a city that he had never seen before and yet he felt curiously at home, as though he had spent some forgotten portion of his life here. The houses were built of stones so big he thought it would take a community a lifetime to lift just one alone. They seemed to be empty, though he felt the promise of habitation well from within, as though the occupants had just recently left for the market and would soon return bringing with them all the trappings of wealth and happiness. Many roads wound through all this, seeming to have no rhyme or reason beyond the sheer joy of being there and leading people off to meet others of their kind they might other-wise never have met. These roads were starred with bright stones, just as were those the Dark Ones had built so long ago, and for a moment all he could do was stare and feel his heart contract inside him so that he did not know whether it would ever beat again.

"Do you recognise this place, Kai-ya?" Zinni asked. "Do you recognise it as that part of you that sends you where you need to go whether you know it or not? Do you see it for what it is? Do you see that it will never give up, that it will rise in many and different forms and that each time it does you must explore it anew or it will run riot, turn on you in your darkest nights and warp all those fine thoughts you hold so dear and which will kill you soon enough?"

"No!" He whirled to face her, not wanting to see the arching roof that cut off this city from the outside world, from the light, that cast him into the darkness he had long moulded but never really understood. "No, Zinni!" He moved suddenly, jerkily, caught hold of her, shook her, pushed her away. "No, it cannot be, I will not look, I will not!" He stepped away from her like a dancer on hot coals. "No, no, no. I will not find what I seek in here. This place has no answers for me, only torment and I will not stay. I will not. Take me back where you found me and I will find my own answers, not those you wish to force upon me!"

"Too late," Zinni said sadly. "Too late, my friend. You are already there."

Kai-ya turned. He saw the inhabitants of all those houses and fell to his knees when he saw who they were. His people. His people, and they drove out before them the humans they had spawned. A hundred Pale Ones tall and immutable in fine robes and carefully curled hair, fifty humans of ten-der age bearing the deformities that marked them from their forebears. Their strange-shaped skulls, foreheads so short and stunted, eyes so many variable colours, limbs short and muscular, made for heavy work, like the Dark Ones, the Dark Ones who had led all astray. Kai-ya leaped to his feet, hands flying to his face. He could feel himself changing, features and body melting, reforming, the land about him changing too, drifting in a shifting of sands so that he stood not in a city but outside the camp of one of the clans.

But what was going on? For he and his Pale companions hid behind outcroppings of rock as their human prisoners ran madly for the safety of the camp of the Dark Ones. He and his companions began to screech and blow war-horns and clash together the swords and weapons they had brought with them. The humans fled, panicked and screaming, and the Dark Ones, the Dark Ones were alert for the sound of attack, they had heard rumblings of trouble from the cities and when they heard the cry of the horns they came out of their huts bearing arms and courage both and fell upon their foes. And these foes pleaded for mercy but the Dark Ones fought for their lives, or so they thought, and in the light of day they were half-blind and did not see who they killed till it was too late and all humans lay dead save one who fled screeching of the murder and injustice done to its kin.

The council of Pale Ones turned away, a job well-done. Countless Dark Ones keened and moaned and went mad with staring and clutching at dead faces they had once known. Kai-ya slowed his steps and looked back, forgot who was guilty and fell to his knees in shame, clawed at a face that was changing again so he knew not who he was or who he had ever been. He cried when he felt the daggers enter him and saw it was his own people turned upon him, the humans turned upon him, the Dark Ones turned upon him. Now he did not know who killed whom and his scream wrenched worlds from their tracks till he was found sobbing and shivering in Zinni's arms.

When he looked up he saw a realm of understanding in her face and pulled her closer so that he could bury his head in her breast once more.

Chapter Thirty-Six

"What was it, Zinni?" he cried. "What did I see? I don't understand, all my memories, all the tales of how it was long ago. We lived in harmony, didn't we? We lived together, didn't we? We loved one another, didn't we?"

Zinni murmured over his head, stroked the pleadings from his brow then caught hold of him and held him away, looked him deep in the eyes, this man that stood almost twice again her height, knew that he was as a child compared to her.

"Is that what you want, Kai-ya? The memories of happiness, the utopian world you hold in that head of yours?"

"Yes." He nodded his head so furiously that it was funny.

"Look behind you."

Kai-ya turned to look. His heart began its beat again for here was the crow he had forgotten in his terror and it held a flame as black as pitch in its eyes, wheeled and dove at him with a vicious squawk. He screamed and threw his hands before his eyes in protection.

He felt its wings and claws battering at his face and flailed at his sudden attacker, wondering why one who had long been his companion now seemed determined to be his enemy. Yet hadn't it been this way for so long? Always his friend was his enemy. Carried inside him.

He spun to face Zinni again, with something new to tell her, but she was gone and all that remained in her place was the flame he had come to know so well. It spoke to him in pictures this time and he saw a land he held in his memories that was so welcome he spread his arms and dived right in.

*   *   *

Dil-ya was unsure when she had made the decision to travel on two legs instead of four, all she knew was that as she approached the mountains at the edge of the world she needed to face whatever was on the other side in this way. Zinni had taught her many things since she had become an ancestor, and one of those was to always trust her instincts. It had been a hard transition for Dil-ya to make, she had been brought up in a society where a group of people called the council made the decisions for everyone else and if you happened to disagree with one of their decrees you were a sinful person and must strive to eradicate the forbidden from your mind.

This particular thought brought Dil-ya to a halt and her constant companion, the little bird that had now gained a plumage of quite wonderful green and blue feathers, fluttered up from her shoulder and circled her head in full burst of song.

"Now where on earth did I get such an idea?" Dil-ya stared without focus at the steadily steepening slope before her. And indeed she could not think, for it seemed to her that she had always known that her people were good with no need to ever disagree with anyone, and that surely no sin had ever been theirs and if it had who then had known to call it a sin?

"Strange," she murmured and continued walking again. "I've never felt so confused before. I always thought the humans were the only ones to sin, but now . . . "

The bird trilled joyfully and fluttered off somewhere, as it was wont to do.

"Now," she continued, barely aware of its disappearance. "Now I find myself wondering . . . wondering if this thing called sin even exists. Yes, that's it!" She brightened; her tall, thin face broke into a wide smile. "I thought my memories were so infallible, the only truth, but it seems they're just as open to . . . manipulation? . . . as anything else."

Her stride lengthened and the summit of the mountain grew ever nearer. Small heads began to grow through the grass and she recognised each one of them as parts of the many bodies her bird companion had once occupied. She saw that it had been many things and all things, that it had killed humans for a wrong only it could see and it had been a human, too, as confused as she and left with only the rage and the murder it brought to assuage a guilt it should never have felt to begin with.

It all seemed so wonderfully jolly to her. She wondered casually if she had just gone mad. The thought did not seem unduly disagreeable to her.

"Hello," she said, dropping to her knees beside one of the heads. It opened its eyes and looked up at her. She saw that they were a beautiful blue, like a spring sky. She remembered the clouds she had watched floating in another land and wondered which land she remembered this time.

"Hello," replied the head that grew from the ground and nodded politely in her direction. "Would you care to open me up and look inside? I'm sure you'll find it most interesting."

"I will, if you think it wise," she said and, not thinking that what she did was in any way strange, she touched the head below its ears and at some urging from its widely grinning mouth found two small levers. She pressed them down and up came the top of the skull with a sick and gristly creaking sound. Inside she saw a mist that cleared to show a hundred pictures all hanging motionless, each one of them containing a different memory. There were pictures of humans killing Pale Ones, just as she remembered in her own head, but there were also pictures of Dark killing Pale and Pale killing human and human living in peace with Dark and on and on till she felt quite awhirl at the possibilities of it all. Then she saw another picture, she saw one where Kai-ya dreamed her death and she fixated on this with all of her soul, heart pounding wildly. She saw him watch her die and turn to Sahla, knew that he had sent her away for this, in full knowledge of what would happen to her. She let go the head with a shrill cry and did not see the next picture that held a far different tale because this was the only one she could remember right now.

"No!" She scrambled away from the still-grinning head, scrabbled for stones and threw them at it. It grinned all the more as they bounced off and fell to the ground, rolling back down the hill with glee at this sudden jaunt.

"No!" She struggled to her feet and ran, ran for the summit, more heads springing up beneath her feet but she did not want to look now, did not want to think the many memories that could be hers if only she allowed herself to see.

"You loved her more than me," she gasped, feet trampling ground and heads alike. "You loved her more than me. Sahla more than me and I hate you for it!"

And then she reached the summit and fell screaming into the emptiness on the other side.

Chapter Thirty-Seven

When Sahla stepped through the door she had no idea what she expected to find, but nothing was certainly not an answer she had entertained. It seemed she had walked into a sea of formless white. Everything around her was so bright it confounded her eyes and she found that the harder she looked for detail the more it blinded her. All she could see were stacks upon stacks of struggling filaments dancing on the stage of her retinas. This was the part of her brain that sorted the world her eyes saw into understandable packages of information. She wondered if what it saw was even remotely related to reality. So entranced was she with this thought that she jumped at the touch of a hand on her arm and turned to see the silent woman staring at her, framed in a crown of white.

"What is it?" Sahla asked of the woman, taking her small and loose-veined hand in hers. "Are you all right?"

The woman cocked her head quizzically and Sahla wondered how it was that even with the veins writhing over her face she was still so beautiful. She also wondered what the woman held within her that so desperately wanted to be free.

Sahla felt helpless before this continued gaze and so she merely held on to the delicate hand and turned back into the white, curious as to what she might find if she started off into it.

"I'm going in," she said to the woman. "You don't have to come with me but I think I'd like it if you did."

She took a step forward, half expecting the ground to prove nothing more than an illusion, but it did not, in fact it seemed to grow more dense at her movement and instead of blinding her offered up a path, formed from the brilliance, that was just one shade darker than pristine.

The silent woman clung to her hand and followed without a murmur. The two of them wandered off into a world that could not be and did not stop to think that maybe it wasn't.

*   *   *

The path continued for a long, long time and it seemed an end would never be reached. A journey Sahla had begun full of what passed for hope in one unaccustomed to it had now descended into a trip of torment. She began to curse the brightness all around her and realise just how uncomfortable its unceasing light really was.

The silent woman, of course, did not say anything, but, as Sahla finished her foul words and slumped cross-legged to the ground, her veins stretched out from her body in little pitter-patters of life and dribbled blood all over the pure path as they slithered along it in search of . . . something.

At first Sahla did not watch. Perhaps it was because of the sight of someone's veins behaving in such a way, peeling through skin and disappearing off into the distance, such a terrible length of them that a mind could only gibber at the fact that the bearer did not fall down dead. Perhaps it was the fact that she could no longer bear to fix her gaze on the endless white that she knew deep inside was her home no more than any other place had ever been. Perhaps it was the fact that it was so much easier just to lay down and close your eyes and pretend that nothing existed, not even yourself, and therefore the struggle was no longer worth it. For who could dare to continue on when there was nothing and no one to continue with?

An excited cry from the silent woman made Sahla wake and look up, out into the big white world. She gasped. Shivered. It had changed. She saw cracks in the walls and the ground, old and full of dust and decay. She grew white herself as she thought how long she must have slept for such an age to take its toll.

"Walls?" she murmured in a voice dull from lack of use. Indeed she barely knew what to say to herself, felt embarrassed and on the verge of tears at the inanities that passed her lips.

"Walls? They can't be. It was a world. What happened to the world I was in?"

The silent woman voiced her wordless cry again and Sahla turned to see what upset her so.

And oh by all the ancestors she *had* been asleep too long, for now her silent woman lifted a face to her that was lined and full of sags so deep that the once-beautiful eyes were nowhere to be seen. Now she was an old and aged hag, but with none of the strength and wisdom this gave. She was a bubbling imbecile, her veins all curled and dry about her, a sickly bile colour dripping slowly and interminably from them and into the ground, poisoning everything around her. Sahla clasped her hands to her face and moaned. Her skin fell away beneath them and her fingers investigated soft and mobile flesh. A cage of iron bars fell with a clang around the two of them and pierced the ground till blood spurted forth in great foaming geysers. She cried aloud and fled forwards with her decaying flesh in tatters to seize the bars of her cage, to try to mould her long-lost dark, but it would not come here in the land of eternal light.

"No." She sobbed in disbelief. Her fingers came away and she fell back screaming for the waste of a life so alone. Then she saw the animals come in three by threes, elk and wildcat, bear and wolf, hare and fox, shackled together, hobbled and limping down the age-cracked path, and each and every one of them was dead. When they reached her cage they gave up their futile act of life, fixed her with dark and watery eyes and toppled before her.

"Why?" she asked of the uncaring whiteness. "Why these? Why all the animals? Why are they all dead?"

But she knew. She knew as soon as she asked it. They had been caged too long just as she and their wounds were hers. She went to her grave for the hundredth time knowing this.

*   *   *

"Worlds are turning, worlds are turning,
nothing is as it seems.
Worlds are turning, worlds are turning,
calling up the in-betweens.
Worlds are turning, worlds are turning,
now's the time for all our dreams."

Somewhere a Zinni sang and drifted to a land whose dreams had ceased save for one lone old man who hovered above an ocean and played still upon his drum. This man, one of oh so many Davikis, looked up at her as she came and his eyes widened in wonderment. She took his hand and the sea below heaved a sigh, lifted slowly in a great and musical swell and created a wave that grew and grew and grew.

Chapter Thirty-Eight

It seemed to Sahla that she grew from the ground like a little tree and she exulted in the sensation of her young and supple branches, bending and swaying in the breeze. She strived to grow taller, nearer the wonderfully warm sun, and yet her time passed so slowly that a leaf could take a day to lift its face to the light and all was so wonderfully calm and peaceful that no sound impinged from the fast and frantic land all about her.

She sensed another presence beside her and knew that this was her fellow sapling, grown from the same great and towering tree as she. This creature spoke to her in low and rustling murmurs and she realised that it held the memories of its mother within it, that nothing was ever lost at all and she reached out a branch to it so that they two entwined and watched for a while as the humans ran and played, fought and loved, stared up into the sky and down at the earth.

The city wherein they stood started life as a small and simple cluster of mud-brick huts, baked to cinder hardness by the scorching sun. The people were small and dark; a little like Sahla once remembered being, though their heads seemed strangely flattened compared to hers. Their lives were simple, full of hunting and eating, sex and children, short-lived and desperate, appreciative and vibrant. Over time they grew larger, leaner, taller, thought great thoughts, bred those animals with which they had once run wild. The city grew, the buildings turned to huge, imponderable brick and those who remained dark in mind if not in stature were hunted themselves. The two trees shivered as the flames licked at their roots and would have killed them both if not for the sky that opened like the word of some goddess and drenched the dead of both the warring races.

And then the sky was closed off and darkness descended on those left behind. In that gibbering madness they looked long and hard into clouded mirrors and struggled to clean and polish the scales that marred the surface. Scales that covered their eyes as surely as any cataract. But they could not and so they buried those mirrors deep and cursed the ground and the creatures that grew from their shattered visions. They would not listen when the scaled snake grew from the land and offered them the chance to see themselves once more, they cried for war, beat and raped both land and selves, caused a world to groan and die, start out all over again. The trees drifted and saw it all, planted this time in a mountain of sacred principle. Here the same old play was acted out once more and the tree that was Sahla mourned. The hollow inside her was no longer full of life and so she cast out all those tiny creatures that dwelt within her, curled up and died.

*   *   *

When Sahla next opened her eyes she cried to see that the beautiful spreading branches were gone, that the gnarled trunk had disappeared, that the young and old tree she had been was no more and she was mortal again, with a mortal's unique cares and miseries, the curse of a brain that had perhaps become too clever for its own good.

Dropping the horribly fleshful hands into her lap she looked up and around. The silent woman lay still nearby and all around them was a murky dimness out of which lurked great hulking shapes that smelled of old and musty spaces.

She blinked and looked more closely. These big dark shapes were none other than the stone buildings she had seen as a tree and she glanced fearfully around, expecting at any moment for the people to come pouring out and cast her as one of the enemy. Hateful as she was of herself and her life she found she had no wish to lose either.

No one came. These houses were empty now and had been for a long, long time. Silence spun a web in the air and it seemed that time had staggered to a halt and fallen down to die a while. Windows glowered like empty hearts with shifting shadows for lost loves, walls humped jagged and broken limbed, roofs opened like cracked eggs to the elements that this city had not felt in so long. Far above, as Sahla craned her neck, she could see the great arch that cut them off from the world outside. Although each and every home was proved by her eyes to be bereft and deserted it seemed to her that she could feel the people they had once held, as though their spirits were prisoners still, trapped and weeping in the ruins of a city they had been too afraid to leave. She pitied them in between the pity for herself and cried inside that they would not speak to her in anything other than formless moans and so there was nothing she could do for them. She wondered that her grief seemed all she had left to her at that moment. Perhaps this was the most precious thing of all and those who lost their grief were the only irredeemable ones.

A sound from her left made her jump and she turned to see the silent woman awake and staring directly at her, a single leaf hanging in her hair. Sahla recognised her fellow sapling and wondered if she remembered, too.

The silent woman held up her hand, the only one she had left, and peered intently at her palm as though she saw something magnificently important therein. Sahla regarded her with puzzlement for a moment before realising that she was referring to the mirrors the people had buried in the only way she could.

"The mirrors!" Sahla exclaimed. "Then you do remember."

The silent woman nodded, still looking at her hand. Sahla thought how like the snakes she had seen were the scarlet veins flailing about her slender form.

"I wonder if they're still here?" Sahla wondered. "I wonder if we looked hard enough we could find them?"

The silent woman nodded again at this and climbed to her feet. She caught hold of Sahla's arm and gently tugged at it.

"What?" Sahla asked, touched that someone should want to help her still, after all she had done. "Do you know where to go, is that it? Do you want to show me?"

The silent woman nodded and Sahla saw pain and grief flicker for a moment in those catatonic eyes. Maybe here was one who needed the mirrors as badly as she and so she let her lead her on into the forgotten city hidden away so well from the world above.

Chapter Thirty-Nine

Dil-ya fell for nearly ten seconds before she remembered she could mould the dark. It was a long time. Out of all proportion to how she normally experienced time. Everything was so quiet, just a gentle rushing, a cool buffeting of soft white clouds and the soft hiss of blood in her ears. She wondered if this was what heaven was like, falling forever in perfect peace, completely free from the effects of gravity on a thick and mortal body. Then she looked down and saw the ground below her, spiralling in nauseating swirls of green and brown, and knew that this was a heaven that could never last.

Quickly she lashed out with her mind, seeking a possibility that could save her just as she and her once beloved husband had done so long ago when they had opened a way into the dreams of a land stricken with war. *What then of this land*, she thought. *Can a land of the dead dream, too, and if it does, do the dreams then dream? And where does it all stop?*

With this thought the dark was moulded and her senses swelled with the sudden surge as the power took her. The land below came into focus. She saw beautiful cities and pastel colours, glittering ice-glass and twinkling torches that lighted streets down which walked Dark and Pale arm in arm with their human offspring. She found her cheeks wet with tears at the sight of them caught unknowing in it all.

She met the ground with a soft step and stood for a moment, dazzled, recognising this wondrous world in some deep part of her soul yet ultimately knowing it had never really been. The bird, she found, had returned to her shoulder and its song was mournful.

"Oh by all the stars," she murmured. "This truly is a land of dreams and we made it all so real, didn't we? But it was never like this, was it? Or was it? I'm so confused." A tear fell from her lashes. "I thought I understood everything but now I feel I know nothing."

Desperate, she moved into the flow of people, caught hold of the first couple who walked by, a handsome Pale man with unusually dark eyes, and his Dark wife with thick black hair and smooth umber skin. Their child was three, four at most. A bright and bubbly human that spoke in an endless stream of 'what's that?' and 'why is this?' and each and every question was answered by someone, whether parent or other passers-by. Indeed Dil-ya found herself answering its need to understand how the ice bridges stayed where they were in the air above the sprawling streets instead of crashing down in a million beautiful shards. She had to shake herself and ask what she had intended to ask.

"This city?" The man seemed surprised by her question, looked at her as one would look at a particularly slow but still-loved child. "Why it's Eden, of course. Or the Elysian Fields, or Tir-na-nog, or whatever you want it to be."

He and his wife shook their heads, smiled at poor, stupid Dil-ya and walked away, flowers springing up where they had stepped. Dil-ya stooped and cupped one in her hand, inhaled its impossibly sweet scent and felt like crying again, for all their dreams of heaven seemed just that, a dream. She had called this up out of the dark to save herself, it didn't really exist.

"How do you know that?"

She looked up, surprised that someone had read her thoughts. She was even more surprised to see the speaker.

"Kai-ya!" she exclaimed and shot to her feet so suddenly that he took a hasty step away from her and began to look nervously about as though concerned that he had inadvertently happened upon an escaped lunatic—if there were such a thing in heaven.

"Kai-ya?"

He looked at her askance. "I think you have mistaken me for someone else."

"No," Dil-ya studied him closely, all of a sudden wary, though she knew not why. He looked the same, despite the long robes and the seed pearls wired into his curly white hair. "No, I don't think I have. I know you, I know you as the man who left me to die so he could turn to another. These things make for memories, Kai-ya."

"I think you *have* mistaken me, madam." Kai-ya made to brush by her. Already he had dismissed her in his mind and this incensed her. She reached out and grabbed hold of his arm, wrenched him up to face her, for she was as strong, if not strongerm than he. She would have her say once and for all.

"Oh no, sir, I have not! I know you well, perhaps better than you yourself. Zinni taught me many things and only now do I see the full truth of her words. This place you hold so dear, these clothes, these pearls you wear in your hair, they are no truth, they are a dream, a pretty dream with its own reality, for I know now that all exists in its own way and you and I are less real here than we are anywhere else. We do not belong. This is a place of forgetfulness, Kai-ya, and yes that is your name. This is a place we would all like to go so badly that I think we created it out of our own minds. But it can never be. Look!"

She pulled him flapping and objecting behind her as she stalked through the city. She tugged at plants and trees, shimmering stones and clever talking monkeys, tore them from their place and threw them down and wherever she did this darkness blazed forth from within, a black hole torn in heaven and in every hole there was suffering, children starving, women being raped, men being murdered by their own kind, forests raised to the ground, their stumps raw and splintered. Kai-ya moaned and held his hands to his eyes as a tiny, emaciated brown thing lifted a face that seemed all eyes to his and extended an arm so frail it snapped when he summoned the courage to take it.

"No," he moaned.

"Oh yes," Dil-ya cried. "Yes, yes, yes. See it all, Kai-ya. This is reality. While you lose yourself in your visions of what was, what might be, what never was, while you think grand thoughts and write weighty tomes, while you speak and you think, all this goes on and you cannot hide it in finery, you cannot pretend it doesn't exist. It's a veil, Kai, a veil. We have to take this heaven to them, to all those miserable people or all this . . ." she waved her arms wildly at Tir-na-nog as the people gathered around her. "All this will never be. Heaven isn't a right, husband of mine, it's a privilege, and by all the gods and goddesses I think not a one of us has truly earned it and for all that you turn off your emotions so you cannot see, the suffering is still there and until you stand and see it you can never ever hope to face it."

"Not true!" Kai-ya screamed and fell to his knees. All around him the people of heaven did likewise. Thousands of silk-gowned entities from a hundred different lands wailed and beat at the ground as they remembered the pain they had caused, the pain they had done nothing to ease. And so the black holes grew and grew, the ice bridges toppled, the children wailed and Dil-ya sobbed for the cruelty she must inflict but it was all for nothing unless this one man, this man she no longer loved, but would never hate, could admit he knew her, could admit he remembered her, could name her.

"Kai-ya," she spoke softly into the crashing of a land. Razor-sharp shards of glass and stone sliced the air but did not touch her. "Kai-ya, do you remember me? Do you remember my name?"

He was still for a long time and in that interminable moment the last shred of heaven ripped apart and blew away. The child that Dil-ya had reassured cast a reproachful gaze upon them both before flitting away.

Then he lifted his head.

He shifted his shoulders and let the robes fall to the ground. A crow shook its head in relief now that the covers were gone and eyed its small and brightly coloured cousin with a wise and unwavering eye. Their mortal carriers had their own affairs to attend to.

"Yes, Dil-ya," Kai-ya said. "I remember you."

He looked up at her and she saw that the last bit of heaven was not gone at all, it burned still in his eyes as a flame of pure night-light. Maybe they were not without hope after all.

Chapter Forty

When Darbo emerged at the other side of the door he found he stood in the middle of a vast, subterranean city of large stone buildings. At first he thought that night lay across this city but then he realised that he was mistaken and that what he had thought to be the sky was in actual fact a great arch of stone that cut off the buildings from the world outside. This did not seem so strange to him, though. After all, had he not come from a city very much the same as this himself? The spires were no grander in their way than these homes built of huge rectangular blocks, merely part of a different era perhaps. Where those who had hollowed out the spires had sought to go up, those who had built this city had sought to stay close to the ground. It seemed that neither way had worked for this city was as empty as those he had left behind.

The four-legged creature at his side whined softly in the dark and Darbo dropped a hand onto its strong, warm back. The touch of the beast made him think of Sahla and he felt those curious tears come to his eyes again. He blinked slowly, sight blurring, mind struggling still to comprehend these new . . . feelings . . . he had awoken when he cut away his vine. Had the vine kept him dead while it kept him alive? Never had he felt this way before, never had he felt such a desperate need to reach out to another being and it was all the more painful for being so denied. Such a paradox, yet he felt that it could only be true and, shocking himself with his wrenching sobs, he felt a sudden temptation to take out his knife and drive it deep into his new-found heart just to see if he could die now, if he could flee this terrible loss that had come upon him when Sahla took herself and her woman friend and left him alone with only the beast for company.

The four-legged creature seemed to sense his sadness for it took his hand in its mouth and pulled him deeper into the city. He allowed it to do so for he had nothing and no one else to turn to right now and to trust in a beast seemed more natural than anything else.

The city was a warren of many levels and at first sight seemed as empty as Darbo's soul had once been. Buildings and larger pillared edifices that may once have been temples of some kind stood shattered and dust-covered, shadows and murk their only occupants. The stones that had once made grand walls were wilted, almost melted, in places. In others they merely scraped at breathless air with all the care and use of a rack full of rusty old swords. Darbo and his companion padded silently through this theatre of the dead, eyes wide and alert for the sound of any movement. Despite the glaring emptiness of the place, with each step they took they grew more and more aware of the fear emanating from every house. People lived here still, had been here so long, forgotten and tormented, that they had become invisible and so must wail in hoarse sighs for those who should come to save them but did not.

"I do not like this, furred one," Darbo murmured to the beast. "This is unnatural. How is it that I can feel these people but I cannot see them? It is impossible. It seems that they are everywhere, I hear their crying and sighing, yet wherever I look only darkness greets me."

The four-legged creature growled low in its throat in response and Darbo felt the snake lift its head inside his chest, felt its eyes blink and grow accustomed to the gloom, began to see things through those eyes as well as his own.

He began to recognise things then and shook his head in a slow and sinuous way, astonished at the tears that rolled, unstoppable now, down his cheeks and melted his lashes to his skin.

"Oh, this," the two moaned. "I remember this. So empty, so empty now. But it wasn't always so."

At the bidding of the snake Darbo caught hold of the tumbled doorframe of a blackened house, stepped carefully over fallen rubble and reached out to pick up the shattered half-skull of a once doll. He wondered that this small part of a human soul still existed. For humans had lived here, of that he was sure.

"It wasn't always so."

The mirrors, the snake mourned as it too looked at the doll. *The mirrors. I offered them the mirrors of their souls; I offered them the chance to see their true selves, the chance to heal all wounds, the chance for the only love there is. I offered them everything. Everything. Salvation for all, regardless of age or creed. But they would not take it. Why? Why would they not take it? Oh, my precious people, why did you leave me? Why did you turn away from me? I loved you so, loved you with the cruelty and compassion you needed. Loved you the only way it can be. Why did you fear me?*

More tears fell.

Have I become so much to be feared, then? Have I become so much to flee from, then?

Darbo screamed and clutched at his chest while the four-legged beast threw back its head and howled in time with the snake's agonised coilings. Darbo felt that the snake would burst from his chest, so miserable was it. He recognised that feeling well, that feeling all caught up inside, for it had been with him all his life, it was that part of him the vine of immortality had locked away and he wished he could tear open his chest and let it out, finally let it out. But he couldn't and so he cried aloud and looked up at the broken roof of the house he had wandered into, reached out and moulded the darkness it held as Sahla had taught him to do and saw it spin around him, felt the whole world spin. He heard the voices of children and their mothers, saw them come bouncing in at the door, one a little girl with the doll—now whole—in her hands. She was so pretty, so full of life, he wondered how the mirror of that beautiful face could crack as he saw it now in the hands of a man who scarcely knew what he did, a man he recognised all too well, and how the little girl screamed and how the man screamed inside as the house fell in a mass of flames and shakings and Darbo turned and looked out of a burning window to see that every house in the city was burning, stone melting and running away, fleeing into the earth as its occupants never could. The snake sobbed and wailed inside him, too much, too much for it to take, and so the vision shattered and the spinning stopped and Darbo sat alone and shaking in a burned out shell of a home far far in the future with a small and battered doll in his hand. He listened to the terror and fear of the trapped ones lost and alone in these ruined homes and started to go slowly mad once more.

Chapter Forty-One

Fainan had been wandering around this curious city many days before he heard the crying. When he did he felt the tears prick at his own eyes for it was so raw and heartfelt that it seemed to come from the very bowels of the earth itself. For a long time he clambered and leaped over tumbledown buildings in search of the ones in so much pain, but try as he might he could not find them. The sound of such constant misery ringing in his ears bore him down, made all the worse by the fact that he could do nothing to assuage or stop it. That night he lay awake listening to it, curled up in the lee of a dust-covered wall, trying desperately not to hear it. As though to spite his efforts the sound grew louder all about him, as though the very buildings and the darkness within them echoed and intensified it. He groaned and held his hands to his ears, thought of Sahla and wondered if she, too, were lost and alone in here. Maybe she was the one so sad. Maybe he would find her the next day, make her happy again. Make him happy again. Make this infernal moaning and crying cease for good. Lost in these thoughts his own tears fell and he began to sing, soft and low under his breath, words of nonsense and bittersweet meaning, untrained melodies of wistful yearning. As he sang it seemed that somewhere his song was heard and a beat as of a heart and the pounding of surf began to swell with ever more strength.

*   *   *

Zinni rode on the crest of a wave to end all waves. Bright turquoise and raging grey was she. In between the scintillant horses of virgin spume sat an old old man. He helped her pick the bones from her hair and cast them out into the ocean that held them both.

"I think," said she, "that new flesh is needed, my friend. A new body for a new world. Oh yes." She turned to Daviki who looked at her with eyes that had once been afraid and were now full of an innocence that bared its soul without regret. "So, old one, are you ready to be renewed? Are you ready to sing with me that final song from which there is no return?"

Daviki did not reply for a long time, instead he turned his head into the crashing waves wherein they travelled, touched but never destroyed. He saw in that restless mass the land he had known all his life, the dream echo of a mountain that was in turn perhaps the dream of something, or someone, else. Zinni did not press him, merely watched him with compassionate eyes. She knew her young well.

"They are all still there, aren't they, wise one?" Daviki asked without turning. Zinni nodded and up from the depths spun the faces of many loved ones, bobbing and darting like shoals of silver-backed fish. Among them were those he had wronged though he had not known it at the time.

Daviki smiled at them and they smiled back.

"Yes," he said. "I am ready for our song."

Zinni reached into his heart and played upon the drum of all drums. She brought forth the sacred song, the song that women know, the song that creates.

*　　*　　*

Kai-ya and Dil-ya stood alone amidst a rushing mass of swirling blue and grey, all that was left of the dream of heaven. It was a sea they did not have to swim against and for a moment both thought how nice it would be to stay here, how much easier it would be to float with neither thought nor care, merely to blend into a great and formless nothingness and leave behind the struggles of mind and body. The squawking and trilling of their avian companions did not reach them and they let their bodies fall back into the comforting arms of nirvana, began to assure themselves that they had destroyed the false heaven and found the real. Already their bodies were shimmering away, becoming translucent, so that tiny dots of spinning light, like faraway stars, could be seen deep within their flesh. They may have laughed at this but if they did nothing came of it and they would soon have drifted away if not for the sword of pain that sliced through Dil-ya at the same time that her beautiful bird dipped its wings and arrowed towards her, singing furiously. It hit her belly with a thump and all the breath shot from her body. She looked down to see a bright eye and a rich green feather disappear deep within her and at this she realised what crime she committed.

She wrenched herself free of the grasping calm and screamed at the top of her voice, for she was body and questing mind and what was this madness that sought to take all this away from her?

Then the crow eyed her well and she thought it smiled at her. It carried the face of an old white-haired man and she smiled back, caught the ghostly Kai-ya by the shoulders and struggled to separate him from nirvana.

But it did not want to let him go.

Hook-ended streamers of enraged heaven coiled and lashed for her and her once loved and now loved again husband. They sank into her flesh and tore it from her body. *We will have you*, they screeched. *One way or another, we will have you. What need have you for this body? For any body, anybody? None at all, none at all. It all leads to pain; it all leads to misery. Deny it Dil-ya, deny it all!*

"Never!" Dil-ya waded into the violent heaven, continued her hauling at the limp and precious body of her husband. "Never! I'll not give my life to you. I'll not give my body to you. This is me, this is what I am." She realised then the root of it all, pulled Kai-ya close and kissed him in forgiveness. The crow cawed in triumph, lifted its wing and soared down to touch them both.

The false heaven screamed its loss as they dropped through the door that appeared in the nothing beneath them and so arrived at last in the city where it all began.

Chapter Forty-Two

Sahla and the silent woman didn't know when the screaming had started but they both wished it would stop. At first it had been just a gentle sobbing at the periphery of their hearing, but just now, in the last few seconds in fact, it had increased to a terrified and angry shriek. It was so loud it shattered the women's balance and many times the two of them missed their step and would have fallen if not for the other being there to hold them up.

They were climbing now. The many terraces upon which the city stood lifted away above them; scatter-stone dwellings stacked one atop the other for as far as the eye could see until the impenetrable arch ended all further contemplation. Yet it was bizarre, because it seemed the higher they climbed, the darker it became and the deeper they journeyed. Sahla wondered if they would ever come across the mirrors they had seen whilst they were trees or whether they, too, had been the hallucinations of a gibbering brain.

"Maybe I could mould them," she murmured to herself, wincing as her voice was lost in a strident wail of terror from somewhere far above and below. The silent woman must have heard her though, because she stopped and turned with that quizzical expression on her face. "Yes," she continued. "They have to be out there somewhere. Instead of going to them, why don't I just bring them to me?"

"Because these kind of mirrors have to be searched for long and hard, my girl." The voice was a new one, loud and hard, piercing, even through the screams.

A man stood on the first and final terrace above them.

Soot he was from head to foot. No white in eyes or teeth, soul or heart. His skin was dull and grainy, his head bald and black, his eyes emotionless orbs of permanent night. He was an emptiness, a void set before them, yet paradoxically full, so full of horrors that Sahla backed away, she could not help it, and the silent woman was left alone to face him.

The man threw back his head and laughed raucously at this. "She is afraid to face me!" he taunted. "How like her. How very like her. And are these the things you were looking for, little one?"

At his word the terraces between them fell away in a vast rumbling of stone-dust and smoke and a pit circled with seven massive mirrors blinked and dazzled into her face. Each one held a horde of faces, accusing, abusing, ignoring. Each one spoke in a deafening confusion of voices, slashed her soul to ribbons and laughed at it for ever daring to think it could live. Each one wanted something of her, hated her, envied her, wanted to be her. She recognised them all, she had been some of them, seen them in her dreams, lived with them, spoken to them. These were her clan, her family, the dead, the ancestors, the eternal screaming occupants of all these underground houses, the people in her mind that threatened to drive her insane. She fell to her knees at this terrible realisation, clasped her hands to her ears and begged them to stop, for they wanted her, for what she had done, for the evil she had visited on them, and she couldn't bear it, she couldn't bear it any longer.

"Leave me alone!" she screamed, shook her head. "Leave me alone!"

"Foolish Sahla," the man sneered. "That is why they hate you. You have left them alone too long."

"No." Sahla snapped her head up. "You lie. I've given my life to others since the day I was born; I've always done what's right by them. I've had no life of my own, I've been feared and hated for the powers I have. I've been so . . ."

"Alone?"

For a moment she met his gaze and in those featureless eyes she saw the only true mirror she could ever have.

She whimpered and let her eyes fall. Too afraid to face the confusion in her soul.

"Come, child," the man turned to the silent woman. "You, at least, are always welcome here. Come cross the abyss to me."

Sahla peered like a feral cat through her tangled hair as the silent woman smiled her sweet smile and leaped out across the yawning mirrors.

"No," Sahla moaned. "Oh no, don't let her die." She climbed agonisingly to her feet, screamed at him. "Damn you, thing from the pit! Don't you dare let her die!" She fixed him with the only strength left to her and for a moment the silent woman hung motionless in mid-air, reflected over and again in the flexing mirrors, then the man laughed and extended his hand. From it whirled the thinnest rope she had ever seen. The silent woman caught hold of it and he pulled her safely across, reeled her in like a fish, turned to Sahla with an offer in his gaze and the rope in his hand.

"Your turn now, Sahla." He smiled a sharp-toothed smile. The silent woman looked at him and then at Sahla. The man laughed once more, his merriment petering away just a little when the silent woman stepped past him and held out her own hand to Sahla.

"Your turn, Sahla," she echoed and Sahla felt her heart stop in her chest at this simple gesture. She knew then that she had to make this jump and she had to make it without the man's help.

The rope came swinging across to her. She snapped a thought at it and sent it slithering down to skate across the mirrors and into whatever waited below.

"I don't need your help," she said in a low and resonant voice. "Her words are enough for me."

And with that she jumped over the edge.

Chapter Forty-Three

She fell forever. The mirrors spun below her, never seeming to come any nearer, twisting and melting so that all the glass spiralled in a huge whirlpool of reflective memories and she saw her life disappear into the centre along with them.

Her falling ceased in that moment of true-seeing and she hung impossibly in mid-air, suspended by a hand of purest dark she had not realised she'd conjured. In that instant she felt like weeping, for she knew that she could stay here for all eternity, caught and hanging as an interminable sacrifice over the pools of her own life. Knew that she could exist like this and would come to enjoy it in a sick and twisted way. As she thought this the hand closed more tightly around her and she screamed and slashed out at it with all her thoughts and all her strengths, with hands and feet and teeth and nails so that it shattered into a million pieces of unwanted torment and she was falling again and this time there was no stopping her. She plunged into the pool of memories with the laughter of the dark man ringing in her ears.

*   *   *

The first thing she saw on the other side of this pool was a perfect dark scattered with jewel-like stars and in the midst of this a door made of fine oak wood ringed with beautiful iron scroll work. She drew herself to her feet and walked towards it. She did not question how it was that she walked and breathed in what was obviously boundless space, just as she did not question where the sacred mountain had gone. It seemed all were one and the same now. All as unreal as the other. She knew that the only reality was in herself, so that was where she looked for the key when she pushed at the door and it would not open. She opened her mind to all the emotions of her life, all the injustices and loneliness, all the fear and sadness, and then wished she had not for they threatened to flood her with their power. She swayed and moaned, put out a hand to save herself, fell once more and rolled on the ground with her head in her hands. Her heart poured from her in great gibbering reels of pain and misery, coloured red and blinding violet with the violence of the feelings she was barely aware she had. How had she thought she was so cold once? They were so strong, so very very strong, whirled and streaked away from her like a million fireflies, out into the space that surrounded and cradled her. And there, in the first and most precious darkness, all the screaming ones that lived in the city she had momentarily left behind, all those parts of herself that had suffered and died over the years of becoming, took form. Part human and part bird, they cocked their heads and looked down at her until she slowly dropped her shielding hands and looked up at them.

They were terrible, beautiful things, bodies made of her own flesh and blood, wings made of her hair and bone, swirled all together so that they dripped scarlet fluids all about her like the veins of the silent woman. They looked at her with big moist eyes and flapped their creaking wings in a vain attempt to take flight.

"Oh you poor things," Sahla sobbed. "You poor, poor things. All that's been done to you and still you want to fly. And here am I, the shaman who should help such as you, and I'm too afraid to speak on your behalf, too afraid to show you the way." She raised her hands again to hide them all away.

The bird-humans clicker-clackered amongst themselves and flapped their brittle wings some more. One of them dropped down to flop beside her and, despite her fear, she forced herself to lower her shield and look upon it.

"Yattle," it clacked at her. "Schubuttle."

"Nonsense," she whispered to herself, and, unknowing, reached out a hand to touch it. It dipped its head a little to meet her questing hand and she found that its skin was dry but strangely alive beneath her touch.

"Arrrrrrr," the bird-human sighed and twitched its wings like a dog who has been scratched in a favourite place. Up above the others clacked in wonder and their wings lifted them a little lower, a little higher.

"Poor thing," Sahla said, and held its heavy head between her hands. Something tingled in her mind, she remembered it vaguely. "Poor sorry part of me, poor battered soul. My blessings to you, creature of the dark places, may you hurry towards the centre of the night and return twice blessed at the hands of the Wise One, the Woman Who Knows, She of the Bones. Let her rock you and mend you and heal you and sing you back to new life."

With that she released the bird-human's head. It laughed a hearty, joyous chuckle, and all of a sudden its eyes came brightly to life, it streaked up into the distant sky, each and every one of its friends following in its wake. Behind them they left a key, hovering motionless in the air, a key of streaming blood and bone, slashed flesh and hair. Hardly daring to believe in what she saw Sahla reached out for it, gasped when it healed at her touch, the blood ceasing to flow and the many scars fading. She felt that now she could put it into the door's lock without fearing what she might loose.

The very moment the key touched the lock she sensed movement from the other side of the door and almost stepped back, almost ran away, almost reopened the many wounds, and then it swung open and this choice that was not a choice was taken away from her.

Two people stood in the gap beyond. Their faces told of the horrors they had faced.

"Kai?" she spoke slowly, softly, as though she expected them to disappear at her words. "Dil-ya?"

"Sahla," Kai-ya said. He looked pale and drawn, she barely recognised him. Dil-ya, at his side, seemed thinner, harder than once she had been. But they were still the same underneath. Still the same. Only now they had grown, as had she, so that she knew the answer she would give to his question before he even asked it.

"Can you forgive me? Us? Can you forgive them all?"

Sahla answered by folding him into her arms. Other arms joined hers in wrapping around him and she knew this was Dil-ya. When Kai-ya stepped back to show what he brought she already knew it in a way.

"Sahla." He held out his arms and in the cup of his palms burned a small dark flame, alive with brilliant golden edges. "Dil-ya and I found this for you."

Hello, Sahla, the flame said. *I've been waiting for you.*

And then it flared high and in its burning she saw a million things, the first of them forgiveness. For she saw them as people now, nothing more, nothing less, each with broken dreams and secret shames. Each with small worries and large agonies, each with a burden of fear and guilt that matched her own and she wondered how many of those tormented souls trapped in the city were theirs and not hers.

In that moment she loved Kai-ya and Dil-ya with a sight so clear it blinded her and when the crow flew to her in a snapping flurry of wings and settled on her shoulder she saw the whole dark at last and how hard won it had been. She saw the false heaven destroyed and now that she knew what she did she turned her attention back to the city she had left behind, called to it and saw it emerge from the veil of space as a realm of spinning mist that gradually solidified.

She and her family stepped through and she spoke as a true shaman once more, spoke to the wounded ones, no longer afraid of the dead.

*   *   *

It took several minutes for Fainan to register the fact that the screaming and crying had stopped, that the wailing and beating of invisible chests had ceased, that he no longer had to block his ears from the sound of so much pain that it was almost a physical thing. In that moment he climbed to his feet and thought of Sahla. Thought of the face and mind he loved so well though he had never held her close save only in dreams.

"Is she well?" he asked of the city. "Is she finally returning to me?" He did not understand the meaning of his words as he spoke them, did not know where they came from, but they felt right. He clambered and ran over wall after wall, stone after stone, knowing that someone hunted for him and that this time she would take him. It was all he had wanted then and all he wanted now. When he reached the edge of the terrace he saw the wolf a moment before it saw him and ran to meet it with joy in his heart.

Chapter Forty-four

The man disappeared the moment Sahla fell into the mirrors and for a while Kelefeni just stood, silent and alone, at the edge and waited. Then she realised that here she would wait for the rest of her life and so she turned her back on the black hole and walked off into the city once more.

As she walked her pain increased with each step. She had never told Sahla of the pain. The terrible, awful pain that accompanied each writhing vein, every drop of blood shed by her bizarre and impossible body. It was this pain that had driven her deep into her mind where neither thought nor speech could be formed, just a numb and mindless terror of a world that had done this to her. Yet all that had changed in just a single moment. When she had spoken those words to Sahla, those instinctive, unbidden words, the pain had suddenly become more bearable, and now, even though it grew in intensity with every second, she continued on. She knew she had something to do, something very important, something without which Sahla would be unable to return. Kelefeni felt that she owed Sahla very much, that without her she would cease to exist. A strange thought, that, but no stranger than anything else that had happened to her recently.

She clutched her maimed right arm closer to her chest, cast a fleeting glance at the ragged wrist where once had been a slender, dextrous hand. It bled still, just as did every other part of her. She wondered how one could bleed so much, suffer so much, and still live. She wondered if she were bleeding for the wounds of each and every human who had ever been. Then she wondered how wonderful this new wondering was.

A sound a little way off to her left caught her attention. A human voice groaning. A low and burbling edge to the cacophony of misery she scarcely noticed anymore.

The sound came again and Kelefeni narrowed her eyes and bobbed her head, peered into the shadows that scuttled like disease carrying vermin along the edges of the street she walked upon.

All she could see was row upon row of empty houses. The sundered rock seemed to her a barbed and vicious echo of her own deformity and she trembled, her entire body tingling with cold electricity at the thought of what hid there in the dark and moaned at her so.

"Aaaaaaahhhhhh!"

It came again and she whimpered softly and hugged herself because nobody else would.

"Aaaaaaaahhhhhh!"

"No," Kelefeni shook her head. "No, no, no. I am not going to look for you."

But she did, despite her solemn vow she crossed the slightly raised street and hopped down to the level of the houses. The sound came from her right now and she turned, ducked her head and stepped into the hollow shell of a building that seemed the source of that which she unwantingly sought.

Inside she saw a man curled up in a ball. He held his head in his hands, fingers clamped so tightly to his flesh it seemed he wanted to tear it apart and rip at what he found inside. He was moaning and sobbing, rocking slowly back and forth, his tears cutting bare runnels in the dust that surrounded him. She recognised him in that instant and slumped to her knees as the wolf she had created from her own tears so long ago padded towards her and sat quietly at her side.

"It's him," Kelefeni chattered to herself in a small and insane voice. "Him. The man in my screens. Oh, I remember him now, though I think I didn't know him at first. I think my pain has driven me mad for so long I can't even see my tormentors when they stand before me. Darbo, she called him Darbo, didn't she? And what am I to do now I have him here? He called me to him, didn't he? Called me to him as his love, then as now, and am I the only one who can save him? I? The one that he maimed? I? The one whose hand and mind he took? Am I now to save him?"

Darbo ceased his crying at the sound of her voice. He sat up and looked at her. An old and battered doll tumbled from his hands.

"Kelefeni? Is it you? Really you?" His heart was in those eyes, *and yes,* she thought, *he does have one, after all.*

"Yes, Darbo. It's me." She smiled at him and the wolf thumped its tail gently. "A fine pair we make, you and I. Fear and pain have undone us both, haven't they?"

Darbo shook his head. A strange light burned in his eyes. "Not fear, not pain, no," he spoke quickly, as though he had too many thoughts waiting for freedom. "Anger, Kelefeni, anger that made me do what I did to you, to the others. I think I killed all those who lived here without ever meaning to. I wish it had all been different, I wish I could take back all the harm I've done, all the misery I've caused."

Kelefeni held out a hand that no longer was to him. "No, Darbo. It had to be. The rage always comes first. And now you're tired, exhausted, beaten down as low as you can go. Now the fear and pain have come to claim you, just as they did me. Yes, it hurts, it always does. Look at my blood, Darbo." He looked. Her seeping veins had already soaked the floor. "Do you remember watching your own, too? This is the reason why, Darbo, this is the reason why." Her broken arm hovered before his face. "Take my hand, Darbo."

He looked from her face to her bloody stump, then back to her face again. His features twisted so that it seemed they would slide clear off his bones, then he fixed his gaze on her arm, lifted a hand so slowly that days rose and set and touched her.

At his touch a spark passed from him to her and a living snake of scarlet—and silver now—reared from his chest and darted for her in a tingling flash of light, turning each and every one of her veins to purest silver. She threw back her head and screamed, lost in a swirling cloud of delicate-knit metallic snow that danced and condensed, coiled down, formed a new hand, a hand of brilliance to replace the old.

The wolf joined her in her screams and took to its heels as Darbo reached for her at long last.

Chapter Forty-Five

When the city reformed about Sahla and her companions the screaming she had left behind increased in volume, as though those invisible mourners knew that she whom they mourned had returned.

Listen to them, the flame that Kai-ya had given her flickered from its place above her head. *They fear you and welcome you at the same time. They know their time is at an end. I felt this way also when I witnessed a new birth. But all life comes from such as this. Do not be afraid, Sahla. Send them on their way, shaman of both worlds.*

Sahla wondered what the flame meant by this but the voices of the undead filled her thoughts, clamouring at her, beseeching her, threatening her, and in their cries she saw all the fears and miseries, all the sadness, all the terrible parts of herself and her clan since time began. She remembered the misshapen birds she had sent off to the Old Wise One and knew that she had to do the same now for these.

And so she reached into that part of her mind so recently laid bare and found the darkness that could bind them up and set them free. With this thought she saw the first of the spirits step forth from his shattered home. He was a tall man, dark of brow and eyes, yet with the white on white hair of the highest caste of Pale Ones. She recognised him as both part of herself and part of Kai-ya and cast tender skeins of darkness around him, pulled him down into the earth where he melted away into dust and bones with a small sigh of wrathful bliss.

So many more followed him, women, children and men, old and young, limping and crying, a constant stream of sepia-toned, hollow-eyed, translucent souls, emerging from house after house, all over the city, fleeing the ruins that had held them prisoner for so long. With heads bowed they came, or gazes raised high in misplaced anger, terrified pride, each came to seek their place in a world they had almost forgotten but always missed. She recognised all as some part of her, of her clan, of her people, of all people. She saw her own childhood eyes stare at her with haunting sadness, her birth-mother's tears hit the ground, Kai-ya's love turn bitterly strong, Dil-ya's quest to save the others turn to isolation from all that she loved, all of these and more she saw in the spirits that came to a halt before her, ready for their judgement. She heard the two Pale Ones gasp softly behind her and knew that they saw all this, too, knew that she drew on them a little when she sent each and every lost soul to its rest.

And then it was over, the screaming was at an end and peace fell upon the city. The houses were truly empty at last.

The first thing she saw when she looked up from the bones of the last of the lost was a man, a beautiful twilight-eyed man as dark as she, though not as stocky of limb as most of her people, not as wide-headed, not as leather-skinned. He was just like her and a wolf was leaping for his throat, fangs bared.

She cried out, fearful for his life.

"Fainan!"

His name? How did she know his name? And yet it must be right, because he looked up and his face broke into a brilliant smile at the sight of her, a smile that warmed her heart and soul and made her feel as though she belonged for the first time in an age.

The wolf did not attack him but sped past, bounded up to Sahla and caught hold of her hand in great gentle jaws, tugged at her to come, come, and she could not greet this man, this Fainan, as he deserved, because her eyes fastened on the house behind him, fastened on Darbo and the silent woman, fastened on the death he was about to deliver the woman who had quickly become her dearest friend, and she ran for all she was worth towards them, summoning the deadly dark as she went, oblivious to the warning shouts of all around her.

*   *   *

"No, Darbo, no!" She hurled the words and the darkness behind them with all the violence of a thrown and quivering spear. They stopped him just as well, threw him back and away from the woman he attacked, tore a shrill scream from his mouth. His head turned and he looked at her, eyes wide in pain and disbelief. In his hand he held the knife she remembered as the cause of so much blood. The silent woman shrieked and writhed at his feet, holding her red-sheathed arm to her chest, veiled from head to toe in a cloud of spitting, hissing silver sparks.

"What have you done to her?" Sahla screamed, forming her thoughts into a barb of solid blackness more tangible than any mortal weapon could ever have been. "What have you done to her now?"

"Sahla, look out!" The cry could have been anyone's but she did not heed it, she could deal with him, oh yes, she could deal with him now. He would never hurt her or anyone else ever again.

He climbed to his feet, stood over the silent woman's thrashing form, lifted the knife. His face twisted and she took it for his usual cold, unfeeling cruelty.

"Bastard," she hissed through clenched teeth and stayed the bolt of dark in her mind, came to a halt in front of him, felt the breath of the wolf on her heels and stared him straight in the eyes, let her hatred fan the air between them so that the screams of the silent woman were as nothing in comparison to the shimmering violence of her rage

"Bastard," she repeated. He quivered and did not dare raise the knife before her gaze. She took joy in that. "I'm not afraid of you anymore. You're nothing to me."

And she let the darkness go. He fell before it with a cry that all the murdered dead of all the worlds could never hope to echo, writhing as the silent woman writhed, tearing at a foul and clinging mass of deepest night, the last and only defence he could offer to throw his knife her way. It landed with a clatter at her feet and then he was lost and wailing amidst a stormcloud of endless possibility that had a million ways to make him suffer.

*   *   *

"Sahla." Feet pounded up behind her and she looked around to see Fainan, Kai and Dil-ya, faces flushed with terror.

"What?" she demanded. "What is it?" For a moment she thought they would chastise her for such brutality, yet how could it be wrong to do this to one such as he? Did he not deserve it?

"The city," Kai-ya said and pointed upwards. "It's falling."

Sahla snapped a gaze at the arch above. Great chunks of rock peeled away before her eyes and cartwheeled to the city far below where they smashed into the ground in vast plumes of dust, pulverising everything that had once stood below. The sound waves were deafening and set her bones and teeth to rattling.

"Damn." She looked at the screaming, no longer silent woman. "Fainan, pick her up, bring her with us. We've got to get out of here."

Fainan stooped to lift her and together they all ran for an exit they were not even sure existed.

Chapter Forty-Six

Great boulders of rock smashed the city to shards all about them. The crow dipped and dived through air suddenly become more dangerous than any storm it had ever flown. The wolf loped ahead, leading the way. Fainan followed close behind, the unconscious Kelefeni slung across his shoulder. Sahla and the others ran in his wake, dodging from side to side, hands held over heads, struggling to keep up with him despite his burden. The rocks seemed almost to be aimed at these three, so dangerous was their path. Buildings trembled and toppled at every corner, pounded beneath the ruined arch that had once protected them. Dust rose from the shuddering impacts in huge plumes, formed cloud upon choking cloud that sought out lungs with horrifying sentience and strove to beat their possessors to the ground to end their days in the place they had helped destroy. The city had no reason to be now, no lost souls to imprison, and its anger knew no bounds.

"Look out!" Kai-ya screamed as a rock the size of one of the buildings spiralled down towards his wife. She looked up to see the threat and stumbled, fell to the ground, stared with wide eyes at the life-ending monolith that approached. Sahla and Kai-ya darted forwards at the same time to pull her back to her feet, dragged her away just before the rock impacted, sending all three of them rolling over and over.

They had no time to recover, the next rock slammed down in their midst. Kai-ya and Sahla cried out, threw their bodies to the side, lifted hands to shield their eyes from razor-sharp stone. Dil-ya moved a fraction too slowly. Her scream was shockingly short.

"Dil-ya! No!" Kai-ya staggered to his feet; stared with wild eyes at the boulder still rocking on the spot his wife had occupied not a moment ago.

Sahla drew herself up. The pain of this loss ripped the words from her lips. It took the arrival of the crow upon her shoulder to remind her of the truth of the matter.

"Kai-ya!" She snapped the words as a command. He ceased his tugging at the rock and turned to look at her. "Leave her," Sahla said. "She's an ancestor, not truly alive, not truly dead. You'll see her again but you can't do anything for her now. You have to come with me or we're both going to die in here."

Kai-ya stared at her blankly. Sahla felt her heart contract with grief for him.

"Please, Kai." She could not keep the emotion from her voice this time. "Come with me. For the love we share."

His eyes clouded at that and tears trickled down his cheeks. "Please."

He stared at the hand she offered. A hundred thoughts seemed to play across his brow, his mouth worked silently, then he closed his fingers around hers as though this were the last time he would ever touch her.

For a moment no stones fell, the dust hung still and attentive, something more than love passed between them and then they blinked, started the world turning again, climbed to their feet and left Dil-ya to her second grave.

*   *   *

Fainan realised Sahla was gone when the woman in his arms fell all of a sudden silent and limp. There seemed, though he knew not why, a strange kind of connection between the two. The sight of the woman so pale made his heart leap with fear.

The wolf, too, seemed to realise something was amiss and turned back as Fainan lay the woman carefully on the ground and smoothed back her golden hair from her temples.

"What am I to do?" he asked of the wolf, neither of them flinching in the slightest when a huge rock smashed to the ground not five yards away. "I can't leave this woman helpless and alone, but I can't go on without Sahla. If I stay here we'll die, if I go back . . . and yet I can't go back . . ." he looked on the face of the woman, marvelled at the silver hand in place of human. "I feel she's important," he murmured and the wolf whined softly. "Important to me in a way I don't understand, yet without Sahla I'm nothing. She's the reason I came here." Another rock spiralled down and another, lifted all three of them several inches off the ground, sent a cloud of dust so high into the air that it took a full minute for it to return to earth. When it did Fainan accepted its umber coat with a quiet grace and looked up at the crack the rock had birthed.

Far above, the arch that had once blocked out all the sky yawned wide and open in a hundred places, admitting more and more of the outside world with each and every stone that fell. Shafts of silvery light reached inside and lit upon the myriad particles coating wolf, woman and man, made each glisten like a molten statue. The wall of the building around them folded softly inwards to show what lay beyond and Fainan let out a breath as recognition flooded him.

It was his spire! He had never left. He walked here still, all this, all that he had seen in the many days that had passed, existed within that magical forest birthed from the serpent's pool back in his room.

"Oh Gods," he gasped. "How did I never see this before? I never left. I never left."

The wolf whimpered and looked up at the largest stone yet to fall,

155

bound straight for Fainan amid his revelations.

"I never left." He smiled like a child. "And now I have to prepare her land for her, just like the serpent said."

And with that he closed his eyes and existed solely apart from the world that tumbled about him. The wolf jumped back with a shrill howl as the boulder that would have killed him shattered in mid air and a shower of scarlet rose petals drifted slowly down to envelope them all.

Branches and vines erupted from the ground all about, pushing cold stone aside and spreading rich green leaves over every inch of land. Flowers opened and bloomed in a matter of seconds, air that had a moment before hung full of dust now resonated to the song of thousands of gaily coloured birds. What was left of the arch above groaned and creaked, grew transparent, shimmered and disappeared, letting light pour in. Yet it was not sunlight but moonlight and the crow that screeched with delight and announced the arrival of the last two travellers was finally home.

*   *   *

Dil-ya blinked salt-spray from her eyes and turned to look at the woman who rode the wave next to her. An old man sat by her side, arm linked with hers.

"Hello, Dil-ya," Zinni said. "You did very well, dear."

"I did?" Dil-ya quickly touched each and every part of her body. "Then it's true?" She looked up. "Death isn't the end?"

"That remains to be seen." Zinni smiled and continued with her interrupted song.

*   *   *

To Sahla it seemed that Fainan stood in two places at one and the same time. Caught in the midst of a mass of vegetation he was a part of the forest he created. Vines and creepers poked from his hair, leaves cloaked him, his eyes, for just a moment, seemed as dark and brown as the rich moist earth, then he changed and he was just a man, a man standing in the doorway of a spire, a lone and lonely spire in a vast expanse of land that had once held so many.

"Kai." Her voice cracked, she could not help it. "What are we supposed to do? Should we see only forest and go hunting for a while? Or should we see the spire, should we go inside and see what the humans have done to it all?"

"I think that choice has already been made for us, Sahla," Kai-ya said and pointed ahead.

Sahla looked. Fainan had lifted Kelefeni to her feet, and, after casting one backward glance at them to see that they were there, he stepped through a doorway and disappeared inside a spire that should not have been amidst a forest that was still growing.

*   *   *

A poor bedraggled creature, its limbs bent at awkward angles, its clothes a shredded mess, its skin blackened and charred, watched as the two people followed the green man and his limp bride into the spire. This creature watched from a single ruined building perched atop a hill overlooking this lovely forest and its oh so slender rocky tower. The building was all that remained of a once great and viciously powerful city.

"What about me?" it whimpered as the door closed behind them. "What about me?"

It turned away, no longer able to watch, and pulled out a knife from the stone it had hidden it behind countless times only to retrieve again and again.

By the light of the moon the creature began to cut at itself and these wounds, it knew, would never heal.

Chapter Forty-Seven

Sahla and Kai-ya stepped inside to find Fainan and the now conscious Kelefeni waiting for them along with the wolf. All three were silent and though Sahla knew in her heart of hearts that they were her friends, for a moment she was afraid and reached up a hand to smooth the crow's feathers. This soothed her a little so that she could recognise their silence as respectful and join Kai-ya in looking around at their new surroundings.

The interior of the spire was a dull grey, specks of disturbed dust spun and swirled, caught in the cold light that shone always, illuminating the millions of walkways and pipes that had not been used since the humans had stolen the secrets of life. The vines that had once wound their way through the walls hung lifeless and limp now, their sparkling sheen gone, torn away in their last desperate attempts to escape the spire that had once sustained them as they had sustained it. Gaping holes in the walls gave mute testament to their final convulsions and in the silence there seemed to be a soft and sighing echo of the great crack and falling of rock in the moment when all had breathed their last.

"Sahla," Fainan broke many silences by stepping away from Kelefeni to speak. He seemed almost in awe of her. She found herself wishing he wasn't. "I made all this for you, just like the snake asked me to. Do you like it?"

Sahla did not know what to say and so said nothing at all. It was obvious that all Fainan could see was the beauty of the forest they had left outside. And whose madness would she prefer? Hers or his? She found that she did not want Fainan to be mad, did not want to feel this attraction for someone whose mind was lost and flailing in a forest only he could see and so she took his hands and told him yes, yes, she loved all that he had made for her and she did not ask about the snake for she did not want to know. No more than she wished to know of the noise that she could hear at the very edges of consciousness as she took this beautiful man's hands. A sound like the rushing of water and deep within it a voice, a voice speaking to them both.

All the answers you'll ever need, my children. I am all the answers you'll ever need . . .

*　　　*　　　*

In unspoken agreement the four of them decided to climb, it seemed somehow the right thing to do, the only thing to do. To bring the humans out of here and into the world Fainan had created.

The spiralling crow led them upwards until they reached the very first of the inhabited circles inside the spire and came to a halt before a door that creaked ajar at Sahla's touch.

The great black bird fluttered in to land on the ground before it, let out a vilely raucous caw in the hollow calm, cocked its head to one side and hopped into the room. The others looked at it but dared not follow. Something told them that this was all horribly wrong.

"Gone," Kelefeni said suddenly, the word as shocking for the fact that it came from her as for what it portended. Sahla turned to her, wanting to ask what she meant, but Kelefeni walked away and around the circle, knocking on each door in turn. One after one they sprang open at her touch, unable to resist the bidding of her silver hand. Ominous shadows swarmed within.

Sahla did not know what else she could do other than walk into the room it seemed only the crow did not fear to enter.

And so she did.

"Sahla . . ." She heard Fainan's warning, heard him hesitate for a moment then come after her, but it was too late, she had already seen.

The occupant of the room may once have been a living creature but now she was no more. The vines, in their struggle for survival, had taken back all those parts of themselves the humans had stolen. One wall of the room had shattered outward under an impact of unimaginable force. Thick, knotted, scabrous grey vines clitter-crawl-clumped over the floor and Sahla took an involuntary step backwards, coming up short against Fainan's chest. But no, they were dead, and so was the woman caught in their coils and dragged halfway back into the wall. She no longer resembled a human though, for a vine twice as thick as she had penetrated deep into her spine in search of the baby lifeline she held inside and she had burst open and rained her flesh and blood all over the floor. But red she was not. The colour of life had no part here. Her ruined remains were as grey as the vines that lay dead about her. Half of her face drooped limply to one side and it was as fine and terrible a sculpture as Sahla had ever seen.

The crow observed all this with a calm eye. Sahla felt its detachment with a small part of her soul and knew that it had expected nothing less, that this was its true nature and she could not hate it for that any more than she could hate the humans for killing her world and the vines for ending all hope of resurrection.

The crow turned its gaze on her and in that black-rimmed eye she saw a lick of a flame once more, a flame that seemed to her to flare out and touch her in searing caress. She screamed and staggered, felt her flesh melting, unaware of Fainan's arms trying to hold her, his voice trying to tell her all was well, it was just an illusion.

The crow darted for her, clawed her cheek, drew blood, sailed out into the gaping centre of the doomed spire. All around, the walls and walkways shimmered and shook, the crow was caught and held in a hundred lightning snapshots of motionless movement.

All four of them were caught with the crow, existing separately in all those different seconds. A flame, real flame now, flicked jerkily from Sahla's heart and grew minutely so that when time started again the conflagration it bore exploded in a great and burgeoning rage and at its centre they saw a vision of a crater the size of the moon outside.

They had but an instant to see and study this before the flames descended upon them with a deafening roar.

"Jump!" Sahla screamed and pulled Fainan over the edge along with her. She saw Kai-ya and Kelefeni do the same and then she was lost in the darkness because now she must bend it to her will or they were all dead.

Chapter Forty-Eight

Behind her eyelids a multitude of colours swirled and she thought for a second how ridiculous was the notion that there was no life in the darkness. Then she was past all that and reaching out with all of her training, all of her natural ability, searching, searching the endless turnings for a place somewhere, somewhere to be safe.

Her body registered the flames lapping around her with something as close to a scream as it could form and she moaned inside and grasped at vari-coloured straws that wriggled and swam from her vision in vast and terrified shoals.

And did it all glow red now, then? Was the spire being formed anew from whence it had first arrived? The heart of the sacred mountain thrusting all forth . . .

Yes! Sahla arrowed in on this image, swimming with intent at last, all else lost to her, fear, pain, nothing to her. This, this was all.

Oh, by all the ancestors, but it was beautiful, this birth, she had never known that flames could be liquid before, never known that such violence, such destruction could be responsible for so much life.

Earth and rock cracked and split, blew apart around her, filling the sky with scatter-black ash and spinning rock, blinding, brilliant clouds of steaming light and supernovas. She lifted her hands to her eyes but nothing could shield her from the fiery rain descending.

Death, she thought, and in its midst she stood inviolate for here was much, much darkness, all for her, all for her, for she had done this, she had known this, too, she had torn apart a world half-dead, she had devoured all in flames of passion, danced and screamed in the blood and ruins. And so she did so again, threw back her head and laughed and leaped, tossed her head and flung her arms high while the flaming lakes parted around her just as they had for another and she reached a hand deep down into it to draw forth the flame that had started it all.

A black flame, burning with the memories of countless times, countless explosions.

We belong together, you, and I, she thought and, *Yes, we do,* the flame thought back at her. *Truly, now. So let us prepare the way, Sahla, let us prepare the flames for the life to come.*

The conjoined thoughts of these two flared forth in a blue-white tidal wave of shuddering gas-light . . .

Fainan had dreamt of falling forever, but had never done so. Until now. It was much as he had imagined it, a quite delightful yet utterly terrifying sense of weightlessness. He looked up at the flames following in his wake, roaring with a voice of millions, saw the crow caught and consumed, living flame leaping upon its back and setting its feathers sparkling alight so that it shone red-hot for a moment before folding its wings about itself and disappearing in a circle of embers.

"Yes!" Sahla's cry followed this death, so well-planned, so orchestrated, that Fainan turned his oh so light and heavy hair to see her, bypassing the struggling, whirling, seed-like forms that were his companions in terror—Kai-ya and Kelefeni—and letting his gaze rest for its final moments on the woman he loved above all else and all others before the flames caught him as they had the crow.

He thought it was because the flames had already killed him that he saw the pale blue glow start around his loved one. He thought he must be dreaming again, the last, desperate ecstatics of a doomed brain, and then he saw it grow, saw countless shades dance within a beautiful veil that enclosed her whole, spread out in a gentle shimmering wave, enveloped him and the others in welcome coolness and advanced on the flames as a lioness stalks her prey.

From far away he heard the wolf howl and thought he could see/sense it running in maddened circles below, then the blue wave touched the flames and the light grew to be so blinding that he had to close his eyes and so he missed the perfect flash that changed the fire, that soared upward like a scream unleashed, blew the top from the spire and sped high up into the air to say hello to mother moon and tell her soon now, soon.

*　　　*　　　*

Kai-ya's eyes were ever focused on the light and he saw all, looked at Sahla with eyes of worshipful love as a single tendril of the light curved back down beneath them all and bore them to the ground with a gentle hand.

That the spire shook now and seemed only half there, caught in a shaft of starlight that spun and raged as a mighty whirlwind, that they, too, were caught in this heavenly, earthly arrow, that the spire held them still and would take them with it if they dared to stay too long, he cared not, all he could see was the flame, the black as pitch flame that burned above her head more fiercely than he had ever seen it in all the days he had spent at the ancient crater in his world of dreams. He saw in her what few are ever given to see.

"I know now," he murmured, even as the others milled in confusion, as the wolf barked in frustration to urge him on. "I know."

He knew the flame would soon be his and it scared him and comforted him at one and the same time.

Chapter Forty-Nine

Overwhelmed by all she had seen Sahla caught hold of each of her friends in turn and hurled them clear of the spire that was built now more of shimmering summer evenings than stone. The last to go was Kai-ya. She saw the flame, flush with new life, reflected in his eyes, and also a recognition of what she had to ask him to do.

"You," he murmured, and reached out a hand to touch her cheek. "It was you all along."

Sahla closed her eyes and leant her head into his touch for one small and perfect moment. The feel of his skin on hers was electric and she felt her heart contract painfully inside for love of him. Unable to bear it a moment longer she put up an arm, eyes still closed, took his hand firmly in hers and held it tight before pushing him away.

"Go, Kai-ya," she said, "and take this flame with you. You know what needs to be done."

"I do," he said and she felt the flame go to him.

All was silent for a moment and she thought he was gone, turned her blind face above, seeing within what she must manifest without or all that she had wordlessly asked of him was ended before it was begun.

"Will you come with me, Sahla?" His voice, so unexpected, shocked her, and she opened her eyes without meaning to. She instantly wished she had not, for she knew then, as she looked in his deep, dark eyes, that she would do as he asked though she had not meant to. She loved him, perhaps more than she loved the others, perhaps differently, who knew? But love him she did and follow him she would. "Will you?"

Sahla, you know you ca . . . the flame glowered sullenly in his hands but she cut it off by pulling him close and kissing him with all the passion they had never been able to share.

"No regrets, Kai-ya." She looked him straight in the eyes. "Whatever happens after this moment, always remember, no regrets. You are what you are and knowing that is the greatest thing of all."

Then she did push him away. The others already outside pulled him back to watch as the spire began its final transformation.

*   *   *

Now Sahla was alone. Saving them from the flames had been only the first of her challenges, there was more to be done to pave the way for new life, there had to be a gateway, and only she could open it.

She lifted her gaze. This time her eyes were fully open for she had nothing to fear now. Up there, up in the place where the spire opened to the night, the blue she had freed wailed and surged into the sky and she saw an image of a mountain that had once been, a mountain she had never seen, a mountain that none of her people had seen in thousands of years. This was the sacred mountain as it had been before the Others, before the Pale, before the Dark, before the mis-led dreams of primeval utopia had been thought by the firstborn, this was a return.

Sahla lifted her hand in salute to this vision and gritted her teeth against the many others that threatened to impinge, because now she was deep in the darkest of darks and here was the root of all, so many possibilities all wanting to be born, each with an infant's selfish, all-consuming desire to be loved, nurtured, fed.

"No," she snarled as the mountain changed before her gaze into a warped and twisted mass of bilious green and the great column of light in which she stood threatened to collapse into a form it should never be. "No, this is what I want, this is what I shall have."

The mountain returned, clearer now, more defined. On its flanks she could see forests like that which Fainan had summoned, covering everywhere and everything. She could see lakes and animals, people moving, babes in slings, hunters with spears, elders with food, alive, but not alive, because she sensed that these were parts of herself she forced on this vision and as she thought this they disappeared and her gaze shifted to the mountain's peak. This mountain had once brought death to those people and the crater it had wrought in so doing came into her view. She floated above it, saw that inside it was soon to burst to life again, that the flames she had killed before were as nothing to these and yet if she wanted what she had just seen she had to restore this terrible capstone to her so long dormant mount or all was lost for good.

She laughed then, because she remembered meeting Zinni for that first time back in the land of ancestors and she knew what Kai-ya meant.

"Come then, flame-mountain!" she called for it and clapped her hands together. The spire convulsed. "My irony is a wonderful thing!"

*　　　*　　　*

Kelefeni screamed. The spire exploded in a fountain of giant spinning shards that seemed to take an eternity to fall, raining slowly down and flickering to nothingness so that blue light in the sky opened out to reveal a mountaintop none had laid eyes upon in living memory.

"Oh Lord," Fainan murmured and lifted his head high. The mountain's summit reared far above, silhouetted against the night, limned in silver by the moon. Perhaps it had been there all the time, just waiting for them to look.

The blue light faded fully before his gaze, smoke and mist drifted along the scarred and endless scree flanks that slanted high into the air. Water gushed forth from cracks at the mountain's foot, staining the ground yellow and white. A low, animalistic rumble shuddered the air and Fainan thought to himself that it would take days to walk up there to discover the secrets. And secrets they were for the smoke came from inside the mountain itself, issuing forth as though this rock behemoth breathed and lived.

"Where's Kai-ya?"

He flinched and turned at the sound of the voice. Sahla stood before him. No trace of the spire remained.

"Kai-ya? He's right here . . ."

He looked around. Only Kelefeni and the wolf returned his gaze.

Sahla's mouth tightened. "I gave him his destination and he's on his way." She turned towards the many fissured cliffs that led to the mountain's top. "Come on," she said. "I have a promise to keep."

*   *   *

"Flame and water," Zinni chuckled and edged her ocean with mischievous red, much to the delight of the old man and young woman that worried no longer. "Flame and water. Who would have thought it, eh?"

Chapter Fifty

As Kai-ya bent into the mountain he found that he missed the crow. He had never thought he would, but he was wrong. Amazing how lonely a journey could be without this one simple avian companion.

He continued climbing and did not bother to look up to see how far he still had to go. He would get there when he got there, not one moment sooner and that would be soon enough. The flame Sahla had given him travelled on ahead of him, flickering blackly like a demonic will-o-the-wisp, and this was one more reason he did not choose to look up because he feared that if he did he would stop right where he was and never move again. In that last short moment with Sahla he had caught a glimpse of how sweet life could be and now he wanted nothing less than to have to leave it.

There would be nothing to leave if you were to go back. The flame hovered closer to him and he lowered his head still farther, fixed his mouth in a firm line and his mind firmer yet.

Kai-ya, you know this. You have known me for a long time, now. You came to me when you were in pain and did I not listen to you? Why then do you refuse to listen to me now?

"I see no reason to," Kai-ya grunted as he negotiated a particularly steep section of cliff. The mountain shook and trembled disturbingly beneath his hands and feet and he wondered what this strangely improbable phenomenon portended. The moon was hidden on the other side of the mountain and he could see little to help guide him. Clouds drifted sullenly across the sky like silver-backed whale pups abandoned by their mother and all about was colourless and hidden as the loneliest recesses of the soul. He thought perhaps the whining wind was the call of all these and then tried not to think anymore for he required all of his concentration to remain alive.

Then how do you propose to know what we must do when we reach the top of this volcano?

"This what?" Kai-ya came to a halt and lifted his head to look at the flame. A stray gust of wind took new strength and flicked his white hair out into the night like a cloak that he could not hide behind. Small flakes of unknown matter drifted down and settled upon his pale skin to complete his mantle.

See? The flame quivered, a slash of deeper black in the growing night. *You do not even know its name. How then do you plan to conquer it?*

"I know enough to be sure of my own abilities," Kai-ya snapped. "I know that Sahla sent me up here to finish her work and she had no doubts that I could do it."

Indeed? Then why do you travel so slowly, Kai-ya? Why do you not notice the night growing darker around you? Why do you not feel the rocks quaking? Do you not feel the urgency rising? Do you not feel the pulse of the land pound as the frightened deer? Do you not share the fear of the land, Kai-ya? Do you not feel it?

Kai-ya turned his reluctant gaze to follow the movements of the flame. It trailed far out into the sky and for a moment he had a ridiculous notion it would fall. All seemed so high up here, so instantly fatal. The lower flanks of the mountain, the land where all had once lived, the land upon which one never even knew of the existence of such sheer and abyssal drops, seemed so far away now.

Come, Kai-ya, the flame urged. *Look below.*

Kai-ya took a deep breath and looked down. He saw the sacred mountain in all its entirety, sculpted by the night into endless troughs and swells, coloured by blue-edged shadows, spreading so far down and so far into the distance that he marvelled that there could ever be an end to it. Yet an end there was, for at a far distant point the flanks spread no longer, the land petered to a halt and changed to rocky rubble that faded slowly away into nothing.

"How?" Kai-ya murmured.

Look closer, the flame hushed lovingly in his ear.

"Gods." And indeed they were, for out there, out in the nothing on which this wondrous mountain perched, were all the stars that his people had ever mapped, all the glowing balls of gas they had envied and called gods for their freedom and cool detachment, all out there creating the ocean for their home to drift in. "Oh, gods! How did we never see this before?"

You never looked.

"Never looked? But we did. We did look. We spent our whole lives looking!"

You only looked for that which you were prepared to see.

"No. No, you're wrong. Our sight is freer than that."

Oh? Then look down. Look at your feet.

Kai-ya did and saw that he floated out in the air with the flame at his side.

"No!" he cried and flung his limbs wildly about. "Help!"

Calm yourself, the flame said with some hint of amusement. *You cannot fall. I won't let you.*

Kai-ya forced his body to be still and found that yes, he was quite safe, and yes, now he could see even more. Stretched out below him the mountain grew a coat, a wondrous coat of trees and grass, all colourless in the night, but there nonetheless, and beautiful on a land that had been barren for so long. This coat raced up the mountain's flanks, each and every side, and in amongst all this he thought he saw movement, like the flitting of fairies from childhood tales. He turned to the flame with a spark in his eyes.

"Is this it, then?" he said eagerly. "Have I done what was required of me? I see life down there. I see creatures running amongst the trees. Have I done it then? Is my life my own at last?"

Do you see the connections? The flame did not respond to his questions. *Do you see how all this,* it sent a spark arcing for mile upon mile to dance on the mountain's flanks, *is connected to all that?* Another spark whizzed off up, out, down and forever into the nothing and the stars it contained. *Do you see?*

"Yes," Kai-ya said, though he had barely begun to grasp it. "Yes, I see."

Then come put me where I belong and see the greatest of all connections.

Kai-ya blinked and found himself clinging once more to the shaking land.

Hurry, Kai-ya. The flame seemed to die a little before his gaze and he wondered how this could be so when the mountain was coming to life all about them. *I do not have long left. I must go back to where I belong or all this life will have run its course in the time it takes you to truly understand.*

"Yes," he said and this time meant it. Could not believe that any death could find him now. "Yes, I will hurry." He dug his feet and hands into the rock, finding holds where no other could. "Yes," he murmured, feverishly pulling his body ever upwards. "Yes, now I have a land to give to Sahla, now I have a land and she will love me for it."

Chapter Fifty-One

Sahla could not believe that Kai-ya could be so far ahead of them. Her heart beat a little faster with concern for him, echoing the ominous rumbling of the land, a rumbling she knew she had caused, a rumbling she knew meant no good and all the good for everyone. Afraid, she wondered if she had done the right thing in sending Kai away, for in so doing she felt she had lost part of herself and surely a person could not give away so much and still thrive.

The mountain was much steeper now, rose like a knife before them, threatened to cast them off at any moment. She dragged herself ever upward, feeling along rocky ridges for any indentation that might offer a hold. Her fingernails were torn and bleeding, all the soft flesh ragged and sore. She could hear the others' laboured breathing behind her and the howls of the wolf abandoned below when the way became too steep. All around her the night closed in like a sentient being, full of dark clouds of sharp choking ash. She missed the hidden moon with all her heart, could not believe that this new capstone could be so wonderful if it closed away something so important.

A shrill scream assaulted her ears and she gasped as her feet slid out from beneath her and for a single, terrifying moment she was hanging from a mountain higher than she could imagine by only her fingertips. In that moment she realised that she had not considered death as an outcome of this, not seriously, and at once her mind was flooded with the warning cries of a hundred dead, ancestors dear to her, and chief among them was Hi-ya, whom she had not heard for so long.

Do you not think my father can do this alone? Look to these others you lead to their deaths before their time. Look to them.

She looked down and saw Kelefeni dangling from Fainan's hand, her small body flapping and twirling like a rag in the wailing wind, her face stretched and wide-eyed with horror. She saw Fainan's shoulders shudder, his grip loosening with every moment.

"What have I done?" she murmured. "Again?"

Quickly she scrabbled at the cliff-face, regained her footholds, sent rocks tumbling downwards. One of these, she knew, would pass by her friends, and as it did she snatched at it with her mind and formed it into a new possibility, moulded it to the mountain in a great jutting ledge and heard Kelefeni's scream trail away as Fainan let her go to land safely just a few feet below.

She looked down over her shoulder to see Fainan staring up at her with a smile across his face despite the blood on his own hands.

"I knew you wouldn't leave us, Sahla!" he cried up to her and then she heard the wolf's howls anew. In them she heard the echo of a lost and tiny voice, a voice saying 'What about me?' She began to climb back down as fast as she could.

"Where are we going now?" Fainan asked her when she reached the ledge upon which Kelefeni lay and he stood.

"*We* aren't going anywhere," Sahla said. "You're staying here where it's safe. I'm going back into the forest. I left something important there, something I have to get back."

"No, you're not." Fainan caught hold of her arm when she would have gone on and she glared at him. He glared right back. "Not on your own. We spent too long finding one another. I won't leave you now."

"Fainan, don't make me regret saving you." Sahla struggled against his grip, though she did not really want him to let go.

"Then you'd best regret it," he laughed. "Because where you go I go."

"Kelefeni, too?" Sahla looked down at the young woman who was studying her hand to the exclusion of all else. "Kelefeni?"

Kelefeni looked up. Her face was pale yet radiant. She held up her hand for the two to see. They gasped. It was almost human again; just one finger remained sculpted from silver now. It seemed that in its glowing tip the face of a serpent bobbed and smiled at them.

"No," she said and turned her head to look out into the ever-blackening sky. "No, I'm not coming. I think what I have to do I can do from here."

Sahla's face fell then. Though but a moment ago she had thought to go back on her own, now the prospect of going without her beloved Kelefeni filled her with dread.

"Oh no," she fell to her knees before her. "Kelefeni, why? Please don't make me leave you here." Even as she spoke these words she knew that this must be, that this was the last time she would see her friend. She reached out and pulled her close while Fainan looked on and shed his own quiet tears.

Kelefeni returned the hug, smiling a small and delicate smile, then she pulled away and turned her gaze out into the sky where it seemed that just for a moment a single pinprick of rushing blue could be seen out there in the dark.

"There," she said, pointing outwards. "Do you see it?"

Sahla and Fainan looked. It could be there. An ocean in the sea of stars. A pure, faraway note of song. A dream perchance . . .

Sahla turned to Fainan.

"Do you trust me?" she asked him.

"You know I do," he said.

"Then hold tight." She offered him her hand and together they leaped off the ledge and fell into the circle of howls offered up by the wolf and transformed into something else by mind of woman.

Chapter Fifty-Two

Kai-ya lifted his head. The land was still for the first moment since his interminable climb to the top. In that endless second he thought he could hear something, something far below, and craned his neck awkwardly to see what might be following him.

He had thought it a wolf's howl, but the idea that the animal had managed to climb up here was too incredible even to consider. Was it possible that the wind had carried its voice up here or had he just imagined it? As though in answer to his wondering the wind chose that moment to gust with an eager violence that—along with the reawakened land—sought to pluck him from his precarious hold and send him crashing to the mountain's foot far below. He laughed a little—at both wind and imagination—he was far stronger than that. It would take more than this land's cries on the wind, however strong, to tear him from this place now.

He turned his gaze upward again and reached out with a hand to find his next purchase. Hold quickly found he pulled his body up almost a full length before sliding his feet into a crack and flattening out again, ready for the next search. He could smell the sulphur in the air, sense the summit so close, a darker shadow against a dark sky in a land already so full of shadows. The grey specks coated him from head to foot and the flame had dimmed so that it could not be seen against the rest of the night but he knew it was still there for he could feel its relentless urging hot against his mind. With one last great effort he heaved his body up the last few feet, planted his hands on the summit, pushed up and arrived, at last, on top of the world.

"And so," he announced to no one in particular as vast fumeroles spouted high and pungent around him. "Here I am. All my life, all these journeys, have brought me to this, and where is the moon to light my way, or her sister, the sun?"

He looked up, expecting to see the moon now that he was atop the mountain and there was no longer anything to block the way. Or maybe if not the moon then the first rays of the dawning sun. Had this world ever had a sun? He had not seen it since his arrival here. Surely there must be something . . .

But no, strain his eyes as he might to west or east there was no sign of either sphere, just a vast cloud spreading for miles above the mountain. And yet, and yet . . . what was that, far away in the distance? Some blue dot burning through the miasma, far away on the horizon, perhaps another star, a forgotten god, a beaten-down goddess. A return?

He felt the flame arrive at his ear. Its hiss of endless burning was impossibly loud up here where the air was so thin he felt his lungs shrink inside him and his head spin with desire to drift a while.

Hurry, it sighed. *Please hurry, Kai-ya. Return me to my home. I'm so tired.*

Kai-ya looked at it in amazement, saw it flare for perhaps the last time, saw that in its depths another blue dot lived, wondered which was the first. Yet the amazement was not for that but for the simple fact that he had never before heard it say please and in that moment he realised that it was just as helpless as he, as them all. He thought that this was the most wonderful thing he had ever known.

"All right," he murmured and reached out a hand to touch it. Crazily it seemed to take shape, a woman's face, familiar perhaps. "It's all right," he said. "I won't let you die."

And was the transformation not yet complete? Did he see more within it? Did he see one who had saved him, too?

Come then, the flame shivered slightly. *Carry me to my home for I can fly no more.*

Kai-ya, Pale no longer but ashen grey, took it in his hand, cradled it like a newborn, began his walk to the inner edge of a crater that he remembered from many lands and many pain-filled times. A home he had never realised till now.

*   *   *

In the midst of a rushing blue tidal wave three people sat. How it was that they were still untouched despite the distance they had travelled and the violence of their transport was a mystery, but perhaps it had something to do with the woman, the old woman with the youthful eyes who looked upon her two companions and told them what they must do.

"Daviki," she said and returned his drum at long last, putting his heart back in his body so he could feel again and feel properly this time. "Now you are whole again, now you can call up all the shades of your people from the waters, now you can summon those who walk still in the sacred mountain below. You can prepare the dead. Shaman."

Daviki smiled and patted the blood on his chest, touched the old woman on the cheek and smeared the blood wide.

"Yes, I can, Wise One, yes I can." And with that he took a deep breath and plunged down beneath the waves, leaving the two women to watch the silvering shapes that darted in his wake and took on faces and forms that each had known once upon a time.

"Dil-ya," Zinni said after a long silence.

Dil-ya looked up at her Goddess. The only one there was.

"Your flame is calling. Go to him."

Chapter Fifty-Three

Sahla and Fainan drifted to the ground like a pair of summer seeds and the wolf greeted them with a howl of delight before turning its tail and darting away. Back into the forest.

"You think it wants us to . . ." Fainan started.

"Follow it," Sahla commanded, already negotiating her way down the slope.

Fainan followed her and the forest welled quickly before him. It seemed much thicker now; barely recognisable as the one he had called forth. Now, as they entered its fringes, it was dark, much darker than it had been, the leaves and branches overhead thickly intertwined, the canopy all full of grossly gnarled forms and slick inky leaves. The sky overhead was fully black, no stars or moon shone and the tiny glowing spark that Sahla called into existence to light their way did not seem nearly half enough to Fainan. He thought for a moment to tell her to douse it and that they would continue by feel alone for it seemed that light was not something the land wanted them to use right now.

"What did you leave behind, Sahla?" he asked while he struggled to force his way through trees and undergrowth that did not seem to want to let him past yet parted for Sahla and the wolf in a way that scared him.

"I don't know," she murmured, though he did not know whether she had heard his question and was answering him or was merely voicing her many fears aloud. "I don't know, I really don't. Why am I here? I left it behind so long ago now, I thought I'd finished, thought I'd done it, done all that I needed to. What did I forget to do? What did I forget to do?"

In the depths of the forest something moved along with them. Fainan flicked his gaze from side to side and wondered what these dark shapes were, too many shadows to be their own, too many movements, too precise, too considered, to be solely wind in branches.

"Sahla," he said softly and reached out to touch her, to slow her down, before she disappeared entirely into the trees without him. "We're not alone."

Sahla stopped. Ahead the wolf continued on. She looked at Fainan and he saw the pain in her eyes. It struck him to the core of all he was because he saw that her pain had never been tangible, never been clear and clean, never been a suffering that other people could see and understand and therefore she had been more alone than anyone could ever comprehend. There had been no help for her, ever, and she still, even now, did not believe there ever would be.

"I know." She searched his eyes; he felt she was testing him. "I know we're not alone. I've seen those shadows, in one form or another, for every day of my life. They're the only company I've ever had and I wish to all the ancestors that they would leave me be, leave me alone . . ." she bent her head and he hesitated for a moment before reaching for her. That moment was too much, the light she had summoned dimmed and she lifted her head, lashed out at him, took him by surprise, sent him falling back into the moist and springy earth.

"Why won't you leave me alone?" she screamed, looking at him as though she loved him and hated him at one and the same time. Then she turned and loped off after the wolf and Fainan lay there with his head spinning and his eyes brimming and feared that she was lost to him after all for he had seen the wolf in her and this one would kill him if he pursued, of that there was no doubt.

* * *

Sahla cried as she ran. The silver-backed shape that was the wolf wound through the trees in front of her, sinuous body blurred and indescribably indefinite. She could no longer tell if it were simply wolf, or partly human, partly her, but it led her on and oh, how could she have been so foolish, such a short time ago, to think she knew it all, to think that the pain was at an end and soon she would have the love she so desired, the love she had never had, the love she did not think she was truly capable of. *It is too hard,* she thought, *too hard to care anymore. All are gone now, left behind, uncaring, lost to me one way or another. And if I find what is lost, what then, what am I then?*

The shadows closed in on her, whispering their damning messages just as they had always done and she knew she could never win, never beat them. How could joy and strength turn so quickly to pain? How? How?

She moaned and increased her speed, did not feel her legs anymore, felt nothing other than the sensation of the forest flashing around her and the sound of her heartbeat in her ears. *I am nothing,* she thought to herself. *I am no more human than the wind in the trees, nor should I strive to be. I was born for this and this alone . . .*

She lifted her head and howled into the cracked night.

* * *

Kelefeni sat on her lonely ledge and looked up into the sky. A blue crack spread from one side of the horizon to the other and from it, or perhaps because of it, she heard the howl of the werewolf, the tortured human animal, but also a song of great and simple beauty. She smiled when she saw the old man dive down out of the ocean pouring from the crack, the old man who swam straight for her as though he knew her. She lifted her hand, human now, to take his, and dove back into the water once more to gather the others below.

*   *   *

Kai-ya stood at the edge of the crater, the heart of the volcano that had erupted once, so long ago, and birthed this world, his world, the world he only now truly loved.

"So here, my flame, friend I think you are, now," he said, and let it go so that it dropped down into the dark and empty depths. "Return to your home and return mine to me. I've waited too long for this already."

He watched it till he could no longer feel its soft murmuring in his mind and when this ceased he felt such a sense of loss that he stumbled to his knees and cried out because he thought he had erred, had done the wrong thing in giving it away. He hauled himself back up and hung half down into the crater as though to see one last glimpse, to call it back, to own it once more. And then he saw the billowing cloud of flame so far down, yet rapidly approaching. The scream in his throat died as a thought for he saw Dil-ya's face in there, and Sahla's, saw the faces of any and every woman and he knew them all.

The dreams are at an end, Kai-ya, my friend, she said, *the dreams are at an end. It is time for me to waken once more.*

"Mother," Kai-ya sobbed and thought of his loves in the moment before he threw himself into the flames and flared so briefly.

A violent fiery blast tore the top off the mountain and sent a river of destruction down into the forest below.

*   *   *

Fainan lay where he had fallen for an endless tormented moment during which he felt a million sharp white teeth tear him limb from limb. He moaned softly to himself. Oh, the pain would be great, so very great, and yet the reward, oh yes, the reward, now that would be worth it.

For a love such as this, no price was too high to pay.

He leaped to his feet, branches and barbs tearing at his skin, and let loose a wild cry from his lips.

Another wolf sped off into the forest.

*   *   *

The howl ended and the Sahla-wolf looked up to see a shabby and crippled human totter to a halt before it. Its clothes were tattered and covered in blood, dried and fresh, its limbs, torso and face were covered with a criss-cross hatchwork of wounds and scars that wept and bled and made the wolf's mouth salivate and the woman's mind wail with pity.

Weak, the wolf thought. *Prey.*

Pain, the woman thought. *Misery.*

Let us end it, thought these two.

The wolf tensed to leap. The human creature shambled closer, looked at the wolf with tear-filled eyes.

"Sahla?" it said and fell to its knees, flung its arms around her and sobbed into her fur.

The wolf flickered and a woman's form came into being. Sahla was human and she shuddered to be so but lifted Darbo's head all the same and looked into his eyes to be sure it truly was he. They were the same icy blue she remembered so well, but melted now and she saw the ember of a flame reflected therein.

"Darbo," she sighed and pulled him close. He moaned and clutched at her in desperation, burrowed into her like a small animal seeking warmth, knocked her to the ground so that she rolled with him. "Oh, Darbo, what has become of you?"

"You left me," he sobbed. "You left me and took the others. Why did you do that?" He looked up at her out of bloodshot eyes. "Why did you do that, Sahla? All I wanted was to be loved."

"That's what we all want, Darbo," Sahla said and caught a glint of metal in the corner of her eye. "That's what we all want."

And then she held him tight and whispered words of love and in that moment she heard Fainan's half-human, half-animal cry and knew he had followed her and wanted her still.

"Look, Darbo," she murmured into his hair and they two looked up together to see Fainan hover between wolf and man for a single moment before settling on neither and pad-walking forwards to offer his love, too, a love they accepted with open arms.

It seemed to Sahla that she knew them both, saw deep into their minds, and they were one and the same and she felt safe, at last, in those arms.

Darbo's knife, chipped and blunted now, fell harmlessly away and tears watered the ground while a great crack as of a million thunderstorms serenaded them.

The flames took them while they embraced.

*   *   *

An ocean-song in the sky descended and took the volcano lady's fury into itself, drowned and soothed it in sparkling waters, fed the sacred mountain so long gone dry and finally receded so that it remained only in scattered lakes and rivers on whose banks plants already sent forth tentative shoots to test of this new world.

Of the rock spires there was no sign. Of the forest that had once stood here, there was no sign, of the people who had once walked here, in dreams and in life, there was no sign. Overhead the sky was a soft, pale blue, the sun a gentle orb in the sky. The moon hung still, cool and unrepentant for the task she must always perform. The breeze seemed barely a breath. All hung motionless as attention was focused on a single lake where the heart of this missing forest had once stood

For a moment nothing stirred, then something chimed, an eyeblink of darkness fluttered into life over the lake and the water stirred, rippled, fountained high into the air. Two hands emerged, twined together, droplets of water falling from them in shimmering veils to robe the bodies that followed.

A male body and female body to whom nothing mattered save the hard won love they shared.

*   *   *

Somewhere an old woman laughed herself awake at this new possibility and turned back to the dark in between darks to count the bones of her children once more.

Printed in the United Kingdom
by Lightning Source UK Ltd.
2105